DAWN
UNDERCOVER

Also by Anna Dale

Whispering to Witches

DAWN
UNDERCOVER

Anna Dale

BLOOMSBURY

First published in Great Britain in 2005 by Bloomsbury Publishing Plc
36 Soho Square, London, W1D 3QY

A CIP catalogue record of this book is available from the British Library

Hbk ISBN 0 7475 7407 3
Export pbk ISBN 0 7475 8032 4

All papers used by Bloomsbury Publishing are natural, recyclable products made
from wood grown in well-managed forests. The manufacturing processes conform
to the environmental regulations of the country of origin.

Typeset by Dorchester Typesetting Group Ltd
Printed in Great Britain by Clays Ltd, St Ives Plc

3 5 7 9 10 8 6 4 2

www.bloomsbury.com

To Marianne
and the Mayfield Road mob

Chapter One

The Portent

Dawn Buckle had been waiting for ages. She shuffled forwards so that the toes of her plimsolls peeked over the edge of the kerb, and stared forlornly at the lollipop lady on the other side of the road. The lollipop lady, who could be glimpsed every few seconds through a stream of traffic, had leaned her pole against a lamp-post and was popping yet another toffee into her mouth.

'Thirteen,' murmured Dawn, who had been keeping count. The lollipop lady chewed her sweet, unaware that an eleven-year-old schoolgirl had been waiting to cross the road for almost a quarter of an hour.

A further five minutes went by (not to mention six lorries, one bus and thirty-two cars) and Dawn continued to stand in the same place, her fingers squeezing the strap of her satchel nervously. She had been late for school numerous times since the start of the summer term and, although her teacher had never seemed to notice, there was always a chance that one day Dawn would be spotted sneaking into the classroom a few minutes after everyone else. If she was caught, Dawn knew that the punishment would involve a ruthless scribble next to her name on the house-point chart. So far this year Dawn had only managed to win one house point, and she was rather anxious to hold on to it.

Dawn had tried waving at the lollipop lady to attract her attention, but her flailing arms had gone unnoticed. She had whistled to the best of her ability (producing not much sound and rather too much spittle) and she had shouted as loudly as she could (unwisely choosing the moment when a double-decker bus was trundling past). Not one of her efforts had worked. She had not even succeeded in scaring away a pigeon sitting on a telephone wire above her head. Dawn felt a flicker of disappointment, but she was not really surprised. Over the years, she had become accustomed to being treated as if she wasn't there. Being ignored from dawn to dusk was tremendously puzzling and, at times, exasperating, but Dawn was quite a cheerful soul and she tried not to dwell on it.

An outburst of raucous laughter made Dawn turn round. Her heart lifted when she saw two boys, dressed in the crimson uniform of Rustygate Primary School, wending their way towards her.

'Hi, Paul. Hi, Gavin,' said Dawn.

Paul bumped his bag against her shoulder which, she

supposed, counted as a sort of greeting. Dawn did not particularly like the Evans twins, but she knew that their arrival meant that she might actually make it to school on time. Dawn glanced hopefully at the other side of Semolina Road. She saw the lollipop lady stuff her bag of sweets into a pocket of her luminous yellow coat and seize her pole.

Dawn's pulse quickened.

With no apparent regard for her own personal safety, the lollipop lady marched into the road, causing several vehicles to slam on their brakes. Then she halted dramatically in the centre of the thoroughfare, turned round and thrust her open palm towards the windscreen of a two-seater sports car.

'Stop,' she said firmly, her peaked cap slipping down over one eye. 'Stop, please.' The dark green MG Midget slid gracefully to a standstill. 'It's safe to cross now, my angels,' said the lollipop lady, brandishing her pole.

She smiled beatifically at the waiting motorists as Paul and Gavin swaggered self-importantly across the road. Dawn brought up the rear, happily plodding across the tarmac in her well-worn plimsolls. She had almost reached the opposite kerb when a sudden movement in the green sports car caused her to turn her head. The sun's rays bounced off its windscreen, making it difficult for Dawn to see the driver's face clearly. She squinted and gave a little gasp of amazement. The driver was goggling at her.

It was not a straightforward stare, either. The driver's gaze was so intense that Dawn felt herself blushing furiously. She hurried after the Evans twins and almost tripped up the kerb in her haste. *How strange*, she thought as she paused on the pavement. Dawn was astounded that someone had actually taken an interest in her. Not knowing whether to be alarmed or excited, she watched as the lollipop lady strode back across the road. The traffic began to move again. Nearest to Dawn, the sleek, green MG Midget began to creep forward. It reminded Dawn of a crocodile gliding sedately through water, keeping a beady eye on its prey. She shivered and hurried into a patch of shadow cast by an awning outside a newsagent's.

Dawn watched the reflection of the sports car in the shop window as it rolled slowly past, the sunlight flashing on its silver hubcaps. Its hood was up and its windows closed but she caught sight of someone with their face turned towards her. *They're still watching*, thought Dawn, and the back of her neck prickled uncomfortably. She held her breath and only released it when the green MG had gone.

It was the first time that Dawn had ever had chocolate for breakfast. As she sat on a bench in the playground of

Rustygate Primary School, she broke off several chunks at once, pushed them between her lips and let them melt into velvety lumps on her tongue. Her eyes didn't blink once in three whole minutes. She was in a state of shock.

A typical day for Dawn involved a lot of waiting, listening, following instructions and traipsing around on her own. She was actually quite talkative, but the trouble was that no one was ever very interested in what she had to say. Dawn spent most of her time trying to get people's attention. Usually she failed dismally, but this morning had been different. She had gained somebody's interest with absolutely no effort whatsoever. At first Dawn had been embarrassed, then a little pleased. Now, she felt rather perturbed. She stuffed another chunk of chocolate into her mouth.

No one ever stares at me, thought Dawn. *No one usually notices me at all. My teacher can't even remember my name.*

And it was true.

Dawn was not an outgoing child. She was timid, bland and nondescript. Slightly on the dumpy side, with a round, pallid face, hair the colour of milky tea and a sprinkling of hairs in each eyebrow, it could not be said that Dawn was very striking to look at. She wore crumpled, baggy clothes and was never without a pair of mushroom-coloured knee socks and battered plimsolls. People always tended to look through her or over her head, but never directly *at* her.

On the rare occasions that Dawn's teacher, Mrs Kitchen, spoke to her most forgettable pupil, she addressed her as 'Deborah' or sometimes 'Denise'. Dawn's protestations fell on deaf ears. Nevertheless, she refused to give up hope that, one day, Mrs Kitchen might actually get her name right.

Dawn drifted through life without anyone giving her a second glance. She did not complain about the situation, but sometimes she felt a bit lonely. With no friends to speak of, apart from Clop who was made of wool and didn't really count, she felt rather left out of things.

One of life's optimists, Dawn found it impossible to be downhearted for very long. She clung to the hope that something exciting was going to happen to her one day – but so far nothing had. She had never won a competition or found so much as a penny lying on the pavement. Even the nit epidemic had passed her by.

From her seat on the wooden bench, Dawn watched the pupils of Rustygate Primary dash and dawdle into the playground. She licked her chocolatey fingers and scrunched up the empty wrapper. Dawn did not usually pop into the newsagent's on her way to school, but after the incident with the green MG she had needed something tasty and comforting to calm her nerves. She had selected a large slab of nutty chocolate, waited at the counter for a couple of minutes until the shop assistant realised she was there, and dropped one pound and eleven pence into his hand. Dawn had hurried to school, eager to eat the chocolate before the bell sounded. As she had trotted along Semolina Road she had kept an eye out for the green sports car which, to her relief, did not reappear.

Dawn had often longed for people to notice her, but now that it had happened she felt uneasy. (She also felt slightly sick, but that was to be expected after gulping down an enormous bar of chocolate.) She squinted up at the bright blue sky where the sun was a shimmering, spiky white blob. It was hot already, despite being so early in the day.

I'm lovely and toasty sitting here, thought Dawn, and she glanced at her arms to see if she had the beginnings of a sun tan.

'Oh!' she said, trembling with excitement at the unusual spectacle of three ladybirds lined up beside a freckle on her wrist. 'Look at that! *It must be a portent.*'

Dawn was familiar with portents because Mrs Kitchen regularly interrupted her lessons to point them out. A stray dog in the playground meant that something dreadful was going to happen, glue spilled in the shape of an earwig forecast the onset of bad weather and the sight of an OFSTED inspector with a clipboard heralded the arrival of one of Mrs Kitchen's splitting headaches. Whereas her teacher's portents were always bad, Dawn had no doubt that her little trio of ladybirds was a *good* omen. *Maybe*, she thought, *just maybe …*

The school bell rang and Dawn got up from the bench, grabbed her satchel and went to join the others queuing up in their classes in front of the school building. *I always hoped it would and now it is*, Dawn told herself. She ignored the pain in her toe inflicted by one of Paul Evans's size five trainers. Dawn felt almost giddy with happiness. *Something … with a capital 'S'*, she thought (*drawn with brand new black felt-tip, coloured in purple and sprinkled with glitter …*), *is about to happen to me!*

While Dawn's classmates jostled each other and fidgeted, she stood stock-still, as if her plimsolls had been bonded to the tarmac. Every few seconds, past a line of bobbing heads, Dawn glimpsed the double doors through which the rest of the school had filed five minutes ago. The only class left in the playground was Mrs Kitchen's.

Dawn was well practised in the art of waiting. In a queue, she was usually to be found at the tail end, and she did not mind a bit. Being patient came as naturally to Dawn as breathing in and out.

In front of her, bags were wielded as weapons, scabs were picked and plaits were pulled, but Dawn stood statue-like, with only a slight, uncharacteristic trembling in the region of her knees, caused by her expectation that Something was going to happen. The class waited for Mrs Kitchen to appear through the double doors.

Only she didn't.

An instantaneous hush fell upon them as a stranger with a long, blonde ponytail breezed through the doors and halted at the head of the queue.

'My name is Miss Cambridge,' said the young woman brightly. 'I'm afraid your regular teacher, Mrs Kitchen, is incapacitated.'

'Huh?' said Paul Evans. 'What's that mean?'

'Has something *horrible* happened to her?' said his twin Gavin hopefully.

Ah, thought Dawn (her vocabulary being slightly wider than theirs). *Our teacher is ill. That's all.*

Miss Cambridge smiled indulgently at the twins and her azure-blue eyes sparkled. 'So, I'll be taking your lessons today.'

'Cor!' said Paul and Gavin together.

'If you'd like to follow me.' Miss Cambridge turned and walked briskly towards the double doors and the class trailed obediently behind her.

Only Dawn noticed the distant familiar figure of Mrs Kitchen in her lemon crocheted cardigan walking rather buoyantly in the direction of the teachers' car park, tossing her keys in the air with unmistakable abandon.

Strange, thought Dawn and her knees trembled so

violently that her mushroom-coloured socks slithered down her calves and draped themselves around her ankles.

Registration was uneventful and, to Dawn's immense disappointment, the rest of the morning progressed much like any other. For one heart-stopping moment, she thought that she might have achieved ten out of ten in her spelling test, but leaving out the second 'a' in 'parliament' proved costly. Had she attained the maximum mark she would have been awarded her second house point of the year. And that, thought Dawn, would have qualified as being quite exciting.

The afternoon was just as ordinary. She did not even come close to scoring a goal in netball – but that was not really surprising as she spent most of the lesson sitting on the substitutes' bench next to Butterfingers Burton. Apart from someone asking to borrow her pencil sharpener in maths, which, on any other day, would have thrilled her beyond measure – absolutely nothing happened.

Not that the day was *dull*, exactly. Miss Cambridge was friendly and unflappable and her style of teaching made a pleasant change from that of Mrs Kitchen, who often looked bored and could be very irritable on Mondays. For a supply teacher, Miss Cambridge seemed extremely interested in her pupils. She asked them lots of questions, and every now and then scribbled something in a small notebook. Naturally, she ignored Dawn's hand whenever it shot up in the air.

By the time the afternoon bell rang, announcing that school was over for the day, Dawn's faith in her portent had dwindled somewhat. However, her belief that something momentous would happen was still strong enough to give her a spring in her step on her way home and, consequently, she arrived outside her house four minutes earlier than usual.

Number eight, Windmill View, was an unremarkable semi-detached house with peeling yellow paintwork and a large, dented dustbin as the centrepiece in its tiny front garden. Dawn felt a rush of love towards its pebbledashed walls as she unlatched the front gate. She had lived in the house ever since she could remember and she knew every brick, crack and damp patch.

'Hello-o!' said Dawn as she unlocked the front door. As usual, she made it over the door mat without anyone responding to her call. Still clasping her door key in her hand, Dawn trod quietly into the hallway and ventured into the living room, which was in its usual state of complete darkness, apart from the eerie greenish glow coming from the television set in the corner.

'Hi, Gramps,' said Dawn, accidentally snagging the curtains with her satchel and letting a glimmer of daylight into the room.

'Huh? Whassat? Oh, it's you,' said Ivor Buckle,

transfixed by the television programme he was watching. He produced a handkerchief and blew his nose without releasing his hold on the remote control. 'There's a mighty big jackpot up for grabs today, Dawnie.'

Dawn glanced at the screen and saw a quiz-show host barking a question at a worried-looking contestant.

'He doesn't know,' said Ivor, leaning forward in his armchair. There was a crackle of static as his unruly eyebrows touched the screen. 'Hasn't got a clue,' he said, thumping the cushion on his lap, his face turning purplish. 'Have you ever seen such a numbskull? The answer's flamin' obvious!'

Dawn squeezed past her grandfather's armchair. Peering carefully in the gloom, she managed to avoid a biscuit tin and two empty bottles of ginger beer which were lying on the carpet.

'Like a cup of tea, Gramps?' asked Dawn as she pushed open the door to the kitchen. The venetian blinds sliced the afternoon sunlight into strips which made a pleasing pattern on the bare white walls. Dawn dumped her satchel on the floor and filled the kettle.

'Cocoa, Gramps?' she said.

'I KNEW IT!' roared her grandfather's voice from the other room. 'HE PLUMPED FOR THE WRONG ANSWER. The dozy great nit. Could have walked away with thousands – an' all he won was a year's

18

supply o' shoe polish.'

'What about a snack?' said Dawn, slotting two slices of bread into the toaster. 'Gramps?'

Receiving no reply, Dawn returned to the living room. She thought for a moment and then said very slowly, 'Gramps – if you felt the need for some refreshment, would you prefer a) a cup of tea b) a mug of cocoa c) a boiled egg and soldiers or d) a custard tart?'

'"D",' announced Ivor instantly, turning to face Dawn. He adjusted his black beret so that it flopped rakishly over one ear. 'I'm tempted by "c", but I think I'll stick with my first answer. Yes, "d". I'll have "d". He cleared his throat and smiled. 'Thank you, Dawnie.'

Dawn's grandfather turned up the volume on the television as a muffled chiming sound throbbed in the air. Then a melodious tinkle started, accompanied by a booming clang moments later. The floor began to vibrate as an orchestra of noises filled the house.

'Blimey! Half past four? Is it that time already?' said Dawn's grandfather, hurriedly switching channels. 'Phew,' he said, settling back in his armchair to watch another quiz programme. 'Nearly missed the openin' titles. That was close.'

After depositing a custard tart in her grandfather's left hand (he ate it in two bites), Dawn busied herself in the kitchen. She made scrambled eggs with a dash of mustard and a sprinkling of Cheddar cheese, tipped the mixture on to two slices of toast and added a sprig of parsley. Then she poured a glass of banana milk, spooned a large helping of chocolate blancmange into a bowl and placed her culinary creation on to a tray. Washing up took only a couple of minutes because Dawn was something of an expert at it. Steam was still rising from her scrambled eggs when she slung her satchel over her shoulder, picked up her tray and crossed the linoleum floor. Dawn paused by the kitchen door to check that she had not left a mess, but there was not so much as a crumb on the work surface to show that she had been there. Squinting in the dim, flickering light that emanated from the television set, she successfully navigated the living room and entered the hall.

Just as she was about to climb the stairs to her bedroom, Dawn heard a muffled chinking noise. She took a few paces backwards and rested her tray on a little oval table beneath some coat-hooks in the hallway. Then she opened a door to her left and padded down a flight of stone steps, pausing when she reached halfway.

The cellar was a vast, cool room with naked brick walls and several threadbare carpets covering its concrete floor – and it was filled to capacity with clocks. Everywhere that Dawn's gaze fell, there were shelves full of mantel clocks, walls covered with cuckoo clocks, tabletops loaded with carriage clocks, rows of stately grandfather clocks and display cases bulging with pocket watches. Dawn's father, Jefferson Buckle, was seated at a workbench tapping at a metal disc with a small hammer. It was this chinking sound that she had heard from the hall.

'I'm home, Dad!' called Dawn, but he did not seem to hear her. She supposed that her voice must have been drowned out by the clamorous ticking of his enormous clock collection. She hurried down the final few steps and made her way across the cellar floor, passing a kitchen dresser with its open drawers stuffed with assorted clock parts. She kept her distance from a wall of cuckoo clocks because their doors were likely to burst open at any moment, it being almost five o'clock.

'Hi, Dad,' said Dawn, stopping beside his work-bench. 'I didn't think you'd be home yet. I thought you were checking out antique shops today.'

'What?' said Jefferson. He looked up at the wrong moment and bashed his thumb with the hammer by mistake. 'Ow! Dang it. Oh, it's you, Dawn. Did you want something?'

'Not really.'

'I'm quite busy,' said her father, running his grimy hands through his ash-blond hair until it was slick and greasy-looking. 'Sorry, what was it you wanted?'

'Nothing,' said Dawn. 'Is that a new one?' She pointed to a little carriage clock on his workbench.

'She's a beauty, isn't she?' Dawn's father lifted up the

clock and stroked its rosewood case lovingly. 'What a stunner, eh? Picked her up from a funny little junk shop over in Bow. Only cost me fifty quid. She's got a twin chain fusée movement. Haven't got her to work yet – but I'll soon find out what makes her tick.' He laughed heartily at his own joke. Dawn laughed too – even though she had heard the joke umpteen times before.

A tortoiseshell clock on a nearby table began to make an ominous whirring sound. Dawn placed her hands over her ears. The clocks were about to strike the hour.

Through her slightly splayed fingers, Dawn heard a new noise. It was a heavy crash and it came from upstairs. After a moment's hesitation, she said, 'See you later, Dad,' and lolloped up the cellar steps as fast as she could manage. As she reached the top step, she heard a loud boom as the first grandfather clock began to strike.

Before the other clocks could follow suit, Dawn's mother, Beverley, yanked Dawn into the hallway with one hand and slammed the door of the cellar with the other.

'THAT infernal hullabaloo is the LAST thing I want to hear when I walk in the front door, especially after the HELLISH day at work that I'VE just had.' She let out a strangled yell, before smiling apologetically at Dawn. 'Nice day at school, dear?'

Dawn opened her mouth to reply but her mother did not give her time to answer. 'NEVER grow up, Dawn.

Do you hear me? Going to school is paradise – PARADISE – compared with the awful DRUDGERY of paid employment.' Beverley sighed and stared at herself critically in the hall mirror. 'I look a disaster,' she said, repositioning a long auburn curl. 'I spent a fortune on this perm and my hair is just as shaggy and lifeless as it was before.' Dawn's mother blinked back tears. 'And my face! It looks like a deflated balloon. At this rate, I'll need a facelift before I'm forty.'

'No you won't,' said Dawn. 'That's rubbish, that is. A good night's sleep would get rid of those bags under your eyes, and with a bit of make-up, you'd look just as glamorous as those newsreaders on the telly.'

'Oh, darling, how sweet of you!'

'I'm only saying what's true –'

'You've made Mummy a lovely tea. I suppose I can sneak a few bites while I catch up with some paperwork. How thoughtful. Thank you, darling.'

Dawn stood, aghast, as her mother balanced the tray of scrambled eggs and chocolate blancmange on one hand and disappeared into her study.

'Oh,' said Dawn. 'Er … you're welcome.'

Dawn used her patchwork quilt as a tablecloth. She draped it over an old tea chest which contained her modest collection of toys, and set her tray on top of it. Then she pulled up a big furry cushion and seized a knife and fork. The omelette she had made had a perfect golden underside and was crammed with potato wedges, diced peppers and a finely chopped onion. It tasted delicious and had only taken twenty minutes to make.

'Yum. Much nicer than scrambled eggs,' said Dawn with her mouth full.

Once she had finished her meal (there was only a scraping of blancmange left so she had opened a tin of rice pudding instead), Dawn unlaced her plimsolls and sat on her small, creaky bed. Usually after school, she read a book or studied for a spelling test or dreamed about having a long, elegant name like Cassandra or Jocasta or Persephone – but on this particular day, she did none of these things. Instead, she wondered who had stared at her that morning while she was crossing the road, and more importantly, *why*.

Dawn was accustomed to being ignored by strangers. People she knew barely spoke to her and even her own parents did not pay her much attention. Her grandfather was the person with whom she had the closest relationship. They had had a long, involved conversation once (during a power cut) and had developed quite a bond. However, in recent weeks, owing to his new obsession with quiz programmes, Dawn's grandfather tended to speak to her only when he wanted to impart a bizarre nugget of knowledge.

Dawn clasped her knees and stared at the forget-me-not motifs on her faded wallpaper. She was deep in thought. For perhaps the first time in her life, she had attracted the interest of a perfect stranger, and she found this amazing event most intriguing. It was *almost* as wondrous as her portent.

Something seemed to click into place in Dawn's brain and she breathed in sharply. Could the two incidents possibly be connected?

The gentle growl of a car engine reached Dawn's ears through an open window in her bedroom. She slid off the bed, idly pulled up her mushroom-coloured knee socks, leaned against the windowsill and looked out on to the street.

Dawn gave the loudest gasp of her entire life. There was a dark green sports car parked outside. Two seconds later, the doorbell rang.

'I knew it!' said Dawn. 'My portent was right. *Something*'s about to happen!'

Chapter Two

Something With a Capital 'S'

Sitting on the top stair, with her head resting against the balusters, Dawn listened. She heard mumbling voices and footsteps in the hallway. Doors opened and closed. Bursting with curiosity, Dawn stood up and trod softly down the stairs in her socks. When she reached the hallway, the door to the living room gave a click and conveniently swung open a fraction. Dawn managed to distinguish the odd word or two from the room beyond.

'Turn the volume down? Are you *mad*?' *That was Gramps*, thought Dawn.

'I don't care WHO you say you are. I'm up to my EYELASHES in paperwork.' *Mum's voice undoubtedly*.

''S got a twin chain fusée movement. Hang on a minute, I'll fetch it.' *That was Dad*.

A moment later, Jefferson Buckle emerged from the living room, a broad smile on his face. He brushed past Dawn's shoulder without a word, crossed the hall and vanished down the cellar steps. Dawn felt a shiver of excitement when a strangely familiar female voice drifted into the hallway.

'Perhaps we might ask your daughter what she thinks.'

'What? Oh ... very *well*,' said Dawn's mother in disgruntled tones. She appeared in the doorway, took a deep breath and cupped one hand around her mouth. 'DAWN!' she shouted in the direction of the stairs. 'COME HERE A MINUTE!'

'I *am* here, Mum,' said Dawn from a couple of paces away.

'DAWN ... GET YOUR SKATES ON!'

Dawn stretched out one arm and tugged gently on her mother's sleeve. 'I'm right here,' she said placidly.

The sight of a ten-foot cockroach would not have caused Beverley to jump any higher in the air. At the same time, she let out an ear-splitting shriek.

'Must you always skulk about?' she hissed, when she had recovered her composure.

'Sorry,' said Dawn.

Beverley grabbed her daughter's elbow. 'We've got a visitor,' she said, 'and she wants to speak to *you*.' Dawn noticed that her mother looked rather bewildered.

With the curtains pulled back, the living room looked like the perfect place for a dust-mite convention: the carpet was speckled with biscuit crumbs and a towering heap of TV listings magazines took up two seat cushions on the sofa.

Ivor Buckle was slumped in his armchair with a grumpy expression on his face. He was desperately trying to read the lips of the quiz-master on the television. Dawn's mother must have wrested the remote control from his grasp and hit the mute button. Its lower half could be seen protruding from underneath her arm.

'Here she is,' said Beverley, steering Dawn towards a young woman standing by the fireplace. Dawn blinked. Although she had changed her appearance markedly, the woman was instantly recognisable.

'Hello, Miss Cambridge,' said Dawn.

'Call me Emma,' said Dawn's supply teacher, smiling kindly. 'So nice to see you again, Dawn.' Her handshake was firm and businesslike. Dressed in a stylish linen trouser suit and black, open-necked shirt instead of the buttercup-yellow shift dress she had worn earlier in the day, Emma looked less like a teacher and more like a highly paid lawyer. Her girlish ponytail had been replaced with a tightly braided French plait, and her new, officious look was enhanced by the smart tan briefcase which she carried in one hand.

'Is that your sports car parked outside?' asked Dawn.

'It is,' said Emma, her blue eyes glinting.

Aha! thought Dawn. *That settles it. So, Miss Cambridge – I mean, Emma – was the one who stared at me while I was crossing the road. But if she found me so interesting, why did she ignore me when she taught my class? And what is she doing here now?*

Dawn was puzzled. She had not behaved badly at school, nor had she shown any signs of being super-intelligent. What other reasons could a teacher have for visiting one of her pupils at home? Her mouth sagged open in wonderment.

'Don't gape, Dawn,' said her mother irritably. 'Now, pay attention. Miss Cambridge wishes to ask you a few questions –'

'Me?' said Dawn eagerly.

'Don't interrupt,' snapped Beverley. 'Apparently, she's been looking for someone with your ... er ... natural talent. Miss Cambridge works for S.H.H. –'

'I didn't say anything,' protested Dawn.

'No. I mean she's from *S.H.H.*,' said Dawn's mother.

'S.H.H. is an organisation, Dawn,' said Emma patiently. 'S.H.H. stands for Strictly Hush-Hush.'

'Oh,' said Dawn.

'Here's my little beauty.' Dawn's father bounded into the room. He held his newly purchased carriage clock in the crook of his arm. 'What do you think then, eh, Miss Oxford?' He thrust it under Emma's nose. 'Just look at that gilded dial!'

'It's Miss *Cambridge*, Jeff,' hissed Dawn's mother, 'and she's not interested in your *stupid* clock.'

'It's exquisite,' said Emma with a glowing smile, 'and

29

it reminds me, Mr Buckle, that I really shouldn't take up much more of your family's precious time – but if I could just have a few words with Dawn ...'

'Oh, of course,' said Jefferson happily. He began to clear the sofa of magazines. 'Sit here, Miss ... er ... er ...'

Emma sat down, patted the seat next to her and raised her eyebrows at Dawn.

'Five minutes,' said Beverley sternly as Dawn settled herself on the sofa. 'I've got an awful lot of work to get through this evening.'

'Well, Dawn, I suppose you're wondering what this is all about,' said Emma, resting her briefcase on the floor.

Dawn nodded. She was smiling so much that her jaw was beginning to ache. Never before had she felt so excited. Somebody actually wanted to *talk* to her – and the conversation might possibly last for a whole five minutes.

'Strictly Hush-Hush is just what it sounds like,' continued Emma pleasantly. 'It's a secret intelligence organisation. I belong to a department called P.S.S.T., which stands for Pursuit of Scheming Spies and Traitors –'

'You've got four minutes left,' said Dawn's mother from the middle of the room, where she stood stiffly with her arms folded and her lips pressed together.

'Thank you, Mrs Buckle,' said Emma politely. Her startlingly blue eyes refocused on Dawn. 'I'm a recruitment officer. I'm in charge of finding people who would be willing to work for our organisation.'

'I thought you were a supply teacher,' said Dawn, feeling quite confused.

'Ah,' said Emma, biting her lip. 'No, I'm not. I may have given that *impression*. Your headmaster allowed me to borrow one of his classes for the day – only after I'd shown him my P.S.S.T. identity card, of course. I've been scouring the schools in every London borough for the past two weeks.'

'Why?' asked Dawn.

'Just following instructions,' said Emma. 'The Head of P.S.S.T. asked me to find a very special type of child to help him solve a particular puzzle – and, well, I think I've found her.'

Crikey! thought Dawn. *I think she means me.*

'What do you say, Dawn?' said Emma softly. 'Would you like to join the team at P.S.S.T.? It would only be for a few weeks, and the summer holidays begin in a matter of days, don't they?'

'This Friday,' said Dawn.

'So you wouldn't miss much school …'

Dawn listened numbly. It was a very glamorous thing to be taken out of school before the end of the summer term. Permission seemed to be granted by Dawn's headteacher, Mr Rolls, only if the pupil was going on holiday to somewhere that was difficult to spell – like Reykjavic or Albuquerque. The Buckle family always spent their holidays in Gosport. Emma's offer could be the only chance Dawn would ever get to finish the school year a few days early.

'I have to tell you, Dawn,' said Emma gravely, 'this job that my boss would like you to do … it's not without a certain element of *risk*.'

Dawn's heart began to thump very fast.

'Of course,' said Emma, 'I have the utmost confidence that you'll be able to cope with … with any *obstacles* that might arise.' She gazed admiringly at Dawn. 'I can honestly say that I've never come across anyone with so much *potential*. Your talent is quite staggering, Dawn. You have a very special gift.'

'Er … er … two minutes and twenty seconds,' said Dawn's mother, whose face had turned quite pale.

'Finest set of bun feet I've ever seen,' murmured Dawn's father, perching next to his daughter on the armrest of the sofa. He seemed to be mesmerised by the carriage clock in the palm of his hand.

POTENTIAL. TALENT. VERY SPECIAL GIFT. Dawn blinked rapidly. Emma's words resounded in her ears louder than a cellarful of clocks. *I didn't know that I'd got any of those things*, thought Dawn. *Nobody's ever mentioned them before.*

'What do you say, Dawn? Would you like to join the team at P.S.S.T.?'

'Um …' Dawn paused. She was not used to making momentous decisions. *And this one's a biggie, all right*, Dawn told herself. She would never have imagined that a few ladybirds could have predicted such a thrilling opportunity. A few hours ago she had dared to hope that she might win a second house point. Now, here she was, on the verge of joining a secret intelligence organisation.

Dawn was so excited she could barely breathe; she was frightened, too – but it was a delicious type of fear that made her tingle all over.

'Yes!' she said. 'My answer's yes!'

'That's splendid,' said Emma warmly. She lifted her briefcase on to her knees and delved inside it, producing a sheet of thick mauve paper with 'P.S.S.T.' printed in gold between two heraldic unicorns. Beneath the initials were several paragraphs typed in black ink. There were three dotted lines on the bottom of the page.

Emma handed the sheet to Beverley, who said, 'Less than one minute,' in an uncertain voice. Slipping an identical sheet from the briefcase, Emma reached past Dawn and gave it to Jefferson to read.

'We've drawn up a special contract,' said Emma briskly. 'We'd love to accept Dawn into our organisation but, of course, we wouldn't *dream* of taking her without your permission.'

Holding the sheet of mauve paper at arm's length,

and frowning at it as if it were an annoying insert that had fallen from one of the TV magazines, Dawn's mother scanned the contract. As her eyes darted down the page, her expression relaxed.

'Hmm,' she said when she had finished reading. A smile sneaked across her face and was quickly suppressed. 'So Dawn would be out from under my feet ... I mean she'd be *taken care of* for the whole of the summer holidays?'

'P.S.S.T. may not require Dawn's services for the entire duration –' began Emma.

'Oh.' Dawn's mother seemed disappointed.

'But I'm afraid it's a possibility.' Emma rose to her feet and touched Beverley's shoulder tenderly. 'I understand how you're feeling. Naturally, you're concerned about being parted from your child for such a long time ...'

'Yes, naturally,' said Dawn's mother.

'I can assure you that Dawn will be well looked after,' continued Emma. 'As P.S.S.T.'s recruitment officer, I'm personally responsible for the welfare of all our employees. I'll do my best to keep a very close eye on your daughter.'

'You're sure,' said Beverley accusingly, 'you're absolutely POSITIVE that you've got the right person? I mean, this contract mentions ESPIONAGE and SLEUTHING.' She shook the sheet of paper so that it made a curious whup-whup noise. 'They don't teach Dawn THOSE kinds of subjects at Rustygate Primary. Well, not as far as I'm aware. I haven't had time to acquaint myself with the latest version of the National Curriculum. I'm RATHER a busy person, you see.' Beverley's face reddened. 'I don't want you getting my hopes up … only to dash them cruelly … Oh!' She hesitated and gave a nervous titter. '*Dawn's* hopes, I mean …'

'You mustn't worry, said Emma in reassuring tones. 'Your daughter fits the job description perfectly, Mrs Buckle.'

'Woo!' exclaimed Dawn's father. He whistled through his teeth and stared, bug-eyed, at his copy of the contract. 'Bev!' He looked up briefly at his wife. 'Cop a load of clause twelve! They're going to pay our kid a *wage*.'

'Don't get excited, Jeff,' cautioned his wife. 'If you read a bit further I think you'll find that it hardly amounts to a fortune.'

Jefferson's face sagged when he realised that his wife was right. 'Is that *all*?' he said, pressing his finger against the contract. 'That's peanuts, that is. Still,' he said, shrugging, 'it'd be enough for a pocket watch and a couple of nice pendulums.'

'I believe my five minutes are up,' said Emma, glancing at her watch. She smiled radiantly at Dawn's parents. 'May I ask if you've reached a decision?'

'I'm in two minds,' said Dawn's mother. 'I'll have to think …'

'What's to think about? Got a pen?' said Dawn's father, staring expectantly at Emma. In 0.03 seconds, she produced a gold-plated fountain pen and Jefferson rushed towards it, almost losing his balance on the slippery heap of magazines which he had dumped on the carpet. He snatched the fountain pen, pressed his carriage clock into Emma's hands with the words, 'Hold this a mo,' and scribbled on one of the dotted lines at the bottom of the contract.

'If you'd be kind enough to sign the other copy as well, please,' said Emma sweetly. Dawn's father nodded and plucked the second contract from his wife's grasp.

'My pleasure,' he said, signing his name with a flourish.

'Mrs Buckle?' prompted Emma delicately.

'Yeah, how about it, Bev?' Dawn's father waggled the pen in front of his wife's nose. 'We'll be a few quid richer … and this nice lady will see that Dawn's all right.'

'Well … I don't know … it's a bit *irregular*, Jeff.' Dawn's mother seemed flustered. She dragged her fingers through her wavy auburn hair and shot a guilty look at Dawn. 'But perhaps it *would* be for the best.' She turned to Emma with a pained expression on her face. 'The school holidays always pose a problem. Having your child at home all day can be very … inconvenient when

36

you're as busy as I am. Work commitments … you know … appraisals, reports, meetings coming out of my *ears* …'

'Yes,' said Emma, nodding fervently. 'It must be very difficult.'

'It would be a load off my mind,' said Beverley, her fingers reaching for the fountain pen, 'if I didn't have to worry about Dawn day in day out.' She took the two mauve sheets of paper from her husband and, leaning them against her thigh, added her signature twice.

'Super,' murmured Emma.

Dawn watched the proceedings from the sofa. There was a curious buzzing in her ears and she felt light-headed. She stared at the three adults as they passed pieces of paper back and forth. Finally, Emma signed the contracts swiftly on the third dotted line before sliding one sheet of mauve paper into her briefcase and presenting Beverley with the other.

'We each have a copy of the contract now,' said Emma.

'So – it's all sorted!' Jefferson nudged his wife and grinned.

''Bout time,' bellowed Dawn's grandfather from his armchair. 'I'll 'ave the remote control back now, thank you very much.'

A vibration in the floorboards told Dawn that it was

midnight. She stopped pacing around her tiny bedroom and lifted an ear-muff (essential headgear for a Buckle who wanted an undisturbed night's sleep). When the last stifled bong had died away, Dawn continued to walk restlessly from wall to wall in her bare feet. A moment later, she stubbed her toe on a carelessly positioned suitcase and, clutching her injured foot, she sank on to her bed. A spring in the mattress twanged in a consoling sort of way. Dawn patted her patchwork quilt fondly and blinked back tears.

This is going to be the last night that I'll spend in my own little bedroom for quite some time, thought Dawn sadly. She drew her knees up to her chin and stretched her nightdress over them so that the sleepy owl motif on its front became strangely elongated.

Emma had promised to arrive just after breakfast the next morning, which meant that Dawn would be leaving Windmill View in less than eight hours. She knew that it was important to get some sleep, but her body was obstinately refusing to settle down for the night. Her heart was pounding, her arms and legs would not stay still and a hundred thoughts were zipping around in her brain. Dawn switched off her bedside lamp and everything in front of her eyes was reduced to a shade of grey as moonlight flooded the room. She groped around for Clop – who was a rather grubby, knitted donkey – and held him close. When he made a peculiar crinkling noise, Dawn realised that she was also hugging her packing list.

It had taken her no more than an hour to pack her red suitcase. She had filled it with several pairs of underwear, every single mushroom-coloured knee sock that she owned, a kilt in Black Watch tartan, a corduroy skirt, two short-sleeved blouses, a pair of cotton pyjamas, a cardigan, washing things, a book entitled *Pansy the Goat Girl* by Jean Hightower and a battered geometry set. Dawn had purposely left a small space in the suitcase, which Clop had already tried out for size.

Dawn sat up, adjusted her ear-muffs and sank back on to her pillow. She tugged her patchwork quilt up to her armpits and stared at the shadowy swirls in the Artex ceiling.

'What do you think, Clop?' she said anxiously. 'Am I doing the right thing?'

Clop seemed to give a positive response and inferred that, perhaps, Dawn would like to lean a little less heavily on his rump.

Dawn blinked sleepily. *It's an adventure,* she told herself. *I'm going to have an adventure like that girl, Pansy, in the book I'm reading. Only I don't expect that my adventure will involve goats. Although it might be nice if it did.*

Chapter Three
The House in Pimlico

'Shall I or shan't I?' Dawn asked Clop.

She looked him in the eye, which was just a couple of stitches, and gave a knitted ear an affectionate squeeze. Dawn detected a look of weary annoyance on her donkey's face as she removed him from her suitcase for the seventh time in as many minutes. *It's so difficult being eleven*, thought Dawn, and she sighed heavily.

'I'm on the cusp of womanhood, you know,' she told Clop. His blank expression seemed to suggest that he did know, actually, but he wasn't particularly interested. *Am I too old to take my favourite toy with me?* Dawn asked herself. Something told her that the people at P.S.S.T. would be less than impressed. 'But I'd like you to come,' said Dawn. 'It would be comforting to have a friendly face around.' It struck Dawn that Clop did not look very friendly at that moment but, nevertheless, she squashed him next to a pair of mushroom-coloured socks and closed the suitcase lid.

A few minutes later there was a knock on her bedroom door.

'Oh,' said Dawn, who had just reopened her suitcase and was holding Clop around his middle. She threw him quickly into the case and he collapsed on to her sock collection. 'Er … come in,' said Dawn shyly.

'Mornin', Dawnie,' said her grandfather, tugging politely on his black beret as he shuffled into the room. He had tucked his pyjama top into a pair of grey flannel trousers.

'Gramps!' said Dawn. She felt highly honoured. Her grandfather rarely made a trip upstairs.

'Came to wish you luck,' he said, scratching an overgrown eyebrow. 'It's nearly eight o'clock, Dawnie. Miss Whatsername'll be here in two ticks.'

'I know,' said Dawn. Her stomach gave a terrific lurch.

'You've packed an' everythin', I see.'

'Mmm,' said Dawn, patting her suitcase. She attempted a brave smile but could not prevent her chin from trembling.

'Now, now, none o' that,' said Ivor kindly. 'You'll be just fine.'

Dawn said nothing. She felt dismayed. Her excitement seemed to have fizzled away and, suddenly, she found that she did not want to leave. Kneeling beside her suitcase, she closed its lid and began to fumble with the straps.

'All right, Dawnie ... listen up.' Her grandfather raised a knobbly finger. 'There's a few gems o' knowledge that I learned off the telly, yes'erday ...'

Dawn listened patiently as her grandfather informed her that the capital of Guam was Hagatna, an ocelot was a type of wildcat, William Shakespeare wrote thirty-eight plays and pteronophobia (spelt with a silent 'p') was the fear of being tickled with feathers.

'Mind you don't forget none o' them facts,' said Dawn's grandfather sternly. 'You never know when they might come in useful.'

'OK, Gramps,' said Dawn.

Through her open bedroom window Dawn heard the chink of a drain cover and the low purr of an engine as a car pulled up outside. She dashed to the window just as the clocks in the cellar began to strike the hour. The MG Midget's soft roof had been folded down and Dawn saw Emma Cambridge switch off the ignition and remove her sunglasses before stepping out of the car.

'Time to go, Dawnie?' said her grandfather.

Dawn nodded, a lump in her throat preventing her from speaking. She put on her plimsolls, tying them carefully in a double knot, and picked up her small suitcase.

'You'll be a'right,' said her grandfather as they made their way downstairs. 'Be a nice 'oliday for you.' He patted her shoulder. 'It'll beat a week in that grotty ol' guest house in Gosport, anyway.'

Emma was waiting in the hall, politely declining Jefferson's invitation to inspect his clocks in the cellar. 'Ah,' she said when she caught sight of Dawn lingering on the bottom stair. 'Here you are!' She smiled warmly. 'Would you like me to stow your luggage in my car while you say your goodbyes?'

'Thanks,' said Dawn as Emma relieved her of her suitcase.

'Bev-er-LEEE!' yelled Dawn's father.

Somewhere in the house a door slammed. Dawn's mother appeared a few seconds later, dressed in a smart business suit and sipping a mug of coffee. She was just in time to receive a handshake and a word of thanks from Emma before the young woman disappeared through the front door with Dawn's suitcase.

Three pairs of eyes focused on Dawn. She felt a little uncomfortable.

'See ya, kid,' said Dawn's father.

'Behave yourself,' said Dawn's mother. She pecked her daughter anxiously on the cheek.

'Wha's the capital o' Guam?' said Dawn's grand-father.

'Hagatna,' replied Dawn.

'Tha's my girl!'

'Bye, house,' said Dawn, looking over her shoulder as

the MG sped away from number eight, Windmill View. 'Bye, dustbin. Bye, lamppost. Bye, tree.'

Emma crossed her hands on the leather steering wheel and took a right turn into an adjoining street.

'Bye, road,' said Dawn forlornly as she lost sight of number eight's chimney pot.

'You'd need an *awfully* high-powered telescope to get a view of a windmill around here. Don't you think so, Dawn?' said Emma light-heartedly.

'Yes,' said Dawn. She was quite fond of her road's name but she had to admit that it was not very appropriate. Windmills were rather scarce in Hackney.

As they cruised along familiar streets, Dawn found herself pointing out places of interest. She drew Emma's attention to the loose paving slab which everyone seemed to trip over, the starlings' nest above the launderette, and the only roof in the whole borough without a television aerial. Instead of ignoring Dawn's commentary, as most people would have been inclined to do, Emma acted as if she were enthralled, murmuring '*Wow!*' and '*Really?*' whenever her passenger paused for breath. Dawn was delighted to be listened to for a change, and it made her feel a bit less sad about leaving her home behind.

In a matter of minutes they had driven through Hackney, and Dawn stared in fascination as they passed through streets that she did not recognise. The scenery changed gradually; noisy roadworks, shopping parades and grimy pavements heaped with plastic sacks became grand palatial buildings and leafy parks.

Dawn caught sight of her reflection in a wing mirror, and grinned. Her hair was leaping and wriggling around her face. She had never ridden in a convertible car before and she found the constant blast of air exhilarating. She wondered what other new experiences lay in store for her. Emma had volunteered very little information about P.S.S.T. so far. Curious as to what kind of work she would be expected to do, Dawn decided to ask Emma a few questions.

'What do the letters in P.S.S.T. mean, again?'

'Pursuit of Scheming Spies and Traitors,' answered Emma, pressing a finger on the bridge of her sunglasses and sliding them to the top of her nose.

'Scheming Spies and Traitors?' said Dawn apprehensively. They didn't sound very pleasant. She supposed that pursuing them would involve a certain amount of running. Dawn wasn't very good at running. On school sports day she was frequently the last child over the finish line.

'There's no need to worry, Dawn,' said Emma, taking a sidelong glance at her charge. 'You'll receive plenty of training beforehand ... Not that you'll need many hours of instruction – you're a natural.'

'A natural what?' said Dawn.

Emma's coral-pink lips formed an amused smile. 'A natural *spy*,' she said.

'Me? A ... a spy?' Dawn was amazed.

'You were born to the profession,' Emma assured her. 'You possess all the basic skills and attributes.'

'Do I?' said Dawn, completely clueless as to what they were.

'Let me explain,' said Emma as she guided the car along a wide, tree-lined avenue. 'You've got one of those special faces that are instantly forgettable.'

The remark was spoken in an admiring manner, as if it were a compliment, so that Dawn's feelings were only *slightly* hurt.

'You have a slow, ponderous gait,' continued Emma, 'that enables you to wander anywhere you please without being detected; you've got what we call a quirky eye ...'

Emma must have noticed Dawn's swift lunge towards the wing mirror to ascertain which of her eyes was the quirky one. Immediately, she put Dawn's mind at ease.

'If someone has a quirky eye it means that they are especially *observant*. They spot unusual things that other people tend to miss.' Emma steered the MG smoothly round a corner. 'Remember when we were driving through Hackney earlier and you told me about the starlings' nest and the roof without a television aerial?'

'Yes,' said Dawn.

'Both are examples of things which are in plain sight of everyone. The majority of passers-by would overlook them, but an alert individual like you would see them straight away. With the sort of qualities that you've got, Dawn, you'll *cruise* through your training programme.'

Profoundly shocked by the revelation that she had been selected to become a spy, Dawn slumped against her seat and lost interest in the sights and sounds of London. At the edge of her vision, colours seem to swell and merge, and the roar of the traffic faded to a mild, innocuous drone.

She hadn't really given much thought to the career path she would choose when she was older, but of the occupations which Dawn had considered, 'spy' was definitely not amongst them. She wondered what a spy actually *did*. Quite a bit of skiing, snorkelling and driving rather fast, judging by the James Bond films she had seen. It occurred to Dawn that perhaps she should have brought her roller skates with her.

'Nearly there,' said Emma, drawing to a standstill at a set of traffic lights. Dawn stopped trying to imagine what a spy's typical day might be like, and watched a gaggle of schoolchildren in boaters and blazers cross the road in front of the car. 'Your teacher, Mrs Kitchen, was a dear old lady …' began Emma.

She'd probably give you a clout if you called her that to her face, Dawn thought.

Emma drummed her fingers on the steering wheel and smiled. 'When your headmaster asked her if she'd mind giving up her class for the day, she was only too happy to oblige. Said it would be *her pleasure*.'

I'll bet she did, thought Dawn.

The traffic lights changed to green and the MG continued its journey. Glancing to her left and right, Dawn noticed that the buildings were becoming even more magnificent. They had marble steps, gold doorknockers and porches that looked like they belonged on stately homes. Despite their impressive grandeur, none of the houses looked half as welcoming as her own pebble-dashed semi in Windmill View.

'Where are we now?' asked Dawn.

'Just about to enter Pimlico,' said Emma, driving the sports car over a railway bridge.

The houses in Pimlico remained rather splendid, but they were smaller, plainer and far less imposing. They passed a café with a foreign-sounding name, outside of which were dozens of neat, round tables shaded with large red-and-white umbrellas. Dawn would have liked to stop there for a bite to eat. She had spent so long deciding whether or not to put Clop in her suitcase that she had omitted to have any breakfast.

'Here we are,' said Emma as she turned the car into a quiet road called Vanbrugh Gardens, and parked beside a row of five terraced houses, each three storeys high and built with dark grey brick. Behind a line of shiny black railings were minuscule front yards, filled with troughs and pots overflowing with colourful blooms: golden honeysuckle vied for space with bright pink fuschia, trailing mauve aubretia and red miniature roses.

Emma raised her sunglasses so that they rested on top of her head. She sprang lithely out of the car, unlocked the boot and strode along the pavement with Dawn's suitcase in one hand and her tan briefcase in the other. She passed two houses and paused outside the third, which had a long-haired black cat with white paws sitting on its doorstep. Emma glanced over her shoulder at Dawn, who had not budged from the passenger seat.

'Best foot forward!' she said encouragingly.

Dawn was baffled. She had thought that she was being taken to the headquarters of P.S.S.T., but this tall, narrow house with its old-fashioned sash windows and neat front yard crammed with flowers did not look like the offices of a secret intelligence organisation. She had expected an enormous office building with a barbed wire fence, and maybe two or three ferocious-looking guard dogs. Dawn glanced at the black cat squatting on the sunny doorstep. He did not strike her as being remotely fearsome.

Emma opened the front gate, knocking the stalk of a magnificent sunflower. Its heavy head swung to one side, revealing a sign behind it that read 'Dampside Hotel'. Dawn grinned when she realised her mistake.

Oh, she thought. *I understand. This must be where I'm staying for the next few weeks. We've stopped here to drop off my suitcase, I suppose, before we move on to P.S.S.T.*

Dawn undid her seatbelt, climbed eagerly out of the car and hurried towards the hotel. Emma was waiting for her on the doorstep. She had set down Dawn's suitcase and was stroking the black cat. He rubbed his head against her hand, then flopped on to his side, purring loudly.

Dawn was just about to crouch down and pet the cat when she noticed something in the nearest window. Through tendrils of honeysuckle, she saw a small square card with 'NO VACANCIES' written upon it. They would have to seek accommodation elsewhere. She felt a little disappointed not to be staying in the smart grey-brick house with its colourful flowers and rather appealing furry inhabitant.

Dawn was wondering whether or not to mention the 'NO VACANCIES' sign, when Emma stopped making a fuss of the cat and straightened up. She raised a door-knocker shaped like a lion's head and rapped five times in staccato fashion on the black front door. Almost instantly, the door was opened by an unsmiling woman with deep-set, dark eyes.

'Can I help you?' said the woman.

'I'd like two rooms, please,' said Emma.

'Two?' said the woman sharply. She seemed taken aback. Then her piercing eyes settled on Dawn. 'Oh,' she said, her eyebrows arching. 'Two rooms. Of course.' The woman opened the door wide. 'Step this way.'

'But ... but the sign says ...' blustered Dawn. She was puzzled. Why had the woman offered them two rooms when the card in the window clearly stated that none were available? After a moment's hesitation, Dawn followed the two women and the cat over the threshold.

It took about half a minute for Dawn's eyes to become accustomed to the subdued lighting inside the house. She seemed to have arrived in a reception area. A thin, dark red carpet covered the floor, and the walls were papered in dull gold with a fleur-de-lys design. To Dawn's left was a low mahogany table with a tatty sofa and a couple of armchairs arranged around it. In one of the chairs sat an elderly man who seemed to be wrestling with a copy of the *Financial Times*. Straight ahead was a lift with tarnished gold gates, and to Dawn's right, behind a reception desk, stood the formidable woman who had answered the door.

She was petite and olive-skinned. Her sleek hair was held back neatly with a hair-slide and she wore a black, Chinese-style silk dress with large scarlet flowers printed on it. The woman had the most penetrating pair of eyes that Dawn had ever seen, and just at that moment, she was focusing them on Emma as the two women spoke together in hushed tones.

Dawn decided to join them at the reception desk and the cat accompanied her. As she approached, the dark-eyed woman stopped talking in mid-sentence. Dawn found this unsettling. She wasn't used to people curtailing their conversations when she appeared. They usually rambled on for ages, completely unaware that she had materialised beside them.

'My name is Mrs Oliphant,' said the woman, addressing Dawn, 'and I am the hotel manager. I do hope that you'll have a pleasant stay with us at Dampside.'

'Er ... thanks,' said Dawn politely. Avoiding Mrs Oliphant's gaze, which she found a trifle unnerving, she let her eyes stray to the wall behind the desk. There she saw a row of brass hooks with numbers above them ranging from one to ten. Most of the hooks had large gold keys hanging from them.

'If you'd like to sign in,' said Mrs Oliphant briskly, 'before I give you the keys to your rooms.' She opened a book with a padded leather cover and slid it towards Emma.

On the desk, attached to a chain, was a gold-plated fountain pen, very similar to the one which Emma had produced so speedily in the Buckles' living room. At the top of an empty page, Emma wrote her own name in purple ink before adding Dawn's below it.

'Very good,' said Mrs Oliphant, closing the book with one hand and reaching behind her to pluck two keys from their hooks with the other. Offering Emma the keys, she said, 'Your rooms are on the first floor. I hope you will find everything to your satisfaction. Luncheon will be served between the hours of twelve and two.'

At the mention of a meal, Dawn's stomach gave a noisy growl.

Mrs Oliphant's eyes narrowed. 'Hungry, are you?' she said. 'Didn't you have any breakfast?'

'No,' answered Dawn in a small voice.

'I see.' The woman lifted a little brass bell from the desk and rang it. A high tinkling sound reverberated around the reception area, and a few moments later a young man with an amiable grin and springy ginger hair appeared through a door marked 'STAFF ONLY'. Dawn thought that he looked quite smart, even though his black bow tie was slightly skew-whiff and there were crumbs down the front of his starched white shirt.

'One of our newly arrived guests requires breakfast,' said Mrs Oliphant. 'See to it straight away, please, Nathan.'

'Okey doke,' said the young man cheerfully.

Mrs Oliphant frowned. 'It will need to be delivered upstairs.'

'Right-o,' said Nathan, giving her the thumbs-up.

'*Delivered*,' she repeated with emphasis, '*upstairs*.'

Nathan looked blank for a few seconds. Then his eyes lit up as if he had just realised something. He winked at Mrs Oliphant.

'Gotcha,' he said, before bending down to scoop up the long-haired black cat. 'Come on, Peebles. Work to do.'

Dawn watched Nathan stride away with the cat's disgruntled face peering over his shoulder. She felt excited. Every time that somebody noticed her or listened to what she was saying, Dawn experienced a warm, buzzing sensation in her stomach (quite different from the loud gurgle that told her she was hungry). She wondered what Nathan would prepare for her breakfast. Hoping for sausages, Dawn picked up her suitcase and followed Emma to the antiquated lift.

The gates squeaked as they were opened and closed. Inside the lift, there were two buttons which had 'Ground' and 'First' printed on them. Dawn prodded the button for the first floor and after a slight judder the lift carried its passengers upwards. Dawn was curious as to why there was no button for the second floor. From the outside, the house had appeared to be three storeys high.

The first-floor corridor was windowless and smelt faintly of dried rose petals. Dim lights glowed inside small, fringed lampshades along the walls. The floorboards creaked under the soles of Dawn's plimsolls as she approached a few wooden doors with plastic numbers fixed to them. She wondered which of them would turn out to be her room.

To Dawn's surprise, Emma marched past every single door without attempting to unlock any of them. Instead, she stopped in front of a full-length mirror at the end of the corridor. Dawn was bemused. Emma had not struck her as being a particularly vain sort of person.

'Quickly!' said Emma, beckoning to Dawn.

When she reached the mirror, Dawn stared at her own reflection in bewilderment. Then she glanced across at Emma, expecting to see her preening herself. But she was not. Bizarrely, her gaze seemed to be focused on the empty corridor behind them.

'What are you looking at?' asked Dawn.

'I'm checking to see if the coast is clear,' said Emma. Then she bent her right leg and gave the skirting board a kick.

Ignoring Dawn's appalled expression, Emma reached out and touched the mirror in front of her. To Dawn's amazement, it moved. Emma pressed the mirror a little more firmly and the panel of glass turned on its axis, revealing a set of stairs behind it.

Chapter Four

P.S.S.T.

The cases went first. Neither made much of a thud as they landed on the plush, spongy carpet beyond the mirror. Having tossed their luggage through the slender gap, Emma grabbed hold of Dawn and pushed her past the swivelling mirror and on to a landing which separated two flights of stairs.

Dawn asked to be told what was going on, but Emma stayed tight-lipped until she had returned the double-sided mirror to its original position. Dawn heard a quiet click as the glass fitted into place. The corridor on the first floor was lost from view.

'Sorry to manhandle you like that,' said Emma as she bent down to pick up her briefcase, 'but I didn't want us to be seen by any of the hotel guests. The existence of this staircase has to remain under wraps, you see.'

'Where are we?' said Dawn, looking around her in confusion. The decor was so different on this side of the mirror that Dawn wondered if they had passed into a neighbouring building. The carpet was a deep, midnight blue and the walls were as pale and smooth as butter cream. 'Are we in the house next door?' she said, gazing up at a resplendent chandelier.

'No,' said Emma. 'We're still in the Dampside Hotel – only we've arrived in a part of it that not many people know about. You've just come through a secret entrance, and those stairs over there,' she said, gesturing towards the staircase which climbed upwards, 'will lead you to the headquarters of P.S.S.T.'

Dawn couldn't quite believe her ears. 'You mean P.S.S.T. is *here* in this hotel?'

'Yes. Our offices occupy the whole of the second floor.'

'*Really?*' said Dawn, struggling to accept what Emma was telling her. It seemed most improbable to her that a branch of secret intelligence could be based on the uppermost level of a modest little hotel.

'S.H.H. and its various departments are scattered all over London in unexpected places,' said Emma. 'Each location is a closely guarded secret and the departments can only be accessed by those of us who know where the hidden entrances are to be found.'

Dawn prodded the mirror. Then she leaned her weight against it, but on neither occasion did it swing open.

'How do you make it work?' she said.

'See that nail in the skirting board?' said Emma, pointing to a bump an inch below the mirror. The nail was the size of a cherry pip and had been painted the exact same colour as the strip of wood in which it was set, camouflaging it nicely.

'Er … just about,' said Dawn, squinting at it.

'A good, hard smack on the head of the nail causes the mirror to revolve,' said Emma.

'And is there a nail on the other side of the wall too?' asked Dawn.

'That's right,' Emma said. She checked her watch before stooping to wrap her fingers around the handle of Dawn's suitcase. 'It's almost nine thirty. We'd better step on it, Dawn. The others will be wondering where we've got to.'

Dawn began to follow Emma up the stairs. Then she stopped and leaned over the handrail. It was an awfully long way down to the very bottom step. She wondered if there might be some more hidden entrances on the lower floors of the hotel, seeing as the stairs seemed to reach all the way to the basement. When Dawn raised the subject with Emma, she discovered that she was right.

'There's one in the kitchen,' said Emma. 'A wall in the pantry opens like a door if you know which pot handle to pull down.'

At the top of the stairs was a narrow corridor, its

floor covered in the same lustrous blue carpet. Dawn wandered along the corridor, distracted by a number of doors to her left and right. Each had a brass plate upon it inscribed with words such as 'Forgery and Fakery' and 'Concealment and Disguise'. They sounded extremely intriguing. The door labelled 'Codes and Devices' was slightly ajar and Dawn glimpsed a crumpled pinstriped jacket thrown over the back of a chair.

She trod past 'Agent Recruitment' and 'Top Secret Missions' until she reached Emma, who was waiting outside a door marked 'Clerical Affairs'. Behind the door, Dawn could hear a relentless tapping sound, punctuated every now and then by a soft *ting*.

Emma knocked smartly on the door.

'Enter!' said somebody crisply.

Pausing for a moment to pull up her socks, Dawn did as she was told.

Inside an orderly office, between two filing cabinets, she saw a woman sitting in a very upright position with her knees tucked under a desk. The woman had a hollow-cheeked, bony face, pencil-thin eyebrows and a large nose. Her brown hair was parted straight down the middle and tied at the nape of her neck with a velvet ribbon. She was sitting so still that Dawn might have mistaken her for a waxwork if her fingers had not been flying over the keys of an old-fashioned typewriter on the desk in front of her. She was so absorbed in her task that she did not pay any attention to the two people who had just come in.

Emma cleared her throat. 'Good morning, Trudy,' she said, resting her hands lightly on Dawn's shoulders. 'Allow me to introduce our latest recruit: Miss Dawn Buckle.'

Trudy continued to type for another minute or so before lifting her fingers from the typewriter keys and looking across at Dawn. Her threadlike eyebrows shot up her forehead.

'Gracious heavens,' she said. 'I thought you'd be bringing a teenager – not a little pipsqueak like that. What's Red going to say when he sees her? She can't be more than eight years old.'

Emma gave Dawn's shoulders a little squeeze. 'Dawn, this is Trudy Harris. She's our secretary here at P.S.S.T.'

'Hello,' said Dawn. 'I'm not eight, actually. I'm eleven.'

Trudy started to type again. *Ting* went the typewriter as she reached the end of a line. 'Eleven!' she said contemptuously, hammering at the keys. 'That's far too young to be a spy. This whole idea is doomed to failure. We'll all lose our jobs, and Angela will never be heard of again.'

Emma sighed heavily and took Dawn's hand. She led her over to a door at one side of the office, which said 'Head of P.S.S.T.' on its brass nameplate. Giving Dawn

60

an encouraging smile, Emma rapped on the door.

'Come along in, do,' said a jovial voice from within.

Just as Emma was about to turn the door handle, Trudy cried out angrily and ripped a sheet of paper from her typewriter. 'Far too many mistakes!' she declared, screwing up the piece of paper and throwing it in the bin. 'It's your stupid fault,' she said to Dawn. 'You made me lose my concentration. Now I'll have to write to the Head of P.U.F.F. all over again.'

'Ignore her,' whispered Emma as she opened the door and led Dawn into the adjoining room.

It was a cosy sort of office, as messy and disorganised as Trudy's was neat and pristine. There were shelves from floor to ceiling filled with books and assorted bric-a-brac and the windowsill was crowded with spider plants. In the midst of all this clutter was a small, stocky man whose facial features resembled those of a garden gnome. He was sitting behind a desk in a green leather chair and he jumped to his feet when he saw Dawn.

'At last!' he said delightedly.

Dawn was quite surprised. She had presumed that the Head of P.S.S.T. would look like a headteacher or a bank manager. At the very least, she had expected him to be wearing a sober suit and tie. The man was not dressed in a suit and his tie was hand-knitted and bright red. He wore a checked, short-sleeved shirt, which was tucked into a pair of corduroy trousers, and his feet were clad in open-toed sandals.

'It's a pleasure to meet you, Miss Buckle,' said the man, walking round his desk. He reached forward and shook Dawn's hand gently, as if he were worried that too much pressure might break her fingers. 'Um … do you mind if I call you Dawn? My name is Redmond Jellicoe. Most people call me Red. I'm in charge of this little outfit.'

'Hello, Red,' said Dawn, sinking into the nearest seat. It was a relief to be greeted with such warmth after Trudy's unfriendly welcome.

Beaming at her, Red perched on a corner of his desk. 'You know, Dawn,' he said, 'I was beginning to lose hope. When I asked Emma to find a child with spying potential I knew that she'd have her work cut out, but when she hadn't come across anyone after two solid weeks of searching I thought I'd have to pull the plug on the whole operation.'

'It was pure luck, really,' said Emma, opening her briefcase. 'I was on my way to a prep school in Pentonville when Dawn happened to cross the road in front of my car. I knew, from the moment I saw her, that she was the one.'

'Jolly well done. You did a first-rate job,' said Red, his eyes skimming over the contract which Emma had slid from her case and placed in his hands. 'Good. Signed by both parents, I see. This all looks to be in order.

Excellent.' He put the contract to one side and glanced at a clock on his desk. 'I've asked the others to assemble in the Top Secret Missions room at ten o'clock sharp,' he said to Emma. 'Could you make sure that everything is ready for the meeting?'

'Certainly, sir,' she said. Then she turned on her heel and left the room.

'That Cambridge girl is a thumping good recruitment officer,' said Red, smiling kindly at Dawn. 'Only twenty-two. Just graduated from Clandestine College. Wanted to join A.H.E.M. but they turned her down – the dunderheads! Their loss is our gain, don't you think?'

Dawn nodded vaguely. She didn't have a clue what he was talking about.

'Oh, what a nincompoop I am!' said Red, scolding himself. 'There can't have been time for Emma to tell you very much about S.H.H. and all its departments. I'd better put you in the picture, hadn't I?'

'Yes please,' Dawn said eagerly.

Red rubbed his copper-coloured beard in a thoughtful manner. 'S.H.H. is, of course, an acronym,' he began. 'The letters stand for Strictly Hush-Hush. It's an organisation that safeguards the security of our country. Its main objective is to gather secret information which will protect Britain against its enemies …'

Before he could continue, the door to his office gave

a creak and started to open slowly. Eerily, it seemed to be moving of its own accord. Dawn watched with widening eyes. Then a feline face appeared at ankle level and Peebles sauntered into the room. He had a look of determination on his face and a small, bulky package attached to a harness around his middle.

'Ah, Peebles,' said Red. 'What have you brought, then, eh? I wasn't expecting a delivery.'

The cat ignored him and walked over to Dawn's chair, the package wobbling on his back. He sat down beside her plimsolls and miaowed with feeling.

'It appears to be for you,' said Red. 'Did you order room service?'

Dawn was astounded. 'Is it ... is it my *breakfast*?' She bent down and untied the parcel carefully. Then, holding it in her lap, she unwrapped two warm bacon sandwiches. 'Thanks a lot, Peebles,' said Dawn. She stroked the cat's silky black head and a purr rumbled in his throat. 'Wow,' said Dawn as she picked up a sandwich. 'I didn't expect my breakfast to be delivered by a cat!'

'Needs must,' said Red. 'Members of the hotel staff aren't allowed on this level of the building. Peebles is very useful. He brings the morning's post and can manage items of stationery, and also light snacks. Unlike us humans, he doesn't need to use the secret entrances. Finds his way underneath the floorboards somehow. He can squeeze himself through the tiniest of gaps and scale almost anything. Peebles is a much-valued member of P.S.S.T.

'Now ... where was I?' Red's brow furrowed. 'Ah, yes. I was telling you about S.H.H. – it's divided into several smaller departments and P.S.S.T. happens to be one of them. Each department specialises in something different, but it's all to do with espionage. You know – *spying*.'

Dawn nodded. 'Mmm,' she said, her mouth full of soft bread and crispy bacon.

'There are six departments altogether. Three are engaged in what we call "fieldwork". That is to say they all employ their own band of spies and regularly send them on missions. The other three departments are behind-the-scenes, so to speak. They provide the first three departments with information and all the paraphernalia that the spies need to complete their missions successfully.'

'What kind of department is P.S.S.T.?' asked Dawn, butter dripping down her chin.

'The "fieldwork" kind,' said Red, 'along with A.H.E.M. and C.O.O.E.E.'

'P.S.S.T., A.H.E.M. and C.O.O.E.E.,' repeated Dawn to herself.

'A.H.E.M. stands for Acquisition of Hugely Enlightening Material,' explained Red. 'Their team of spies are responsible for gathering information. Then there's C.O.O.E.E – Covert Observance and Obstruction of Enemy Espionage. *Their* spies try to stop enemy agents from finding out secrets about *us*.'

'Uh-huh,' said Dawn. She realised that Peebles was drooling on her plimsolls and slipped him a morsel of bacon fat.

'And then,' said Red, straightening his woollen tie proudly, 'there's P.S.S.T. – which stands for Pursuit of Scheming Spies and Traitors. You see, Dawn,' said Red, his voice dropping to a whisper, 'not everyone is loyal to his or her own country. Some people are quite prepared to betray their fellow citizens and help our enemies.'

'Why would they do that?' said Dawn.

'Any number of reasons,' said Red. 'Some are disillusioned with the way this country works, some are blackmailed into it ... and some are just plain greedy. A huge wad of banknotes dangled under a person's nose can be *extremely* persuasive! These people are known as scheming spies and traitors, and it's our job to sniff them out.'

'What kind of people are they?' asked Dawn.

'All sorts,' said Red, gravely. 'It's a sad truth, Dawn, but traitors can be found just about *everywhere* – some have even been known to worm their way into S.H.H.! A traitor in S.H.H. can be a very dangerous thing indeed. Imagine it, Dawn: they could get their hands on classified files, reveal the secret location of their department, and even engineer the failure of a mission.

'Only two years ago we intercepted the Chief of S.H.H.'s own secretary, Mavis Hughes, trying to smuggle confidential documents out of the country. She soon found herself banged up in prison, and won't be seeing the light of day for a very long time. Ah, I tell you, Dawn, members of S.H.H. who have turned bad are the worst type of foe imaginable. They're devilishly cunning and extremely hard to catch.'

'I think I understand,' said Dawn. Her brain was beginning to ache. 'A.H.E.M. spies for the good guys, C.O.O.E.E. tries to stop the bad guys from spying on the good guys and P.S.S.T. tries to catch the bad guys who are pretending to be good guys.'

'That's it in a nutshell, more or less,' said Red. He seemed pleased.

'So, what are the other three departments?' asked Dawn, tickling Peebles under his chin. 'Is P.U.F.F. one of them? Trudy mentioned it. I think she was writing a letter to someone ...'

'Deirdre Feathers,' said Red, smiling fondly. 'She's in charge of that department. Deirdre and I were in the same class at Clandestine College many moons ago.'

'Clandestine College?' said Dawn.

'Yup,' said Red. 'It's a university for school leavers who've got their heart set on a career in S.H.H.

Anyway, Deirdre was something of a swot. Always had her head in a book. Soaked up information like a sponge. I had a hunch that she'd make a name for herself in P.U.F.F. It conducts research,' explained Red. 'P.U.F.F. stands for Procurement of Useful Facts and Figures.'

'What about the other two?' said Dawn.

'C.L.I.C.K. stands for the Creation of Ludicrously Ingenious Codes and Keys. Its staff think up different ways for spies to send secret messages. Lastly, there's P.I.N.G. – Production of Incredibly Nifty Gadgets. That department's responsible for inventing amazing devices which help spies to carry out their work.'

'Is it difficult to be a spy?' asked Dawn, wondering what subjects were taught at Clandestine College.

Red did not answer. 'Have you finished your breakfast?' he said.

'Almost,' said Dawn. Red waited for her to gulp down the last chunk of her sandwich. Then he called her over to the window.

'Have a gander down there, Dawn. Who do you see?'

'Er …' Dawn hesitated. She was not used to being put on the spot. 'A … a man eating a bag of crisps.'

'Good,' said Red. 'Who else?'

'An old lady with a shopping bag. A … a woman pushing a buggy.'

'Nice, ordinary people,' said Red, 'going about their

business.'

'Yes,' agreed Dawn.

'Ninety-nine times out of a hundred, that's exactly what they'll be,' said Red, 'but then there's the other one per cent.'

'What do you mean?' said Dawn.

'Any of the people you just described to me could be a spy,' said Red, settling on the corner of his desk again. 'Spies are a fiendishly clever breed. Only a very special type of person can slip seamlessly into a neighbourhood and fool everyone into thinking they're perfectly normal. On the surface, spies appear to be regular, ordinary members of the public, but in actual fact they're completely phoney. All they're interested in is carrying out their mission.'

'Does it take very long to learn to be a spy?' asked Dawn. She sat down and lifted Peebles on to her lap.

'Ah,' said Red. 'Now, there's a question.' Creases appeared on his forehead. 'In my humble opinion, Dawn, spies are born, not made. A person could study all their life at Clandestine College and never make the grade. On the other hand, I could pluck somebody from the street and they could pick up all the skills in no time at all. It would depend on how naturally gifted they are!' Red made a steeple with his hands and gave Dawn a meaningful look.

She squirmed in her seat, and felt herself blushing.

'Emma told me that I've been chosen to be a spy.'

'Yes, you have,' said Red, 'and there's no need to look so worried about it. You've got bucketloads of talent. In fact, I've never seen anyone more suited to the occupation. Now,' said Red in a businesslike manner. 'We've got a few minutes before I introduce you to the rest of the team. Are there any questions that you'd like to ask me?'

'Um,' said Dawn. She stared blankly at Red's toes, which were poking out of his sandals, and tried to think of something intelligent to ask. If Red thought that she was smart enough to be a spy, she had better not come up with something dumb. 'Where are S.H.H. and C.O.O.E.E. and P.U.F.F. and A.H.E.M. and C.L.I.C.K. and P.O.N.G.?'

'Actually, it's P.I.N.G.,' said Red.

'Oh ...' faltered Dawn. 'Well, Emma told me that they're dotted all over London, in surprising places.'

'That's correct,' said Red. 'They're concealed in a variety of buildings. C.O.O.E.E., for example, has its home in a West End theatre, and A.H.E.M. is tucked away in a rather famous museum.' Red tapped the side of his nose, and winked. 'Keep that information to yourself, though, Dawn. Each address is a closely guarded secret.'

'Why?' she asked.

Red's countenance became grave. 'The information stored within these walls would be a gold mine to our enemies,' he said, 'and the same goes for every other department of S.H.H. At P.S.S.T., we keep files on every single employee, not to mention data detailing every mission that P.S.S.T. has ever been involved in. On top of that, spies visit us regularly. If our enemies knew what they looked like, every mission would be a total disaster. You can't survive undercover if your face is known.'

'I see.' Before Dawn could think of anything else to ask, a black Bakelite telephone on Red's desk began to ring shrilly.

'Would you excuse me for just one moment?' said Red. He picked up the telephone receiver. 'Jellicoe speaking,' he said brightly into the mouthpiece. His face sagged. 'Of course, Chief. Yup. I take full responsibility. The situation has reached crisis point? Well, no. I think that's a touch alarmist.' Red tried to sound light-hearted. 'Everything will sort itself out.'

Dawn felt awkward. Usually she quite enjoyed eaves-dropping on other people's conversations, but only when they had no idea that she was listening in. She gathered Peebles in her arms and walked over to the window.

On the other side of the road, a boy was trying to drag his dog away from a lamppost. The boy looked hot and bothered as he pulled with all his might on his pet's lead. Dawn guessed that the dog must be hiding an impressive set of muscles under his straggly coat; either that or he was extremely stubborn, because he was refusing to budge an inch. The boy gave up the struggle and leaned against some railings. Then he looked across at the Dampside Hotel and his eyes found Dawn's window. She froze. Red would probably not be pleased if a member of the public spotted her. She backed away from the window and stole an anxious glance at Red, who was still talking to the person on the other end of the telephone.

'Now, Chief,' said Red smoothly, twiddling the telephone cable around his finger. 'Surely, there's no need to visit us again so soon. You were only here a few weeks ago. That reminds me – I don't suppose you've changed your mind about my little request ... so it's still a "no", then, is it? S.H.H. can't afford to provide *any* extra funding ... My own fault? Slapdash and negligent? Squandering money like there's no tomorrow?' He loosened his collar and swallowed several times.

Dawn heard a tinny voice blaring from the earpiece of the telephone. It sounded rather angry.

'Yup,' said Red solemnly. 'Gadget budget? Oh ... er ... I think we've got enough to tide us over ... Four pounds ninety. Ah. You're right, Chief. Yup. That does leave us in a bit of a predicament. I don't suppose ...' Red pulled a face and held the receiver at arm's length as a torrent of abuse poured forth from its earpiece. After about a minute, he resumed the conversation. 'You're definitely not of the opinion, then, that Murdo Meek ... Case closed as far as you're concerned. Right, I understand. So, how would you suggest I run my department, Chief? ... That's *my* problem. I see. But the money will have to come from somewhere ... Perhaps I should consider *what?*' Red leaped off his desk. 'ABSOLUTELY OUT OF THE QUESTION!' he fumed. Then he glanced at Dawn and covered the mouthpiece briefly. 'Be with you in a jiffy,' he whispered.

Dawn crouched down and tried to pacify Peebles. He had jumped out of her arms when Red had raised his voice and was squatting underneath her chair, his tail lashing from side to side.

'There certainly won't be any need for *that*,' said Red firmly to the person on the other end of the phone. 'I'm positive, Chief. In fact – I have something in the pipeline already. Now, if you'll excuse me, I have a very important meeting ... Goodbye. Thank you *so* much for calling.'

Red replaced the telephone receiver on its cradle and grinned sheepishly at Dawn. 'That was the Chief of S.H.H.,' he said. 'Philippa Killingback. We ... er ... don't always see eye to eye.'

Yes, thought Dawn. *I sort of got that impression.*

Red picked up the clock on his desk. 'Oops! Look at that,' he said. 'Five minutes past ten. We're late for the meeting. Better get a wriggle on, eh? The rest of the team will be waiting for us.'

Chapter Five

The Spy Who Didn't Come Back

As they approached the Top Secret Missions room, Dawn tidied her hair and did up all the buttons on her cardigan. She wanted to look her best when she was presented to the entire workforce. Having been told that P.S.S.T. was responsible for pursuing all the scheming spies and traitors in England, she presumed that there would be a horde of people congregated in the room.

By Dawn's reckoning, the employees of P.S.S.T. would be a disciplined, hard-working, dynamic bunch. Judging from the lack of noise coming from the room, they were probably all sitting quietly, with notepads at the ready, waiting for the meeting to begin.

Red turned the door handle and, as the door opened a crack, Dawn heard a lone voice pronouncing, 'Ninety-one, ninety-two, ninety-three ...' It sounded as if somebody was doing a head count. The door opened wider, and Red and Dawn stepped into the room.

It was practically empty! The rows of chairs which Dawn had been imagining were not there, and the enormous group of people was absent also. At a table in the middle of the room sat six individuals. Dawn noticed that Emma and Trudy were amongst them. They were both rather rosy-cheeked and seemed determined not to look at one another as if they had just been arguing over something. Instead of notepads, each person was holding a china teacup, all apart from a woman who was doing some knitting and a bald-headed man who appeared to have fallen asleep.

'Ninety-eight, ninety-nine,' said the elderly woman, counting her stitches as she went. Her needles continued to click briskly until she happened to glance up and see the two new arrivals. Then she abandoned her knitting to prod her slumbering colleague between the shoulder blades. 'Jagdish, wake up! They're here. Meeting's about to start.'

The sleeping man twitched and gave a loud snort before staring blearily in Dawn's direction. 'Is that her?' he said. 'She's not very big, is she?'

'Good things come in small packages,' said the woman, eyeing Dawn keenly. She was a hunched little lady with grey flyaway hair, earrings that looked like buttons and a pincushion hanging on a piece of braid in the place of a necklace. 'Hello, sweet pea,' she said kindly. 'I'm Izzie McMinn. I've been saving you a seat.'

She patted a spare chair beside her. 'Emma, dear, is there any more tea in the pot?'

Whilst Dawn sipped from her cup of lapsang souchong, the people around the table introduced themselves. Izzie McMinn explained that she was the dressmaker at P.S.S.T., and that it was her job to create all manner of outfits for spies to wear on their under-cover missions. (She also revealed that the shapeless expanse of wool between her needles was destined to become a balaclava.)

The bald-headed man who had been slumped on the table in a comatose state identified himself as Jagdish Pappachan. He showed Dawn his long, elegant fingers which were stained with ink and told her that he was a forger, capable of rustling up a fake passport in fifteen minutes and copying any signature in the world.

A wiry old man with a weather-beaten face and a stubbly chin said that his name was Socrates Smith. He had been a spy up until a few years ago, and was now employed as a tradecraft specialist. His job was to instruct and advise P.S.S.T.'s current crop of spies: showing them how to use newfangled gadgets, the latest codes and other useful devices.

Dawn had taken it for granted that Emma and Trudy would be present at the meeting, but one person whom she had *not* been expecting to see was Mrs Oliphant.

Dawn remembered being told that hotel staff were

not permitted on the second floor, but she soon learned that there was one exception to this rule because, as Edith Oliphant explained, she was both the manager of Dampside *and* the person in charge of security at P.S.S.T. It was her job to decide which people should be allowed on to the premises and she was also responsible for ensuring that the hotel guests did not suspect that P.S.S.T. had its headquarters in the building.

'This is all of you, is it?' said Dawn, trying not to appear too disappointed. She was still having trouble accepting that P.S.S.T. was only just large enough to form a netball team. How, she wondered, could such a tiny band of people possibly deal with every scheming spy and traitor in the country?

'Not quite,' said Red, from his seat at the head of the table. 'We have a few absentees. Nathan Slipper, for one.'

For the briefest moment, Dawn thought she saw Edith wince slightly at the mention of the young man's name.

'Nathan's just graduated from Clandestine College,' said Red brightly.

'With mediocre grades,' chipped in Edith, her face impassive.

'And I've hired him as Edith's second-in-command,' said Red, examining a pile of folders on the desk in front of him, 'on a temporary basis, of course.'

'He's got three months to prove he's up to the job ... or he's out,' said Edith severely.

Red selected a turquoise folder from the pile. 'If I decide to make Nathan's position permanent, he'll be allowed to roam about on the second floor like the rest of us but, until then, this level is strictly out of bounds to the lad. Now,' he said, sorting through the sheets of paper in the folder, 'I think we'd better get this meeting under way.'

'What about the others?' said Socrates in a surly voice. 'There are three more missing from P.S.S.T., don't forget. It's about time you told the kiddie about Miles and Bob and Angela.'

At the mention of these three names, the room fell silent.

Red frowned. 'I was just coming to that,' he said.

'How *are* the boys?' asked Izzie, lacing her fingers together. 'I do hope they're on the mend.'

'Miles's legs are still in plaster, but his condition is stable,' answered Red. His expression grew more serious. 'Bob hasn't recovered yet, unfortunately. The doctors say it could take months.'

'What's the matter with Bob?' whispered Dawn in Izzie's ear.

'The poor lamb's been struck dumb,' muttered Izzie. 'Lies in his hospital bed and just stares at the ceiling. Won't speak a word. It's a dreadful shame.'

'I won't beat about the bush,' said Red, getting to his feet. He walked over to a wall with a large map pinned to it. 'One of our spies is missing and the other two are lucky to be alive. I'm inclined to think that we're dealing with a formidable foe, here – and we shouldn't rule out the possibility that the villain we're looking for is Murdo Meek –'

'Codswallop!' said Socrates with a scowl. 'Meek's been dead for ten years. I was there when he jumped to his doom! You were there, too, Red – or has that suddenly slipped your mind?'

'Of course it hasn't!' said Red crossly. 'But I can't ignore what Angela said just before she disappeared. I know it sounds preposterous, but we should at least entertain the idea that Meek might still be at large.'

Socrates made an impolite noise. 'You're off your trolley,' he mumbled.

Choosing to disregard the old man's comment, Red drew everyone's attention to the large-scale map of a village which was on the wall behind him.

'Cherry Bentley,' he said darkly. 'That is where we will find the answers – and now I'll explain precisely how I propose to root them out.'

The meeting seemed to go on for hours, and Dawn spent most of it with her legs tightly crossed because she was desperate to go to the loo. It had been a mistake to polish off the cup of tea, she decided in retrospect. Every five minutes or so she put up her hand to ask permission to leave the room, but no one interrupted the meeting to ask her what she wanted.

Red remained on his feet for the entire time, a stick of chalk in one hand and a sheaf of paper from the turquoise folder in the other. Every now and then he scribbled some words on a freestanding blackboard. For Dawn's benefit, he started by explaining the events leading up to the mysterious disappearance of the spy called Angela and the accidents which befell her colleagues, Miles and Bob, a few days later.

Angela Bradshaw had spent almost forty years in the espionage business and, of the three spies employed by P.S.S.T., she was by far the most experienced. According to Red she had completed more successful missions than Dawn had had hot dinners. Despite her impressive record, however, it seemed that someone had finally got the better of her because, twenty-four days previously, on the first of July, Angela had vanished without a trace.

The first of July had been a Saturday and Dawn remembered it well. She had spent the morning making an obstacle course for a family of ants in her back garden. In the afternoon, she had gone to a jumble sale with her father. He had bought an old wristwatch and she had come away with a red plastic saddle for Clop – which, disappointingly, he had refused to wear.

While Dawn had been busy assembling tunnels made from hair curlers, ladders made from drinking straws, and various other ant-sized obstacles, it seemed that Angela had been returning from a mission in Essex. She had been on her way back from Colchester after trailing a member of Her Majesty's government who had been acting extremely suspiciously for some time. It turned out that there was a perfectly innocent explanation for his furtive behaviour. He had been organising a surprise party for his wife's fortieth birthday. An extravagant affair, it was to take place in Colchester Castle with all the guests dressed up in medieval costume.

Once Angela had discovered what the Cabinet minister was up to, she had jumped into her car (a Volkswagen Beetle) and begun to drive south towards London. Unfortunately, she had only covered a few miles when the Beetle's engine started to splutter. After stopping at the side of the road, raising its bonnet and tinkering about with the engine, she had decided that with any luck her car would just about make it to the nearest settlement, where there was bound to be a garage of some description. She turned off the dual carriageway at the very next junction and headed for the village of Cherry Bentley.

She'd had to push her car for the last half mile, but eventually Angela had found a garage and a sympathetic mechanic called Gert, who had taken one look at the conked-out Beetle and announced that it would take the best part of the afternoon to fix. Gert had suggested to Angela that she might like to while away a few hours exploring Cherry Bentley, being sure to visit the Garden and Allotment Show which was currently taking place in several marquees on the village green.

Red had received a chatty phone call from Angela at five minutes past twelve explaining that, owing to engine trouble, she was going to spend the rest of the day mooching about in Cherry Bentley. 'It's about time I had an afternoon off,' she'd said.

The next telephone call that Red received from Angela had been quite different.

It had come an hour and a half later. Her voice had been breathless and panicky and she had only managed to utter a few words. As a matter of course, every telephone call that Red made or received at P.S.S.T. was recorded on tape. Then the conversation was typed up by Trudy and filed away, and the tape was erased. As it was such a brief and puzzling call, Red had kept the recording of Angela's voice. Taking it from his pocket, Red proceeded to play the tape on a little Dictaphone for everyone to hear:

'Murdo Meek. I've just heard his voice – plain as day. He said, "Mrs Arbuthnot's cucumber has won first prize again, I see." *He's not dead*. He's here in the vegetable tent. MURDO MEEK!'

Angela had not phoned again. Nor had she turned up at P.S.S.T. The rest of the staff had received a postcard from her a few days later – but after careful examination Jagdish had declared it to be a forgery.

Red removed the postcard from the turquoise folder and allowed Dawn to read it. Written in blue biro, it said:

My dear colleagues,

I may have misled you into thinking that I had heard the voice of an old adversary of ours. Of course, I did not hear anything of the sort. I am worried that I am going gaga and feel that it is about time I jacked in my job and retired to Barbados. I am not one for goodbyes so I hope you'll forgive me if I don't wish each of you farewell in person.

Respectfully yours,
Angela

Red had consulted the Chief of S.H.H. immediately and she had agreed with the rest of P.S.S.T. that Angela could not possibly have bumped into Murdo Meek, as he had died a decade earlier. However, when the Chief heard about the bogus postcard she did admit that it might be sensible to send another spy to Cherry Bentley to see if any trace of Angela could be found.

Miles Evergreen was given a false identity (Jimmy

James) and a spurious occupation (window cleaner). He was despatched to the village forthwith and instructed to leave no stone unturned in his search for Angela. Unfortunately, after only two days, his window-cleaning career came to an end, as did his mission, when he fell off his ladder and broke both legs.

Bob Chalk was the next spy to be sent to the village. He posed as an artist called Hugo Toogood and spent his first day strolling around Cherry Bentley, making sketches of various buildings and snooping about. However, the very same evening, he was discovered slumped on the floor of a telephone box in an hysterical state, and ever since then he had been incapable of uttering one intelligible word.

That was when things had started to look very bleak indeed. No trace of Angela had been found and there were no spies left to send. In addition to which, P.S.S.T.'s funds were getting worryingly low. Red decided to appeal to the Chief of S.H.H. to give them extra cash so that they could afford to continue their search for Angela – but Philippa Killingback had turned down his request. She had concluded that clumsiness and incompetence had caused Miles and Bob to end up in hospital and there was nothing more sinister about it than that. When Red insisted that there must have been foul play involved, Philippa had scoffed at the idea.

Red had refused to be beaten. He decided that if he

made a few cutbacks in the department, he might be able to scrape together just enough money to send one more spy on one more mission. He could not afford to hire a top-notch agent – and anyway, all the spies who worked for C.O.O.E.E. and A.H.E.M. were occupied with missions of their own – so he interviewed some recent graduates from Clandestine College, hoping to find a high flier amongst them. Disappointingly, none of them were up to scratch.

Red had begun to despair. He knew that this would be P.S.S.T.'s final opportunity to find out what had happened to Angela in Cherry Bentley. He was becoming more and more convinced that her disappearance, Miles's accident and Bob's funny turn were all linked in some way. Somehow, he just *had* to find a spy skilled enough to get results. Then it occurred to him that Miles and Bob were both highly qualified agents and yet someone in Cherry Bentley had identified them straight away and put them both out of action; Angela had been a spy for almost forty years yet she had vanished like a puff of smoke.

Red had come to the conclusion that it would be pointless to send another spy using the same strategy as before. He would have to think of a different angle from which to approach the problem. The new plan would have to be fresh and original. In fact, it would have to be nothing short of ingenious.

Eventually, the idea had come to him. *He would use a child spy.* To his knowledge, no one had ever enlisted the services of anyone under the age of eighteen in the entire history of S.H.H. The person or persons lurking in Cherry Bentley would never suspect a child of being on the payroll of P.S.S.T. It would be simple for the child spy to infiltrate the village and find out exactly what was going on.

At this point in the meeting Red asked if there were any questions, and half a dozen hands were immediately raised. Luckily, Dawn's hand, which was flung into the air rather wildly, accidentally struck Red on the nose and so her request was dealt with first.

On her way back from the toilet, Dawn heard the sound of raised voices coming from the Top Secret Missions room. When she opened the door she discovered that everyone seemed to be talking at once. Socrates was bellowing the loudest and, every now and then, he banged the table with his fist. The only person who did not appear to be taking part in the discussion was Izzie. She had picked up her knitting again and was murmuring numbers to herself.

'What's all the commotion about?' whispered Dawn, taking her seat next to the elderly dressmaker.

Izzie rolled her eyes. 'They're arguing over who should accompany you on your mission. I'm afraid I couldn't go, dear. There'd be nobody at home to look after Gerald, Twinkle and Fluff.'

'Your cats,' guessed Dawn.

'No, dear. My red-kneed tarantulas.'

Socrates rained a few more blows on the table. 'Stands to reason that I'm the obvious choice,' he shouted, prodding his chest proudly. 'I'm an old hand when it comes to working undercover. Dawn'd be as safe as houses with me. What do you lot know about going on a mission, eh? Diddly-squat – that's what!'

'He's always loathed his desk job,' confided Izzie, leaning closer to Dawn. 'Had to retire from spying after his hip replacement. Couldn't cut the mustard after that, you see. I knew he'd jump at the chance of being your chaperone. Bless him.'

'I'm not one to blow my own trumpet,' said Jagdish loudly, 'but I've got bags of experience at baby-sitting. I have five grandsons – and I'm very good at wiping noses, reading stories and other such things.'

'It's a shame,' said Izzie out of the corner of her mouth, 'but he's not the man for the job. Poor old Jagdish suffers terribly with hay fever. He'd be sneezing from morning to night in that little country village.'

'As recruitment officer,' said Emma, tossing her blonde plait over her shoulder, 'I feel that the role of Dawn's guardian should fall to me. We've built up a good rapport and I'd like to be the one to keep an eye on her.'

'You'd have to pretend to be her mother,' said Edith loftily, 'and you're far too young for that. Whereas *I* am –'

'Completely loopy,' said Trudy, staring at everyone in disgust. 'Just like the rest of you. Little girls go to ballet classes or piano practice: they do *not* go undercover on perilous assignments. This plan is insane! It will never work.'

'Hey!' said Red, struggling to make himself heard above the furore. 'Could everybody calm down a moment and let me speak!'

His words went unheeded.

'QUIET!' barked Edith, turning her laser-like eyes on each person in turn. Her stern tone of voice and unsettling stare seemed to frighten everyone into silence.

'Thank you,' said Red. He shook his head disapprovingly. 'All this argy-bargy is a waste of time. I've already decided who will be going with Dawn on her mission.'

'Who?' they all demanded.

'You!' he said, and he pointed a finger at Trudy.

Chapter Six

Bedtime Reading

When Red revealed who Dawn's escort was going to be, there was a collective gasp of amazement and Izzie dropped a whole row of stitches.

'She's swooning! Somebody catch her!' cried Jagdish as Trudy's eyes rolled upwards and she started to slide off her chair.

Reacting the quickest, Emma was the first to reach the limp-bodied secretary. She cushioned Trudy's head in her lap and asked someone to fetch a glass of water. 'Must've been the shock,' said Emma, feeling Trudy's pulse. 'She fainted clean away, didn't she?'

'Oh, dear,' said Red. 'I thought she might take the news a bit better than that.'

Oh, dear, indeed, thought Dawn miserably. She found Red's choice of chaperone very disappointing – and she wasn't the only one.

'That's a stinker of a decision,' said Socrates crossly, and several of the others agreed with him. 'What, may I ask, was wrong with me?'

Red walked over to the blackboard and underlined the name 'MURDO MEEK', which he had written in big, capital letters. '*If*,' he said, 'this man is still alive, and *if* he's somewhere in Cherry Bentley, he might well recognise you. The whole mission could be compromised if you set so much as a foot in that village.'

Socrates looked furious. 'Murdo Meek is dead and gone,' he said, 'without a shadow of a doubt. Anyway,' he grumbled, 'that night in December was darker than the inside of a railway tunnel. If Meek did get a look at me, it probably wasn't a very good one.'

'My mind's made up,' said Red firmly. 'Trudy will be joining Dawn on the mission, and I'm also planning to enlist the help of Nathan. He'll be very useful for delivering messages.'

'Nathan?' said Edith in a shocked voice. 'Are you sure you've thought this through? The boy's not over-burdened with brains.'

'I've got every confidence in him,' said Red. 'Besides, none of you others could go so I was a bit stuck for choice.' In response to an outburst of protests, Red spelled out why this was. 'Edith will need to remain at her post, guarding these premises, Jagdish's nose begins to run if he so much as looks at a blade of grass, Izzie can't leave her spiders, both Socrates and I might be recognised by Meek, and Emma will be too busy taking over Trudy's duties.'

'What?' said the secretary, who had just regained consciousness.

'*Me?*' said Emma.

'*Her?*' said Trudy drowsily. 'No! I absolutely forbid it.' She struggled into a sitting position. 'My files will be all messed up!'

'My typing leaves a lot to be desired, sir,' said Emma, gazing imploringly at Red. 'Couldn't you reconsider? I'd much rather be sent to Cherry Bentley.'

'No!' shouted Red. He was getting quite over-wrought. 'You're too young to pass as Dawn's mother, whereas Trudy is the perfect age.'

'But we don't look alike,' wailed the secretary.

'Perhaps not,' agreed Red, 'but once Izzie has worked her wonders ...'

'I'm not disguising myself as some old frump,' said Trudy flatly. With Emma's help, she managed to get to her feet. 'I happen to take a pride in my appearance.'

Is there something wrong with what I'm wearing? thought Dawn, glancing at her brown cardigan and her comfortable plimsolls. She had made a special effort to look nice on her first day at P.S.S.T. and could not understand why Trudy had implied that she had not bothered to dress smartly.

'What do you think, Izzie?' said Red. He turned towards P.S.S.T.'s needlewoman. 'Could you rustle up a few stylish outfits for Trudy? Nothing too drab, you understand.'

'Aye,' said Izzie, her beady eyes flicking up and down Trudy's skinny figure. 'Something in linen, perhaps ... and I've some fine material from that fancy department store. Let's see ... yes ... and half a dozen balls of cashmere wool –'

'Cashmere?' said Trudy, lifting a slender eyebrow. Then she frowned. 'No, no, no. I will *not* be involved in this hare-brained scheme! The idea of sending a child on a mission is absolutely ludicrous.'

'I prefer to think of it as "daring",' said Red, 'and if we don't go through with it, Angela's fate may never be known.'

'Angela,' said Trudy, biting her lip. She sank into her seat with a sorrowful look on her face.

Red gave his secretary an encouraging smile. 'You'd be *ideal* for this job,' he said, and in case she didn't realise quite how 'ideal' he thought she'd be, he wrote the word on the blackboard and ringed it three times. 'You're intelligent, capable, cool-headed ...'

'Not the motherly type, though, is she?' said Socrates. He still seemed reluctant to accept that he would not be accompanying Dawn himself. 'Don't you need warmth and affection to be a parent? Trudy wouldn't make a very convincing one, if you ask me.'

Izzie gave Socrates a stern look. 'Don't take any

notice of that old gasbag, Trudy,' she said. 'He's just bellyaching because he hasn't got his own way. Plenty of mothers are dour, strict, bossy women. I reckon you could do a fair impression of one of those.'

Trudy glared at her.

'So, you're up for the challenge, then?' said Red gently to his secretary.

She gave a reluctant nod. 'All right,' she said. 'I'll go. If there's even a glimmer of a chance that we might find Angela, how can I refuse?'

'Good,' said Red, sighing deeply. 'That *is* a weight off my mind.' He clapped his hands together. 'Right, folks. Listen up. I aim to send Dawn on her mission on Saturday morning, so that gives us just under four days to get her ready for it.

'Emma, I want you to help me come up with some false names for Dawn and Trudy. Izzie – I'll have to ask you to sew like blazes, I'm afraid. They'll need a dozen outfits each for their new personas. Jagdish, can you get cracking on some forged papers? And Socrates – you'll have the most important job of all. I need you to teach Dawn how to be a spy.

'That's all, then, chaps. Let's get to it!'

After the meeting, Socrates lumbered out of the Top Secret Missions room with a scowl on his face. He spent the rest of the day behind the door labelled 'Codes and

Devices', refusing to open it to anyone but Peebles, whose entrance was only permitted at lunchtime and then only if he was carrying the right sort of sandwiches. The old man's hermit-like behaviour prompted Dawn to ask the others what he was doing. She received two explanations. Red insisted that he was probably very busy preparing Dawn's training schedule – and Izzie said that he was sulking.

It did not really matter that Socrates chose to keep himself to himself. Dawn received plenty of attention from the other members of P.S.S.T.

She spent the first few hours in Izzie's company. In the room assigned to the business of 'Concealment and Disguise' she stood very patiently while Izzie unfurled a tape measure and proceeded to take down Dawn's particulars. The room was strewn with rolls of material and scraps of fabric. There was a wicker shopping basket containing several balls of wool, and numerous knitting needles in a big glass jar. While Dawn happily poked around in an old tobacco tin brimming with buttons, Izzie sorted through a heap of patterns.

Dawn left Izzie slicing through great sheets of material with a large pair of scissors and went to visit Jagdish in the Forgery and Fakery room. She helped him clean his paintbrushes, sharpen all his pencils and load his camera with a new roll of film. Jagdish's room was very brightly lit. There was a huge noticeboard hanging on the wall, upon which was pinned every type of document that could be imagined, from driving licences to bus tickets. In the middle of the room was a vast sloping desk where Jagdish seemed to spend most of his time, a pair of spectacles on his nose and a writing implement between his long, inky fingers.

At a few minutes to five, most of the P.S.S.T. employees began gathering their things together and preparing to go home. Once they had climbed to the bottom of the staircase and sneaked through the secret door in the pantry, they usually left via the tradesmen's entrance in the basement, so as to give the impression that they worked in the hotel – which they did, in a manner of speaking. Emma was the only one who ever accessed the building by its main entrance – and then only on rare occasions when she needed to accompany a guest from another S.H.H. department or, in Dawn's case, a new recruit.

Just as Dawn was about to make her way down the staircase, Socrates emerged from the Codes and Devices room and told her, rather tersely, that she should dip into a good spying manual before their first training session the following day. Then he dropped a book called *Keeping to the Shadows* by Anonymous into her hands.

It was beginning to get dark when Dawn climbed into bed. Nightfall was still half an hour away, but a shapeless lump of leaden cloud had settled in the sky above Pimlico, blotting out the last weak rays of sunlight.

She had been given the key to room four. Twice the size of her bedroom at home, it contained a single bed, a small chest of drawers, a high-backed chair and a wardrobe with a design of squirrels and oak leaves carved into its panels. It would have been a very pleasant place in which to spend the night, if it had not been so stiflingly hot.

Dawn threw back the eiderdown but she did not feel a great deal cooler. She slid off the mattress and padded over the floorboards. Her fingers gripped the underside of the heavy sash window and she managed to raise it a few more inches. In the paved backyard of the hotel, Dawn could see two elderly men, puffing on their pipes and playing dominoes. Apart from Dawn and Emma, they were the only other guests in the hotel. The portly man with the handlebar moustache was called Mr Sparks and his scrawny friend was Mr Hollowbread.

Edith had explained that guests were actively discouraged from staying at Dampside (hence the 'No Vacancies' sign which was displayed almost all the year round). For appearances' sake, a couple of people were allowed to stay every so often – just to keep up the pretence that Dampside was an ordinary hotel, but the fewer guests there were, the easier it was for Edith to make sure that they didn't find out about P.S.S.T. on the second floor.

Thunder grumbled overhead and Dawn heard a succession of little taps as raindrops burst against the windowpane. As she turned away from the window, her gaze rested on a small alarm clock which was sitting on a table next to her bed. Her father had a clock just like it. In fact, he had fifteen. Dawn found herself thinking about home. She could not help feeling a little glum. What would her family be doing right now? Would any of them be wondering how she was getting on?

Dawn cheered up considerably when she saw Clop lying on the bed with his legs splayed out like a starfish. She presumed that he was enjoying a much-needed stretch after having been squashed in her suitcase for hours on end. His legs shifted their position slightly when she sat down on the mattress. She leaned over, gently tugged his woolly mane and told him how glad she was that he had come with her – and that he was quite the best donkey in the world. Typically, Clop stared straight ahead as if he had not heard her. Sentimental remarks always seemed to cause him embarrassment. However, when Dawn studied him closely she was fairly sure that his smile had acquired an extra stitch.

Lightning illuminated the room for a split second. A crash of thunder followed. Dawn glanced worriedly at Clop, but he had not even flinched. He wasn't afraid of thunderstorms.

'Neither am I,' she said out loud. Pressing her toes against a rumpled sheet and blanket, she pushed them to the very foot of the bed.

Dawn did not lay her head on the pillow or close her eyes. The turbulent weather put paid to any ideas she had of falling asleep. Intending to do a bit of reading, she switched on her bedside lamp. Then her hand reached out for her book, *Pansy the Goat Girl*, but she didn't open it. Instead, she set it down again and picked up the book that had been lying underneath it. It was the thick, well-thumbed hardback called *Keeping to the Shadows*, by Anonymous, which Socrates had lent to her. The title and author were printed in bold white lettering on a simple black cover. At least, Dawn had assumed that the cover was plain – but when she tilted the book at a certain angle and peered very closely, she could just make out the silhouette of a man wearing a mackintosh and a trilby hat standing rather shiftily in the bottom right-hand corner.

Feeling a flicker of excitement, Dawn ignored the thunderstorm which was raging outside her window, turned to the first page and began to read.

Chapter Seven

Training Day

Socrates did not give Dawn's knuckles a chance to make contact with the door before he flung it open, exclaiming 'Aha!'

Dawn was so surprised that she lost her grip on *Keeping to the Shadows* and it landed on the midnight-blue carpet with a thud. She eyed Socrates anxiously, expecting to be scolded for damaging his book but, to her amazement, he didn't look the least bit angry. In fact, his face was wreathed in smiles.

'Heard you coming!' he announced smugly. 'Clocked you through the keyhole, too! A spy is always on the alert, Dawn. Remember that. Ha!' He tapped his nose with the tip of his finger and threw her a knowing glance. 'I may have been put out to pasture as far as my spying career is concerned, but I haven't lost the knack!'

Dawn smiled and nodded. She was far too polite to mention that Socrates had instructed her to report to the Codes and Devices room at nine o'clock that morning and, therefore, it wasn't really *very* impressive that he had caught her in the act of arriving exactly when she was meant to.

Socrates opened the door wide and waved her into the room. 'OK, Dawn Buckle,' he said firmly, 'let's get started, shall we?'

Dawn picked up *Keeping to the Shadows* and cradled it in both arms. As she stepped through the doorway, Socrates patted its black cover in a reverential manner.

'Marvellous book, that,' he said. 'Contains everything a spy could ever need to know. You've studied it thoroughly, I hope.'

'Er ... yes,' said Dawn. Well, she'd almost finished chapter three.

'Good.' Socrates rolled up the sleeves of his shirt. His nut-brown, muscular arms were as bristly as his chin. 'Take a seat over there,' he said, pointing to a chair and an old school desk.

Dawn crossed the room – which was no mean feat. Stacks of paper were heaped everywhere and she had to step very carefully to avoid them all. It occurred to her that perhaps Socrates should arrange his documents in some sort of order. Then she noticed that every pile of paper had a large stone on top of it, marked with a different letter of the alphabet. What she had mistaken for a jumbled mess was in fact a rather strange and somewhat archaic filing system.

Dawn stepped over a stone with a white 'W' daubed on it and sat down in a creaky wooden chair. She placed *Keeping to the Shadows* on the desk in front of her, next to a notepad with the first few pages torn out, a ballpoint pen, half a ruler, a freshly sharpened pencil and a nub of grey rubber.

'Feel free to make notes,' said Socrates, threading his way through the islands of paper until he reached a shabby wing chair and sank into it.

Dawn wrote the date on the first page of her notepad and underlined it twice, just as Mrs Kitchen had taught her. When she looked up she found that Socrates was gazing at her intently. He shook his head as if he couldn't quite believe his eyes.

'You're something else, Dawn,' he said in admiration. 'I haven't seen anyone with your sort of potential for *years*.' His face seemed to adopt a faraway look. 'You know, you remind me a little bit of Pip. Natural talent oozing out of every pore, that kid had. Came to P.S.S.T. as a fresh-faced twenty-one-year-old and developed into one of the best spies I've ever worked with. You could be just as good,' he said. 'Maybe even better.'

'It's very nice of you to say that,' mumbled Dawn a little bashfully.

'Right.' Socrates cleared his throat. 'Let's get down to business.'

***

As she scribbled at the top of the twenty-seventh page in her notepad, Dawn noticed a dull, aching sensation in her wrist. She had been writing pretty much non-stop for over two hours, and in that time she had learned a considerable amount.

Firstly, Socrates had quashed all the myths about spying. Unlike the silhouetted gentleman on the cover of *Keeping to the Shadows*, spies never ever dressed in mackintoshes and trilby hats; they didn't wear false noses, wigs or stick-on moustaches either and they tried their utmost to avoid leaning against lampposts or lurking in shop doorways. Socrates said that if spies did any of these things they would stick out like sore thumbs and it would be obvious to just about everybody exactly what they were up to.

Instead, spies tried their best to look completely ordinary. By wearing conventional clothes in dull colours, acting naturally and doing nothing to draw attention to themselves, they could go just about anywhere without being noticed. Spies were never too tall, too short, too fat or too thin; they didn't twitch, fidget, burp or pick their noses. They were as close to being invisible as it was possible to be.

Spies were experts at finding out things. Their methods were simple. They watched and listened until they discovered what they wanted to know. Although spies were reliant on their eyes and ears, they also used their mouths to make enquiries. However, they were extremely careful about the questions that they posed. If they asked the wrong thing or if they appeared to be too nosy, they could instantly arouse other people's suspicions.

Like Boy Scouts and Brownies, it was drummed into spies always to be prepared. This meant that if they were pretending to wait for a bus, they should know its number and destination in the event that someone should ask them; they should carry a pen at all times should they need to write anything down, and they should never be without some loose change in case they needed to buy a drink in a cafe – or a newspaper to hide behind. Swotting up on a map of the area in which they would be operating was also a crucial part of 'being prepared'. Spies needed to know the whereabouts of every footpath, farm track and short cut.

Socrates paused for breath. 'Got all that?' he said to Dawn.

She finished drawing a shaky line underneath the words 'Be Prepared' and then nodded her head. She was fairly sure that she'd managed to copy down most of what Socrates had been saying, even though her handwriting was a little messy in places. With some relief, Dawn allowed her aching wrist to drop on to the desk.

'Elevenses!' announced Socrates. He left the room

and reappeared moments later with a bag of crisps and two cups of tea.

Dawn wasn't particularly hungry but good manners made her accept the refreshments that she was offered. It didn't take long for Socrates to gulp down his share. He pulled a face.

'Not exactly haute cuisine,' he said, 'but it fills a hole.' He gasped and clicked his fingers. 'That's another thing you should remember when you're undercover, Dawn: always carry some food in your pocket! I trailed a bloke for a whole day once. Only had three peanuts and a throat lozenge on me. My rumbling stomach made such a din, I'm surprised the bloke didn't hear it and twig that he was being followed.

'Okey-dokey, must get on.' Socrates began to search around the room until he found a stone with 'C' marked on it. There was a wad of paper beneath it, from which he removed a few sheets. 'Let's make a start on "Communications",' he said. 'Should be able to give you a general overview by lunchtime, I reckon. Might even be able to squeeze in codes, ciphers and keys. You've probably read about them already in *Keeping to the Shadows* –'

'Um,' said Dawn, feeling a twinge in her wrist as she picked up her pen.

After what seemed like twenty minutes rather than two hours, Peebles did his own bit of communicating when he miaowed lustily from the other side of the door. Dawn could not believe that her lunch had arrived already. She had been transfixed by what Socrates was saying and hadn't noticed the time whizzing past. As she sat at her desk, munching her cheese and salad cream sandwiches, she reflected on how many different ways there were for spies to send information back and forth.

In the main, spies communicated by sending letters through the post, leaving notes at hiding places known as 'dead letter boxes' or 'drops' where they would be collected later, and by transmitting words or Morse signals on the airwaves using specially constructed radios. (Morse code was an alphabet made up of long signals known as 'dahs' and short ones referred to as 'dits'.)

Anything that was written down was encoded first, as a matter of course. This meant that a straightforward sentence could be reduced to a baffling mixture of letters or numbers which would mean nothing to anyone who wasn't familiar with the code that had been used. When communicating via radios, spies were just as cunning. They transmitted from secluded spots at scheduled times and made sure that they kept their messages as brief as possible so that enemy agents would not have a chance to discover which frequency they were broadcasting on.

Spies seldom made calls from telephone boxes, where they could be easily overheard, but some preferred to use mobile phones rather than cumbersome radios. Socrates, however, didn't rate phones very highly. He thought that telephone conversations were vulnerable to interception and, if phones were stolen or mislaid, they could reveal sensitive data to the enemy.

C.L.I.C.K. (Creation of Ludicrously Ingenious Codes and Keys) was the department of S.H.H. that was responsible for supplying everything spies would need to correspond in secret.

The staff at C.L.I.C.K. were all chess players and crossword compilers with the types of brains that thrived on solving really difficult puzzles. It was they who came up with all the codes and ciphers that the spies used to obscure their messages. A code was a system that replaced words with other words whereas a cipher swapped each letter with another letter. To solve a code or cipher you would need a codebook or a key – not one made from metal which could lock and unlock things, but a confidential piece of knowledge that would enable you to work out how to unscramble the message so that it made sense.

Dawn swallowed the last crumb of her second cheese and salad cream sandwich and wriggled uncomfortably in her seat. The waistband of her kilt felt rather tight. It wasn't just her stomach that felt full, however; her head was stuffed with so many facts that she did not think she could possibly absorb any more.

When Socrates had been explaining about codes, ciphers and keys she had felt her eyes beginning to glaze over. It was all so terribly complicated. She could not prevent herself from sighing with relief when he lifted down a small cardboard box from a shelf and announced that the rest of the afternoon would be spent doing practical work. Dawn pushed her notepad and writing implements aside as Socrates deposited the box on her desk. She removed its lid and her eyes lit up immediately.

There were bottles of ink (blue, black and purple), notelets, postcards, pads of writing paper, stamps, envelopes, a gold-plated fountain pen, something that looked like a rusty biscuit tin and a book with a crimson cover that was almost the size of a telephone directory.

Dawn lifted the book out first. It was called *C.L.I.C.K.'s Compendium* and was in the kind of poor condition that suggested it had been well used. Someone had stuck several strips of black tape along its spine to help keep all the pages together. Dawn opened its cover, upon which were two labels saying 'REALLY REALLY SECRET' and 'NOT TO BE REMOVED FROM THIS ROOM OR ELSE', and discovered that the book was in its thirty-ninth edition.

She began to flick through its pages and found that it was full of different types of codes and ciphers, each of which had been given a name. There was 'Clown' (a complex cipher involving the repeated juggling of letters), 'Easy Peasy' (where the message was hidden letter by letter in front of every 'e'), 'Shopping List' (in which grocery items represented particular words) and 'Ditchwater' (consisting of a longwinded letter, designed to be so dull that the person reading it would give up way before he reached the end, and therefore miss the message cleverly concealed in the postscript).

As Dawn leafed through *C.L.I.C.K.'s Compendium* she noticed that a few pages had had their corners folded over. Socrates explained that these contained the fifteen codes and ciphers which he wanted her to memorise. Dawn considered herself lucky. In total, there were over nine thousand codes and ciphers in the book, so fifteen was quite a modest amount to have to learn.

She set about the task straight away, copying them into her notebook. Socrates gave her several sentences to encode and she managed quite well, only making a couple of mistakes. He suggested that she might like to use the gold-plated fountain pen and she abandoned her ballpoint eagerly. The fountain pen felt satisfyingly weighty between her fingers and its nib glided smoothly across the page.

Dawn found the black and blue inks to be perfectly ordinary, but the purple ink began to fade slowly as soon as she had set down the words on the page, and after a quarter of an hour they had become totally invisible.

Dawn remembered that Emma had used purple ink when she had written both their names in the hotel's guest book downstairs. When she mentioned this to Socrates he had nodded sagely and told her that anyone on official S.H.H. business always used purple ink when signing the hotel's guest book so that they could appear to behave like normal visitors while leaving no record that they had ever stayed there.

The rusty tin may once have held biscuits, but now it contained a bizarre collection of objects. There was a heavy bolt, a toilet-roll holder, a metal spike similar to those found on the tops of railings, a door knob and – strangest of all – a stone finger with lichen growing on it. Dawn was bewildered. She could not imagine why they had been placed together in the tin or what they could possibly have to do with secret ways of communicating. Socrates provided her with an explanation. He told her that they were examples of dead letter boxes in which spies could hide messages and, lifting each object in turn, he showed her how they could be unscrewed to reveal a hollow cavity where a carefully folded piece of paper could be inserted. Dawn was greatly impressed. The stone finger was her favourite dead letter box. Apparently, it had once belonged to the statue of a boy in Kensington Gardens.

When Dawn had finished examining the contents of the tin, Socrates packed everything back into the cardboard box and returned it to its shelf. He glanced at his watch and drew a breath sharply.

'Only an hour left,' he said. 'Still, that should give me just enough time to talk you through one last thing.'

He steered an intricate course through the stacks of paper until he reached a cupboard, the key to which was in the pocket of his pinstriped waistcoat. Having opened the cupboard doors, Socrates bent down and dragged out a large wooden packing case which had labels with the names of various countries stuck all over it. He beckoned to Dawn and she hurried over to him.

'Used to belong to my auntie Florrie,' he said, patting the case as if it were a faithful dog. 'Went all over the world with her, and now it just sits here in this cupboard.' Its locks sprang open under his fingers. 'I call it my gadget box.'

As he lifted its lid, Dawn peered eagerly inside. 'Oh,' she said disappointedly. 'It's empty.'

'Whaaaaat? Course it's not!' scoffed Socrates. His head disappeared from view as he scrabbled around in the bottom of the box. When he next spoke, his voice sounded muffled and echoey. 'I knew we were running a bit low,' he said, his fingernails scraping against the box's insides, 'but I could have sworn there was *something* left. Wait a minute – what's this?' He straightened up for a second and thrust what looked like a large shell into Dawn's hands. It was smooth, white and oval-shaped with dark brown blobs and splotches on it. She looked at it in puzzlement.

'And this is a gadget?' said Dawn, doubtfully.

'Sure is,' said Socrates. 'It's a shell phone.'

'A phone?' she said, trying to peek between the shell's teeth on its underside.

'Uh-huh. Good, isn't it?'

'Do you use it like a normal phone?' said Dawn, staring at the shell in bewilderment. 'Wouldn't that seem a bit ... well ... odd to anyone who saw you?'

'Nah ... It's one of them tiger cowries ... you know – the sort of shell that you hold to your ear to listen to the sound of the sea. You'd look perfectly natural with that clamped to your lughole.'

'Oh, I *see*,' said Dawn, smiling. 'That's quite clever.'

'Mmm. The folks at P.I.N.G. are a pretty smart bunch. They certainly live up to their name. It's an Incredibly Nifty Gadget, all right.' Socrates took the shell from her, squinted at it and pressed it with his fingers. He sighed. 'Shame it doesn't work. Prob'ly been sitting at the bottom of the gadget box for a good few years. I'll tell you what, Dawn, I'll take it home tonight and have a bit of a tinker – see if I can bring it back to life.'

'Thanks,' said Dawn.

Socrates put the shell in his trouser pocket and began to rummage around in the box again. 'Got something!'

he said after half a minute. He drew out a cigarette and a matchbox.

'Gadgets?' she said uncertainly.

'Too right,' replied Socrates. He shook the box of matches, but instead of making a rattling noise, it made no sound at all. 'Miniature camera,' he said, grinning at Dawn. It did not open like a little drawer as most matchboxes did; this one flipped open at one end to reveal a tiny lens, a shutter release button and a wheel that wound the film on.

Dawn was riveted. 'It's amazing,' she said, 'but it must take minuscule pictures. Wouldn't you need a magnifying glass to see them?'

'Yeah,' said Socrates. 'You're spot on. It's a clever little invention. Doesn't produce a negative like most cameras do. Just spits out a strip of titchy photographs called microdots. Each microdot is the size of a pinhead – and to look at it you'd need to use one of these.'

He held the cigarette between the thumb and forefinger of his other hand. 'This,' he said, 'is a microdot viewer.' Socrates showed her how to unfasten each end of the cigarette. It was like a tiny microscope inside. 'Course,' he said, pocketing both items, 'we can't send a kid on a mission with a ciggie and a box of matches – even if they *are* fake. No, no, no, no. I'll have a go at modifying them for you, shall I?'

'Yes, please,' said Dawn.

'Now, what else can I find?' He continued with his search inside the gadget box. 'What the devil ...?' he said, producing a sombrero and a pair of castanets.

'They're gadgets, too, right?' said Dawn.

'Actually ... nope, I don't think so,' said Socrates, examining them closely. 'They must've belonged to my auntie Florrie. She picked them up on her travels, no doubt.' He tossed them aside and had one last, desperate ferret in the packing trunk. 'That's it, I'm afraid,' he said. 'We've got next to nothing left in our gadget budget, so until Red manages to persuade the Chief of S.H.H. to give our department more funds – and frankly I shan't be holding my breath – we won't be able to place another order with P.I.N.G.'

'It's a bit like asking for more pocket money, isn't it?' said Dawn, and she sighed.

Socrates grinned and nodded. 'Yeah ... you can plead as much as you like, but it won't do any good. Philippa Killingback's never going to stump up any more cash for P.S.S.T. Hard as nails, she is. Reckons that after she's doled out each department's annual allowance, it's down to the Head of each one to make the money last. Between you and me, Dawn, I think she's got it in for P.S.S.T. Red won't tell us what our allowance was this year, but the rumour is that it was *measly*.'

'Will Red get into trouble?' asked Dawn, remembering the fiery telephone conversation between him and the Chief of S.H.H. that she had overheard the previous morning.

'Yeah,' said Socrates sadly. 'Could lose his job. We might all be given our marching orders if things get any worse. P.S.S.T. is supposed to catch at least a dozen scheming spies or traitors per year. We've only managed to nab a handful so far. If we don't reach our target …' He drew his finger across his neck and made a noise like someone being garrotted.

'Oh,' said Dawn and bit her lip.

Socrates smiled. 'But don't you worry about us. You've got quite enough to think about for now, what with your test and all.'

'Test?' said Dawn, her eyes popping. 'What test?'

'The one on spying techniques that I'm going to give you tomorrow.'

Chapter Eight

A New Identity

'Armpit,' said Dawn firmly as she planted her right plimsoll on the first blue stair. 'Bungalow, Chutney, Doodah,' she said, timing the utterance of each word with the thump of her feet on the next three steps. She furrowed her brow before climbing higher. 'Er ... Egghead, Flip-flop, Gunk ... now, what comes after "Gunk"?' She barely had enough time to say 'Hurrah' before a massive yawn stretched her mouth open wide enough for a double-scoop ice cream to pass between her lips without even touching them.

Dawn clutched the banister rail and blinked sleepily. She had stayed up into the early hours, revising for Socrates's test and, although she had read *Keeping to the Shadows* from cover to cover, tiredness was making her brain feel fuzzy. This did not help when she was trying to recall the special phonetic alphabet used by spies when they needed to pronounce letters clearly over the radio. It was called the Cumberbatch Alphabet, deriving its name from its creator who was a lowly C.L.I.C.K. employee called Stanley Cumberbatch. Stanley had thought up the alphabet in a launderette one Sunday afternoon whilst waiting for his smalls to stop spinning round and round (as mentioned in the footnotes at the bottom of page one hundred and six of *Keeping to the Shadows*).

Dawn was familiar with doing tests, thanks to her teacher's almost fanatical obsession with them. Mrs Kitchen tended to inform her class when tests were going to happen, so that they would have ample opportunity to revise, but occasionally she liked to spring tests on them without any warning. Dawn had become quite skilled at sensing when these spontaneous tests were going to occur. Friday afternoons were always a good bet. Firstly, Mrs Kitchen would halt in mid-sentence and gaze dreamily out of the window; then she might glance at her watch and give a heavy sigh; and finally she would lean sideways and grope around in her bag. If, when she withdrew her hand, it was holding a crochet hook or a puzzle magazine, Dawn knew that a test would be announced imminently. Then she and her classmates would spend the next half hour with their heads bent over a page of questions while Mrs Kitchen made progress with her new cardigan or tackled a jumbo wordsearch.

Dawn's ability to predict when a surprise test was

about to befall her class was not the only instinctive skill that she possessed when it came to tests. She also had a knack for sensing which questions were likely to crop up on a test paper, and therefore which topics it would be prudent to mug up on before taking it. As soon as Dawn had come across the Cumberbatch Alphabet in *Keeping to the Shadows*, she felt sure that she would be tested on it.

'Idiot,' said Dawn as she mounted another step on the staircase. She was determined to reel off the whole alphabet before she arrived at the door of the Codes and Devices room. 'Jellyfish, Key-ring, Leotard, Muesli ... uh-oh.' She stumbled slightly as Peebles dashed through her legs with a little bundle of envelopes tied around his middle. 'Morning, Peebles!' she called after him. 'Oh, no, I've forgotten where I'd got to! It was something you have for breakfast. Might have been marmalade ... No. Muesli – that was it. Now, I think the word for "N" is a type of flower ...'

Once Dawn had thought of 'Nasturtium' she rattled off the next few at an impressive speed. 'Onion, Puddle, Quicksand, Roundabout, Sausage, Tracksuit, Unicorn ... er ... er ...' She paused on the top stair, panting slightly, and hitched up her knee socks. 'Voodoo,' she said suddenly.

The corridor was empty apart from Peebles, who was busy trying to alert someone to his presence outside the door marked 'Clerical Affairs'. Dawn walked slowly over the carpet, urging herself to remember the last few letters of the Cumberbatch Alphabet.

'Wednesday, Xmas, um … um …' She stopped outside the Codes and Devices room just as the doorknob began to turn. 'Yo-yo … Zilch,' blurted out Dawn half a second before Socrates's rugged face appeared.

The boy with the scruffy dog was there on the street again. When Dawn had seen him the day before, he had been attempting to drag his dog away from a lamppost. Today, the situation was reversed. It was the boy who seemed to be rooted to the spot on the pavement opposite the Dampside Hotel and the dog who was yanking on the lead, eager to progress further along the road.

Dawn kept her eye on them both as she paced up and down beside the window in the Codes and Devices room. Having spent most of the morning seated behind a desk, she felt the need to indulge in a spot of exercise to loosen up her limbs. The test had proved to be quite a challenging one and her body had been taut with concentration for the entire morning.

There had been questions on almost every aspect of spying, from trailing suspects in the dark to picking locks with a pair of tweezers. She had encoded straightforward sentences so that they resembled twaddle and decoded complete nonsense so that it made perfect sense. Question sixty-three had caused a smile to blossom on Dawn's face. It had asked her which, out of the following, did not belong in the Cumberbatch Alphabet: Egghead, Balderdash, Tracksuit, Puddle. She had underlined 'Balderdash' without a moment's hesitation.

Dawn cast a glance at Socrates who was sitting in his wing chair with her test paper resting on a clipboard on his lap. His face was solemn. Every few seconds, with a flick of his wrist, he marked her answers right or wrong. Occasionally he blew out his cheeks, sighed or swept a hand through his stubbly grey hair. Dawn suspected that she might have made a few mistakes but she was fairly confident that she had managed a half-decent score.

'Stop doing that!' yelled a boy's voice from the street. Dawn looked out of the window again. The boy had hooked his elbow around a railing and was trying to stop himself from being pulled off his feet by the dog, whose claws were scrabbling against the paving slabs. 'Haltwhistle, sit!' said the boy with more than a hint of desperation in his voice. To Dawn's surprise, the dog appeared to obey the boy's command – only it couldn't really be described as a 'sit'. The dog had lowered his rear end by only a couple of inches. It would be more accurate to describe it as a sort of 'crouch'. As it turned out, the dog's position was neither a sit nor a crouch. In fact, he was merely bunching his muscles to prepare for a massive leap. He bounded forward like an extremely hairy greyhound springing from a trap; the lead slipped from the boy's grasp, and the dog, followed by his horrified, spindly-legged owner, dashed off down the street.

'Run away,' murmured Socrates.

'Er … yes,' said Dawn hesitantly. 'They have.' She wondered how Socrates could possibly have witnessed the incident with the boy and the dog from his wing chair.

He shot her a bemused look and prodded the test paper with his pen. 'Last question,' he boomed. '"What action should a spy take if he's sure that he's been rumbled and someone is after him?" You've put: "Walk a bit faster and try not to look too afraid." That wouldn't do, would it?'

'I guess not,' said Dawn slowly. Her brain had felt pretty numb by the time she had reached the final question and she was prepared to admit that she hadn't given it much thought.

'If your cover's been blown and you've got someone on your tail you should run away,' said Socrates, 'as fast as you possibly can. You mustn't let yourself be captured.'

'OK,' agreed Dawn.

'Chances are he'll probably give chase and then it will be up to you to give him the slip. That's why it's important to know the area like the back of your hand. If you're having trouble shaking him off, find yourself a big crowd of people and lose yourself in it. That's always worked for me.'

'Right,' said Dawn.

'Apart from that last blunder,' said Socrates, totting up her score, 'your other mistakes were fairly minor. All things considered, you haven't done badly at all. Good effort, Dawn.' He gripped the arms of his chair as if he was going to get up, seemed to change his mind, deftly folded Dawn's test paper until it resembled an aeroplane and threw it back to her.

She caught it in one hand, then smoothed it out and studied a wavy vertical line of red ticks and crosses. There were several comments scrawled by Socrates in the margin and at the bottom of the sheet was a circled number.

'Eighty-one-and-a-half per cent!' breathed Dawn. She felt immensely proud. 'That's got to be worth a couple of house points at least!'

'Nice haircut,' said Red approvingly.

'Thanks,' said Dawn. After the test, she had been summoned to the Concealment and Disguise room and had eaten a lunch of banana sandwiches while Izzie snipped at her hair with a small pair of silver scissors. Instead of a head of lank, rather untidy jaw-length hair, she now possessed a chic, short hairstyle with a feathered fringe. There was nothing remotely flamboyant about it, but Dawn had opened her eyes very wide when Izzie had held up a mirror. It was the closest thing to a fashionable haircut that she had ever had.

'Cute outfit, too,' said Emma.

'Isn't it?' said Dawn, stepping over the threshold of Red's office. She felt a little naked without her mushroom-coloured knee socks and faithful old plimsolls, but she had to admit that her new white sandals (complete with creased straps and worn-down heels to make them appear as if they'd belonged to her for ages) kept her toes nice and cool. It had to be said that her new navy shorts were also far more summery than the woollen kilt she had been wearing earlier in the day. Her new pale yellow T-shirt was her favourite item of clothing, though. Its sleeves, with their scalloped edges, were very pretty, but they weren't the reason that she liked it so much. It was the colour that had won Dawn over. It was almost exactly the same shade of yellow as the front door of number eight, Windmill View.

'You look just perfect,' said Emma.

Dawn smiled – even wider than she had done when Jagdish had been taking her picture a short while ago. She had sat on a stool in the Forgery and Fakery room while he clicked away with his camera, using up a whole roll of film. He was probably developing it at that moment. She couldn't wait to see the photographs of herself after her makeover.

'I feel like a new person … kind of,' she said.

'Good,' said Red, sitting forward in his green leather chair. 'That's the idea!' He rubbed his hands together before sorting through a pile of papers on his desk. 'I think it's time –'

'Excuse me, sir, but Trudy's not here yet,' pointed out Emma.

Red sighed. 'Botheration. There's no point in starting without her. What do you suppose is holding her up?'

'I believe she's having a fitting.'

'Still?' Red looked amazed. 'Goodness me! I wouldn't have thought it'd take more than five minutes to throw on a few togs.' He began to nibble fretfully at his nails. 'We've got an awful lot to get through. Nip across the corridor, Emma, would you, please – and ask Trudy to get over here pronto.'

'With pleasure, sir.'

Before Emma could rise from her chair there came the sound of a door opening in the next room. Brisk footsteps crossed the small space where Trudy did her typing and then someone rapped quite vigorously on the door of Red's office.

'You may come in,' he said. 'Oh, Trudy, it's you. Excellent. My, my – don't you look nice.'

'Nice' wasn't a word that Dawn would have chosen. It didn't seem as if Trudy agreed with his choice of adjective either. She stood in the doorway dressed in a pair of brown slacks, a plain cotton blouse and a baseball cap. The expression on her face was nothing less than murderous.

'I resign,' she said.

There was a pause; then Red exploded into laughter. 'You've got a cracking sense of humour,' he said admiringly. 'Hasn't she, Emma? What a wit!'

'Er … I've got a feeling she's deadly serious, sir.'

'Hah, hah, hah – I don't think so!' Red neatened the pile of papers on his desk. 'Now,' he said, becoming serious again. He stole a glance at the top sheet. 'I bet you're both dying to know what your false names are going to be –'

'I refuse to go on this mission looking like a scruff-bag,' said Trudy, folding her arms in a defiant manner. 'You *promised* me a stylish wardrobe. When cashmere was mentioned I imagined a beautiful roll-neck sweater – not,' she said, lifting a trouser leg, 'a pair of *socks*. I can't possibly be expected to go out in public wearing this hideous get-up. I look like a farm hand, for goodness sake.'

Red and Emma glanced at each other and smiles crept across their faces.

'You're almost there – but not quite,' said Red.

'I don't follow,' said Trudy crossly.

'Sandra Wilson – that's the name we've selected for

you. Originally, I'd visualised Sandra as a teacher of flower arranging, a Brown Owl ... or something like that, but Emma came up with a much better idea.'

'*Did* she indeed,' said Trudy, her face like thunder.

'Yup. Farm hand wasn't a bad guess. The career we've chosen for Sandra does have something to do with agriculture ... or should that be horticulture?' Red grinned proudly. 'You're going to be a gardener.'

Trudy pulled a face. 'And that would involve ...'

'Mowing lawns,' said Red, 'digging, weeding, a bit of pruning here and there. It's the perfect job for someone undercover. You'll be able to infiltrate no end of gardens and – this is the really clever bit – Dawn can be your helper! It's the summer holidays; you're a single mum; nobody will turn a hair if you bring your daughter to work with you .., and while you're doing your stuff in the flowerbeds, Dawn can snoop about. Cunning idea, don't you think?'

'I suppose,' said Trudy grudgingly. 'But I still don't think I'm the right person for this assignment.' She held out her smooth, pale fingers, the nails of which had been painted pillar-box red. 'Do these *look* like the hands of a gardener to you?'

'Not at the moment,' agreed Emma, 'but their appearance can be altered easily enough. Once Izzie's clipped your nails and pressed a little dirt underneath each one ...'

Trudy groaned. 'I hope I'm going to get a pay rise after this.'

'We'll see,' said Red, pushing a few sheets of paper into her hands. 'This is your personal legend.'

'My what?' Trudy said.

'Details about your new identity: your birth date, your family background, favourite pop group, and so on.'

'And here's yours, Dawn,' said Emma, handing over some pages which had been paper-clipped together.

'I want you both to memorise them,' said Red, glancing at the clock on his desk. 'I'll give you fifteen minutes.'

'State your name, please,' said Red, 'in full.'

'Katherine Ann Wilson,' said Dawn, 'but everyone calls me "Kitty".'

'Age?'

'Ten years, five months and nine days,' said Dawn precisely. 'My birthday is the eighteenth of February. I was born on a Tuesday.'

'Where?' said Red.

'In a place called Bury St Edmunds. I weighed seven pounds exactly.'

'Excellent,' said Red, ticking a few things off a list. 'Now, tell me some more about yourself, Kitty.'

'I'm an only child,' said Dawn. 'My mum is called

Sandra. She's forty-one and she looks after people's gardens for a living. She and my dad, Pete, got divorced when I was little. Um …'

'You're doing very well,' whispered Emma.

'My hobbies are stamp-collecting and gymnastics,' said Dawn, squeezing her eyes shut and concentrating very hard. 'My favourite colour is pale pink, I read books by Enid Blyton, I like chips and cheesecake but marzipan makes me feel sick … and I want to be a schoolteacher when I grow up.'

'Very impressive,' said Red. 'Let's hear from your mum, now, shall we?'

Trudy failed to do as well as Dawn. She misremembered Sandra's birthday and couldn't recall her favourite film, but Red seemed to think that with a little extra coaching, she would be word perfect by the morning of the mission.

'It's quite exciting, isn't it?' said Dawn, delighted by her own faultless performance. 'I think I'm going to enjoy pretending to be someone else.'

Trudy grunted. 'I suppose I can put up with these dreadful clothes and the odd bit of gardening, but if I find my files in a mess when I return …'

'There's no need to worry,' said Red calmly. 'I believe I mentioned that Emma will be taking over your duties while you're absent. You're not the sort to let standards slip, are you, Emma?'

'Definitely not, sir,' said Emma.

'Huh,' said Trudy. 'Couldn't manage to put Bob's file back in the right place, though, could you?'

'I've already told you,' said Emma heatedly. *'That wasn't me.'*

'Well, it wasn't any of the others. I've asked them.' Trudy directed her next comments at Red. 'I noticed the file was out of place last week. Not only was it stuffed into the filing cabinet willy-nilly … well, hold on a moment,' she said, briskly walking over to the door. 'I'll fetch it, shall I? Then you can see the damage for yourself. '

In half a minute, Trudy had returned to Red's office with a grey cardboard folder in one hand. She opened it and produced a sheet of thick mauve paper with a gold edging, much like the paper upon which Dawn's contract had been typed. At the top of the paper Dawn could see the name Robert Alfred Chalk, and below it his personal details were listed.

As Trudy held out the sheet in front of her, Dawn was able to crane her neck and read a few words. Bob was thirty-three. He was described as being 'shrewd, determined and fearless'. He'd had over one hundred aliases, and his list of 'special skills', which included aikido and snake charming, was impressively long.

'You see!' said Trudy, pointing at the bottom right-hand corner of the piece of paper – or at least where the corner should have been. 'It's been ripped!'

'Oh, dear,' said Red, examining the torn edge, where a small triangle of mauve paper had been removed. Dawn watched him run his finger along the lowest line of text. Next to the category 'Dislikes, Allergies or Phobias' had been typed the word 'None'. 'I agree,' he said to Trudy, 'that someone's been rather careless, but I don't think there's any harm done. No information has been lost as far as I can see.'

'Nevertheless, it'd better not happen again,' said Trudy, whipping the piece of paper out of his hands and staring pointedly in Emma's direction.

'Golly, is that the time?' said Red, glancing at his clock. Its hour hand had almost reached the number five. 'Time to wrap things up for today!' He opened a drawer in his desk and lifted out a gardening manual. 'A little something for you to read in bed,' he said, handing it to Trudy.

'Thanks,' she mumbled.

'As for my young spy,' said Red kindly, turning to Dawn, 'I think you deserve the evening off. Socrates tells me that you scored very highly in your test this morning.'

Dawn felt her cheeks turning pink.

'Well, Kitty Wilson,' said Red. 'Only one more day to go before you can put all those things you've learned into practice!'

Chapter Nine

Trouble Downstairs

'Operation Question Mark?' said Red, looking flummoxed. He peered more closely at the piece of paper he was holding. 'I don't remember calling it that ...'

'Well, you did,' said Trudy testily. 'That's what you'd written down. You gave me your notes and I typed them up word for word. If there's an error, it certainly isn't mine.'

'Oh!' Red slapped himself on the forehead. 'I know what I did! I was trying to come up with a code name for this mission and I couldn't think of one which seemed to fit. I wrote down "Operation" with a question mark next to it and decided to mull it over in my mind. I must have forgotten all about it,' he said. 'Anyone got any suggestions?'

The room fell silent as everyone thought very hard. Everyone, that is, except Dawn.

She was far too preoccupied with the butterflies in

her stomach to care about the name of the mission. *Her* mission. The mission which she would be embarking upon *tomorrow*. She hugged her stomach as the fluttering sensation grew worse.

Red had called this meeting 'The Final Briefing'. He had gathered together the staff of P.S.S.T. in the Top Secret Missions room first thing on Friday morning. On entering the room, Dawn had noticed that all manner of maps and photographs had been pinned to the walls. It looked like some sort of exhibition. There was a large-scale map of Cherry Bentley, showing field boundaries and footpaths with multicoloured drawing pins stuck to it. Alongside this were aerial photographs of the village green, the church, the local shops and a tumbledown mansion. Three black-and-white portrait shots turned out to be photographs of P.S.S.T.'s unfortunate spies: Miles Evergreen, Bob Chalk and Angela Bradshaw. Although Dawn scanned the walls from top to bottom she failed to find a photograph labelled 'Murdo Meek'.

Red had surprised Dawn by dressing more authoritatively than usual. He had put on a new brown tie with yellow stripes, swapped his sandals for a pair of lace-ups and trimmed his wispy ginger beard. He had also adopted an expression of utmost seriousness.

In fact, thought Dawn, as she glanced around the room at all the members of P.S.S.T. who were racking their brains to think of an apt name for the mission, everybody looked rather grim-faced, now she came to think of it.

'Operation Hopscotch,' said Izzie suddenly.

'Hopscotch! Pah! That's a kids' game,' sneered Socrates.

'That's why I suggested it,' said Izzie. 'I thought it would be fitting to use a name that's associated with children – in honour of wee Dawn. This is the first time a youngster has been sent on a mission, don't you forget.'

'Of course I haven't forgotten,' grumbled Socrates. 'But Operation Hopscotch just sounds soppy. You need something a bit grittier – a word that could inspire you to do courageous things ... like Arrow or Scimitar or Blunderbuss ...'

Red's face brightened. 'Operation Blunderbuss – that does have a certain ring to it ...'

'What is it with you boys?' said Izzie sharply, a frown appearing on her elfin face. 'I won't have you calling *another* of our missions after some nasty weapon. Why can't we choose something nice that doesn't tend to *wound* people?'

'How about Operation Peashooter?' said Jagdish. 'Peas don't really hurt. All they do is sting a little.'

Socrates groaned and put his head in his hands.

'Leapfrog,' said Izzie. 'Now, that's a lovely children's

game. Operation Leapfrog.'

Red shook his head. 'I don't think so, Izzie. It's not very uplifting, is it?'

'How do you feel about Operation Bold Stroke?' said Emma.

'Operation Sunstroke, more like,' mumbled Trudy, 'with me outside all day, mowing lawns and goodness knows what, in this awful heat.'

'Bold Stroke ... hmm,' said Red. 'That's not bad.'

Socrates lifted his head and grimaced. 'I don't like it.'

'Operation Skipping Rope.'

'Operation Broadsword.'

Red and Izzie exchanged scathing glances.

'Operation Nameless,' said Edith woodenly.

Half an hour later, the discussion was over. Red clapped his hands together. 'That's settled then, folks. Operation Question Mark it is.'

The ceiling fan rattled like an old cartwheel above Dawn's head. Its blades rotated lazily. The fan was displacing a fair few specks of dust but it was not generating much of a breeze. As the morning wore on the room became unpleasantly stuffy, but opening a window was out of the question. What Red had to say was far too secret for anyone below, in the backyard or in neighbouring gardens to overhear.

When he had finished talking about 'objectives' and

'strategies', Red stood beside the large-scale map of Cherry Bentley and pointed at different coloured drawing pins with a long wooden ruler. Each pin represented a building or place that was relevant to Dawn's investigation. The tip of the ruler touched on them all – from the red pin which showed the location of the phone box where Bob had been found in a heap, to the yellow pin indicating where Dawn and Trudy would be lodging.

Finally, Red made a confession. He had not informed the Chief of S.H.H. about Operation Question Mark and he had no intention of doing so. The only people who were aware of Dawn's mission were the members of P.S.S.T., and he wanted it to remain that way.

'You mean this mission hasn't been authorised?' Trudy looked appalled.

'Philippa Killingback would have put the mockers on the whole thing,' said Red, '*if* I'd been stupid enough to tell her about it. She thinks Bob and Miles are accident-prone idiots, she refuses to believe that Murdo Meek could still be alive, and she'd *never* agree to the hiring of a spy who's only eleven years old.'

'Are you sure it's wise to go behind her back like this?' said Izzie. 'The Chief is going to go ballistic if she finds out what we're up to.'

'What do you mean, "if"?' said Jagdish, turning his mournful eyes on his colleague. 'Philippa will get wind of it, sure enough – and when she does we'll all be out of a job.'

'It could come to that, anyway,' said Red, 'even if Operation Question Mark *doesn't* go ahead.'

'Whaaat?' said Izzie.

'This department's in trouble,' said Red gravely. 'We haven't caught nearly enough scheming spies and traitors this year, and our funds are almost gone – I had to use the rest of our biscuit allowance to pay for Dawn, and we've got less than a fiver left in our gadget budget. Philippa Killingback wants me to make big cutbacks, and by that she means *redundancies.*'

'So, who's for the chop?' said Socrates gloomily.

'No one,' answered Red, 'if I've got anything to do with it. Just think – if Murdo Meek is in that village and we can bring him in, he'll be the biggest fish we've ever caught. Imagine how pleased that will make the Chief. I doubt she'll be mentioning cutbacks ever again.' Quite suddenly, Red's face assumed a startled look. 'Why, Peebles – whatever's the matter?'

The black cat, who seemed to have appeared from nowhere, had sprung on to the table and launched himself at Red. His claws gleamed like pearls as he sailed, spreadeagled, through the air; then he landed with precision, sinking each claw into Red's checked shirt – and into his skin, going by the massive yell that escaped from Red's mouth.

'Blimey!' said Socrates. 'I've never seen Peebles act like that before.'

'There's something wrong,' said Edith, rising out of her chair.

'Look! He's brought a letter!' said Dawn, pointing to a slip of paper which had been tucked into the cat's harness and was just visible underneath his tummy. She ran round the table and tweaked it free while Emma unhooked Peebles's claws with great care. While she was doing this, Red said 'ouch' at least twelve times – and a few other words besides.

'Who's it from?' said Socrates impatiently as Red took the letter from Dawn and unfolded it. This did not happen quite as fast as it could have done because Red kept fingering his chest and wincing.

'Poor little cat,' said Emma, holding Peebles in her arms. 'His heart's beating nineteen to the dozen ... and look at his poor tail.' The cat's tail was twice its normal size, twitching and curling like a huge, hairy caterpillar.

Red breathed in sharply and held the note aloft so that everyone could see it.

At first glance, Dawn thought that an insect had been squashed in the centre of the page. However, when she looked again, she realised that it was a single word, scrawled very messily in black ink. It read:

EMERJENCY!

'Nathan,' said Edith instantly, making for the door. 'That boy can't spell for toffee. Everyone stay here. I'll find out what's going on …'

'I'll come with you,' said Red. 'You mightn't be able to handle things on your own …'

Edith's back stiffened. Dawn watched with bated breath as Edith tilted her head and gave Red the sort of look that Medusa the Gorgon might have used in ancient Greece to turn people into stone. Instead of telling Red, in no uncertain terms, that she was perfectly capable of sorting out any situation single-handedly (which was the speech anticipated by Dawn and, most likely, everyone else in the room), she nodded politely and said, 'Thanks, I'd welcome your assistance.'

Uneasy glances were cast all around the room, but no one spoke a word until the footfalls of Red and Edith had died away.

'Oh, my,' said Izzie, wringing her hands anxiously. 'Whatever do you suppose has happened? You don't think this is the laddie's idea of a practical joke?'

'Don't be nuts,' growled Socrates. 'Give the boy some credit. Nathan might be a bit of a twit but he's not a complete turnip-brain. It must be a genuine crisis.'

'Well, a fire can't have broken out,' said Jagdish, 'or he would have set off the alarm.'

'Perhaps,' said Trudy, 'the Chief has just arrived on one of her "impromptu visits". You know how she likes to turn up out of the blue and catch us all off guard.'

'Do you think she's been tipped off about Operation Question Mark?' said Emma fearfully.

'Nah. Whatever Nathan's panicking about – it's not the Chief,' said Socrates. 'Let's face it: a visit from Her Highness is a bit of a headache, but it's not something you could really class as an *emergency*, is it?'

'Oh, I don't know,' said Trudy. 'Nathan's scared to death of her. I am, too, come to that.'

'It's not her, I tell you!' said Socrates. 'It's something else.'

Dawn was only half-listening to the theories of her P.S.S.T. colleagues. She had got up from her chair and was hovering by the door, which Red and Edith had left ajar. If she listened very carefully, she found that she could hear something. Although it was muffled and far away, the urgency of the sound was plain.

Unnoticed by the other members of P.S.S.T., Dawn stepped out of the room. She moved along the corridor, as sure-footed and glassy-eyed as a sleepwalker, her ears straining to catch the distant, unceasing hollering. The door leading into Trudy's workspace was open, and once she had entered the room the sound became much clearer. Every couple of seconds, she heard a plaintive sort of yell. Were they calls for help? Dawn could not be sure. In fact, the closer she drew to the window the less they sounded like the cries of a human and the more they resembled ...

Dawn unlatched the window and heaved it upwards. Forgetting to be inconspicuous, she stuck her head out and looked down. There he was! Sitting on the pavement below her with his lead knotted round a railing. It was the scruffy dog from earlier – and he was barking non-stop.

From such a height, Dawn thought the dog looked like a heap of old rags. All she could see was a tangled mass of charcoal-grey fur and, occasionally, a flash of pink and white when he raised his muzzle to the sky and produced a particularly ear-splitting yelp. Dawn glanced nervously up and down the street. People were stopping to stare at the dog and a number of curtains were twitching. She could not see any sign of the boy with the skinny legs whom she had taken to be the dog's owner.

'Hey!' called Dawn to the dog. 'Shh! Stop making so much noise!'

Her pleas were ignored – as were several less polite requests from other people in the street. As well as delivering a volley of woofs, the dog had now got to his feet and was wagging his feathery tail. Clearly, he was enjoying all the attention.

'Enough!' said a voice that expected to be obeyed and, briefly, Edith appeared in the street below, untied the dog's lead and yanked him inside. The dog stopped barking immediately – probably because Edith had clamped a hand around his muzzle, which, thought Dawn, was quite a brave thing to do.

Silence was not restored, however. Before Edith could close the door of the Dampside Hotel, a number of shouts spilled out on to the street. There could be no mistake this time. The voice was definitely human – and young and male and very, very angry.

'Not another one,' said Trudy.

Dawn raised herself on to her tiptoes and craned her neck, but she could not manage to see what Trudy and the rest of P.S.S.T. were looking at. As soon as the tread of feet had been heard in the corridor, everyone had rushed out of the Top Secret Missions room to find out what was going on. Dawn had been the last to emerge into the corridor and she had been dismayed to find that her colleagues had completely blocked her view. They were so tightly packed that she could not manage to squeeze past their hips – and glimpsing anything over their shoulders was nigh on impossible. Eventually, she got down on her hands and knees and crawled between their legs.

The first thing she saw (apart from the carpet at very close quarters) was a pair of brown leather shoes a bit like moccasins and two bronzed legs as slender as broom handles. She raised her head, which enabled her to see the whole boy all at once.

He was probably not much older than thirteen, Dawn decided. Most of the boys in her neighbourhood dressed in football gear when they weren't at school, but this boy was clothed in a rugby shirt and long, buff-coloured shorts with lots of pockets. He had dishevelled, black curly hair which flopped over his forehead, and an impressive sun tan. His mouth was all pinched and puckered into a scowl, but its fierceness was difficult to judge because she could not see his eyes. They were hidden behind a handkerchief which had been fashioned into a blindfold.

'Who's this young scrap, Red?' demanded Socrates. 'And what've you brought him up here for? What's going on, eh? Dawn said something about a dog –'

'First a girl – and now, a boy,' said Trudy, who was positively fuming. 'What other surprises have you got in store for us, Red? Don't tell me! Next week we'll be opening our doors to school parties …'

'My name is Felix Pomeroy-Pitt,' said the boy, trying to do his best to free his arm from Red's tight grasp, 'and as soon as I get out of here I'm going straight to the police!'

'There won't be any need for that,' said Edith, appearing at the top of the stairs. She was struggling to restrain the scruffy dog, whose ears had pricked up at the sound of the boy's voice. The dog was the hairiest creature that Dawn had ever seen. His coat was the colour of mud and soot mixed together and it looked as if it hadn't been brushed for months. He was smaller than Dawn had presumed him to be, with a big wet nose, a short, grizzled snout and a tongue the length of a strip of bacon.

'Haltwhistle!' said Felix delightedly as the dog careered into his owner. 'Are you all right?' he said, reaching out blindly and finding a shaggy ear. The dog sat down and scratched himself. 'Have they hurt you? Remember what I taught you: one bark for "yes", two barks for "no".'

Haltwhistle didn't seem to be able to decide. He yawned, lay down on the carpet and nibbled at one of his paws.

'What a mangy fleabag,' observed Socrates.

'How dare you!' Felix was incensed. He tried to hurl himself at where he imagined Socrates to be standing but Red held him in check. 'I'll have you know that Haltwhistle is a pure-bred Tibetan terrier with a *very* fine lineage,' said Felix, shaking with fury. 'His grandfather *almost* won *Crufts*.'

'Pull the other one!' said Socrates, his voice full of scorn. 'No one in their right mind would stick a rosette on a mutt like that.'

'Whichever breed he is,' said Edith, cutting in quickly before Felix could retaliate, 'your dog is quite

142

unharmed, I assure you.'

'He'd better be,' said Felix, tearing at his blindfold with his free hand. It slipped down his nose, revealing a pair of chocolate-brown eyes and thick, dark brows that very nearly met up in the middle. He blinked for a few moments, glanced at his dog, then stared at the small crowd of people in front of him. Dawn got to her feet and smiled. Although he was frowning furiously, she thought he had a rather nice face.

'Who *are* you people?' said Felix. His darting eyes seemed to skim over Dawn, although she was standing directly in front of him. 'Hey!' He prodded Red accusingly. 'You said if I came with you, you'd tell me what was going on. *I demand to know what you've done with my granny!*'

'The boy's got a screw loose,' said Socrates.

'She's here somewhere, isn't she?' insisted Felix. He took a deep breath and bellowed loudly, 'Granny? Can you hear me? It's John! Don't worry – I've come to rescue you!'

'Goodness me,' said Jagdish. 'The boy is very muddle-headed. Now he's forgotten his own name.'

'Poor flower,' said Izzie. 'He can't be well.' She approached Felix and gazed at him pityingly. 'There, there … we haven't got your granny, dear –'

'Yes, you have,' said Felix, though not as brashly as before. His frown had changed to one of bewilderment rather than anger. 'You *have*,' he repeated, his voice beginning to waver. 'Old Mrs Mudge saw Granny from the bus ... so we walked and walked ... then Haltwhistle picked up her scent ...'

'Excuse me, sir,' said Emma, whose cheeks had been growing pinker and pinker. She looked pleadingly at Red and put her hands on her hips. 'I really don't understand what's going on. Why have you allowed this boy up here? It seems a bit ... well ... *reckless* to me. Surely you're taking an awfully big risk. I think we're entitled to an explanation, sir ... if ... um ... you don't mind.' She bit her lip as if she was embarrassed by her outburst.

'You're absolutely right,' said Red. He heaved a sigh and rubbed his forehead wearily. 'I brought the boy up here because I couldn't think what else to do with him. Together, he and his dog were making enough noise to alert the whole of Pimlico.' Red shrugged in a helpless sort of way. 'You know as well as I do that we can't afford to attract that kind of attention. The only way to quieten him down was to give him what he wanted.'

'A guided tour of P.S.S.T.?' said Socrates contemptuously. He turned to Edith. 'Some Head of Security you are! I can't believe you let Red talk you into this!'

'No,' said Red. 'You've misunderstood. What Felix wants is the truth.'

'Pomeroy-Pitt,' muttered Trudy, who hadn't spoken

for several minutes.

'The name was familiar to me, too,' said Red. 'I realised pretty quickly who he was.'

'So, who is he?' asked Socrates.

'He's the grandson of Angela Bradshaw.'

The corridor fell silent.

'I'm afraid,' said Red, gripping the boy's shoulder tenderly, 'there's something you don't know about your grandmother. For nearly forty years she's been a spy.'

Chapter Ten

The File on Murdo Meek

'You can't be serious,' said Felix, accompanying his comment with a snort of disbelief. 'That gormless-looking girl … the one who gave me the cup of tea … you're sending *her* to find my granny? That's the craziest thing I've ever heard!'

Dawn was rather relieved that she could not see the look on the boy's face. His words were hurtful enough. She had fetched him a hot drink because she felt sorry for him. He had been so shocked when Red had revealed that his grandmother was a spy (and not an author of books on teashop walks as he had been led to believe). Now, she found herself wishing that she had tipped the contents of the china cup over his horrible head.

When Red began to speak again, Dawn twisted her neck slightly so that her one-eyed gaze fell upon his face. The keyhole felt uncomfortably cold and knobbly against her cheekbone but she was far too interested in what was being said to worry about any discomfort. Red was sitting, facing her direction, in his green leather chair. He had his arms folded and was staring across his desk at Felix with a look of barely concealed frustration.

'Dawn's the best person for the job,' said Red shortly. 'Take my word for it, young man.'

'I want you to send a grown-up!'

Dawn switched her attention back to Felix. She saw him toss his black curls arrogantly.

'I don't think you realise quite how much I love my granny. I don't want some dopey girl making a mess of her rescue. How about that pretty blonde woman, or better still the grumpy old guy who looks like a criminal. He's not exactly James Bond, but he'd do.'

Dawn felt affronted. She did not appreciate being referred to as 'some dopey girl' any more than she had liked being called 'gormless'.

Since she had arrived at P.S.S.T. she had been feeling rather good about herself. It was nice to be praised and held in high esteem for a change. The boy's belittling words had made her feel as if her insides had been sucked out – and she was disturbed to realise that the feeling was horribly familiar. It was the same miserable, hollow sensation that she'd felt every time she'd ever been ignored or overlooked. During her short lifetime, she had become well acquainted with the unpleasant twinge – so much so that it had started to feel as comfortable as her old, battered plimsolls. Having been free of the feeling for a few days, however, Dawn found that she was not in any hurry to welcome it back.

'My mind's made up,' said Red in an unusually gruff voice. 'Despite her tender years, Dawn is more than capable of being a first-rate spy. She got an excellent mark in her test the other day.'

'What sort of test?' said Felix keenly. 'I'm top of my class in almost every subject. I bet I could do better than her.'

Felix sprang to his feet and Dawn lost sight of him for a second as he dashed round to Red's side of the desk.

'If you're so determined to send somebody young on this mission,' said Felix, breathless with excitement, 'why don't you choose me? She's *my* granny! *I* should go! I could show you my school report – then you'd see how smart I am. I'm good at games, too. Haltwhistle could be my sidekick. He's a really intelligent dog and I'm sure we'd find my granny in a flash.' Felix was smiling from ear to ear. He gazed hopefully at Red.

'No!' said the Head of P.S.S.T. sternly. 'Not in a million years.'

'But why?' Felix looked flabbergasted.

'You wouldn't be ... you haven't got ... you're just not suitable,' said Red finally. He shifted uncomfortably in his chair.

'What are you talking about? I'd be great! I've seen hundreds of spy films. I'd know just what to do.'

'You wouldn't,' said Red with certainty.

'I would! And I've proved it already!' said Felix. 'Look at this!' He put his hand into one of the many pockets in his shorts and fished out a crumpled postcard. He slapped it down on the desk. 'This arrived on the sixth of July. It says it's from my granny, but it isn't. See,' he said, jabbing at the postcard with his finger, 'it says "Dear Felix". That immediately struck me as suspicious.'

'Did it?' said Red, blinking tiredly.

'Of course! Granny always calls me "John".'

'And why would she do that?'

'Because I asked her to! When I was four I wouldn't wear anything except a pirate costume and I insisted on being called Long John Silver. I was quite a precocious child.'

'That's hard to believe,' muttered Red.

'My family were boring stick-in-the-muds apart from Granny. She was the only one who called me by my pirate name. She still does it now – only she's shortened it to "John".'

'I see.'

'So that's how I knew she hadn't written it,' said Felix, waving the postcard under Red's nose. 'Anyway, I didn't believe that she'd shoot off to Barbados without saying goodbye so I went round to her house, but nobody was in, and then her next door neighbour, Mrs Mudge, told me that she'd last seen Granny going into a house with a black front door a couple of weeks before. Mrs Mudge had been on a number fourteen bus at the time, but she couldn't remember which street she'd been in, so Haltwhistle and I walked the bus route until he finally picked up Granny's scent ...'

'You sure he wasn't just chasing our cat?' said Red dubiously.

Felix looked down his nose. He was obviously far too disgusted to respond to Red's remark. 'So, you see,' said Felix, 'between us – we solved the mystery. You have to admit that I'd make a cracking spy.'

'You've got brains,' admitted Red, 'but to be a spy you'd need an awful lot more than that: stealth, discretion ... the ability to shut up for five minutes –'

'My granny's a spy,' said Felix stubbornly. 'It stands to reason that I'd be good at it, too.'

Red considered this for a moment. 'It's true,' he said, 'that spying talent can sometimes run in the family ... but not in your case, unfortunately.'

Felix pouted. On the other side of the door, Dawn grinned and hugged herself. For a heart-stopping moment, she had thought that Felix might have persuaded Red to change his mind. She was overjoyed that the Head of P.S.S.T. had stuck to his guns and still wanted to send Dawn on the mission.

'Excuse me,' said a disapproving voice. Dawn felt somebody tap her on the shoulder. Instantly she withdrew from the keyhole, straightened up and turned round.

'Practising, were we?' said Trudy, raising an eyebrow. She offered Dawn a slim cardboard folder. 'Took me a few minutes to find it,' she said, *because it had been put back in the wrong place.*' She heaved a melodramatic sigh. 'Goodness knows what sort of state my files will be in when I get back.' Trudy pushed the folder into Dawn's hands. 'Take it, then! It's what you asked for – all the information we have on Murdo Meek.'

PERSONAL DETAILS

```
Assumed Name: Murdo Meek
Real Name: Unknown
Age: Somewhere between twenty-five and
seventy (or thereabouts)
Appearance: ??? (No photograph exists)
Character: Slippery!
Nationality: Might be English (then
again — might not)
Crimes: Too numerous to mention here
(see pages 2,3,4,5,6,7,8,9,10 & 11)
Last Known Whereabouts: Bottom of the
River Thames
```

Dawn did not find the first page terribly informative.

She set it aside and began to read the other sheets of paper in the file. It did not take her more than half an hour: she was a fast reader and, being alone in the Top Secret Missions room, she did not have to suffer any interruptions.

Having finished studying the entire file, she cupped her chin in her hands and reflected upon what she had just learnt.

It was obvious that Meek was a spy of formidable cunning. Described as 'the scourge of S.H.H.', he was an expert at finding out secrets and selling them to the highest bidder. He had been responsible for the disclosure of all kinds of confidential pieces of information. Dawn glanced at the nearest sheet of paper:

```
Sold the blueprints of a top-secret
fighter jet to a foreign power.
```

```
Ruined the career of the Minister for
Education with the revelation that he
had cheated in all his school exams.
```

```
Discovered the mystery ingredient in a
world-famous brand of marmalade.
```

```
Got his hands on the last chapter of
the most eagerly awaited book of the
```

decade and spoiled the ending for mil-
lions of readers.

Found out the secret location of
P.S.S.T., forcing the department to
move its premises.

Meek sounded like the greatest snitch on the planet.
There were over two hundred stolen secrets listed in the
file, but it was admitted that these were probably only
the tip of the iceberg. Meek must have earned himself a
small fortune.

Dawn was interested to read about his traitorous
crimes but she was more than a little frustrated by the
lack of information about Meek himself. Despite poring
over his file she still had no idea what he looked like or
how old he was. She did not even know the name that
he had been born with. Had P.U.F.F. failed to do
enough research – or was Meek just a very elusive person?

P.S.S.T. had almost caught him once. There were
several pages dedicated to this encounter. Dawn sifted
through the file until she found them. Each page contained a different version of the events which had taken
place on the evening of December the ninth, ten years
previously. She picked up Angela's first.

The Attempted Capture of Murdo Meek

As witnessed by: Angela Bradshaw

It was a quarter past seven in the evening and I was on my way home from work. I had stayed late and was the last to leave the premises of P.S.S.T. (located in the Magic Lantern Picturehouse in Marylebone). It was bitterly cold outside and I remembered that I had forgotten my gloves — so went back to get them.

Retracing my steps, I saw the figure of a man standing in front of the door of the Picturehouse. As I approached he turned and saw me. He said something like, 'Blow! I've missed the last showing of Mr Denning Drives North,' and walked swiftly past me. It was dark and I saw no more than a thick overcoat and a turned-up collar.

When I let myself into the Picturehouse, I saw an envelope on the doormat which had not been there when I had left a few minutes before. It was addressed to P.S.S.T. and underneath had been written the words: Painfully Stupid Selection of Twerps. Inside was a Christmas card with two pencilled 'M's at the bottom. I realised that it was from Murdo Meek and that I had probably just bumped into him outside.

I rushed after Meek and, helped by the thick snow on the ground, I was able to follow his footprints until I had the man himself in my sights. I phoned Red to let him know what was happening. Meek sensed that I was trailing him and tried to throw me off his scent, but I stayed with him until he reached an old warehouse by the river. By this time, Red and Pip had joined me. We decided that I should cover the front entrance, Pip should guard the back entrance and Red should go in and look for Meek.

About five minutes later, I heard a gunshot and the sound of breaking glass. Pip phoned me to say that Meek had got past her and was making for the footbridge across the Thames. I left my post and ran there as fast as I could. I found Pip and Red on the middle of the footbridge, looking down at the river.

Socrates was cycling towards us across the footbridge from the opposite bank. Red shone his torch on the water below. It had been so cold that little ice floes had formed in the river. We saw an overcoat and a scarf floating in the water — but no sign of Murdo Meek...

'What's that you're reading?'

Dawn lifted her head and saw Socrates coming towards her, holding a package. She had been so engrossed in Angela's account that she had not heard him enter the room.

'Oh, hello,' she said. 'I was just learning about Murdo Meek.'

'Meek, eh?' Socrates scowled. 'Crafty devil, he was. Too clever by half. Of course, that's what did for him in the end.'

'What do you mean?' asked Dawn.

'Ran rings around P.S.S.T. for years, selling secrets left, right and centre. Thought he was too cunning to ever get caught. Well, one night he got a bit too cocky.' Socrates pulled up a chair and sat down. 'Back then,' he said. 'P.S.S.T. was based in a poky little cinema in Barleycorn Street not far from Marble Arch. Somehow Meek found out where we were and thought he'd rub our noses in the fact that he was such a smarty-pants.

156

Decided to hand-deliver a Christmas card …'

'Oh, yes,' said Dawn brightly. 'I read about that.'

Socrates squinted at the sheet of paper in her hands. 'Yeah … well, you'll know about Angela catching him in the act, then. She must have given him a bit of a shock – but being the professional that he was he fed her a line about missing some film or other. Remember, Dawn, I told you that a good spy can always supply a reason for being where he is.'

Dawn nodded with enthusiasm.

'Having said that, I don't think Meek would've opened his gob if he'd realised who Angela was. Meek was very careful to protect his identity. No one in S.H.H. had a clue what he looked like, but by speaking to Angela he made it possible for her to recognise his voice.'

'And ten years later, she did!' said Dawn.

'Nooooo.' Socrates shook his head vigorously. 'She made a mistake. Murdo Meek is dead! Young Pip saw him jump from the bridge and all of us heard the splash as he hit the water.' Socrates began to sort through the sheets of paper in the folder. 'I'm sure our reports are in here somewhere …'

'I've read them,' said Dawn. 'You were all on the footbridge. Pip, Red and Angela were chasing him from one end and you were cycling towards him from the other.'

'That's right,' said Socrates. 'Nearly came off my bike at one point. The builders had left things in a right mess. The bridge was closed to the public. It was undergoing repairs, you see. Meek was trapped. He had nowhere to go …'

'Except down,' said Dawn grimly.

'Yeah,' agreed Socrates, '*right* down to the bottom of the Thames! He fell thirty feet into a freezing cold river and that was the end of him.'

'How can you be sure?' said Dawn. 'Couldn't he have swum to the bank?'

'He never resurfaced,' said Socrates firmly. 'If our torches missed him, we'd at least have heard him splashing about – and even if he'd made it to the bank he couldn't have climbed up a sheer brick wall, could he?'

'Was his body ever found?' asked Dawn.

'No, but it more than likely floated out to sea.' Socrates frowned at her. 'We haven't heard a peep out of Meek for ten years. He's as dead as mutton, you mark my words.'

Dawn grimaced. She tried not to think about Murdo Meek's body being sucked out to sea with the tide, like a piece of old driftwood.

'Anyway,' said Socrates, patting her hand, 'I didn't come in here to talk about Meek.' He offered her the parcel which he had brought with him. 'These are for you.'

Dawn's heart skipped a beat. Never one to rip open a wrapped gift, she unfolded the brown paper carefully. Inside was the shell phone. Socrates told her that he had restored it to working order. Then he showed her which splodges on its surface she should press in order to contact P.S.S.T., to speak and to end her call.

The other items in the parcel were a silver pencil with a squat plastic bear on the end and a packet of chocolate raisins. 'Ooh,' said Dawn, handling the pencil and the little box of sweets. She guessed at once what they were. Socrates showed her how to prise off the plastic bear and the false pencil nib to reveal the microdot viewer. The packet of raisins opened in the same way as the matchbox had done. She put her eye to it and looked through the tiny camera lens. 'Thanks, Socrates ... they're great!' she said.

Dawn's new belongings were scattered all over her bedspread. In the centre was a sky-blue suitcase which had been given to her by Emma. She was not allowed to take her own battered red one because it had 'Dawn Buckle' written in felt-tip on the inside of the lid. From tomorrow, she would cease to be Dawn Buckle.

'My name is Kitty Wilson,' said Dawn, trying out her new name.

Kitty. It wasn't quite the flamboyant name that Dawn had been hoping for, but it wasn't bad. She was confident that she would soon feel comfortable answering to it. The biggest problem, thought Dawn, was going to be remembering to call Trudy 'Mum'. Trudy was almost a complete stranger to her and she didn't seem to like children very much.

Dawn found herself thinking about her own mother. Her eyes began to mist over and she slumped on to the bed. Suddenly, she felt terribly homesick. *I'm having second thoughts*, she realised in a panic. *I don't want to be a spy after all! I wonder if Red would be ever so mad if I told him I'd changed my mind!*

Miraculously, amongst all the jumble of stuff on the bed, Dawn's fingers managed to find Clop. As she lifted him up, his stitched eyes seemed to fix her teary ones with a stern glare; and when she tried to hug him his head flopped away from her neck as if he wasn't at all keen.

'What's the matter, Clop?' asked Dawn. 'Why are you cross with me? You don't think I should quit … is that it?'

Clop's head fell forward in a sort of nod.

'Maybe you're right,' said Dawn, smiling at her donkey. She felt her confidence returning. 'OK, Clop, you win. I'll go.'

One by one, Dawn picked up all the items lying on the bed and placed them inside the sky-blue suitcase. Izzie must have worked extremely hard: there were all kinds of clothes, including jeans, dungarees, cotton dresses and even a Brownie uniform. Dawn marvelled at how shabby and faded everything looked. Somehow, Izzie had managed to make them appear as if they had been worn many times before, when in reality they were all brand new. Dawn put aside a blue cotton dress and a pair of sandals to wear on the journey the following day.

Around the edges of the suitcase, Dawn tucked everything else: wellington boots, a soap bag (containing, amongst other things, a toothbrush with 'Kitty' on it and a hairbrush with a few bristles missing), a torch, a rag doll, a writing set with the initials K.A.W. printed on the notepaper, a pencil box into which she slipped her microdot viewer, a notebook, her shell phone and her miniature camera.

The evening was beginning to grow cool by the time the case was packed. Dawn changed into her pyjamas and sat tensely on the bed with Clop on her knee. The hotel was deathly quiet.

The noisy boy and his equally vociferous dog had been sent home hours ago. Felix had been given strict instructions not to breathe a word of what he had learnt to anyone. To ensure that he would keep his lip buttoned, Red had told him that if anyone got to hear about Operation Question Mark, he might never see his granny again.

Everyone at P.S.S.T. had left, too; all except Edith who was still prowling about downstairs. Dawn had hoped that Emma might help her pack her suitcase, but after they had eaten together, Emma had rushed off, muttering something about a last-minute shopping spree. Peebles was also disappointingly absent. She imagined that he was probably lying low somewhere, trying to recover from the shock of having his home invaded by a loud-mouthed dog.

'It's just you and me, Clop,' said Dawn.

Before she got into bed, she folded all her old clothes and put them in her red suitcase along with thirteen pairs of mushroom-coloured knee socks, *Pansy the Goat Girl* and the rest of her belongings. She had been forbidden to take anything of her own on the mission. As she closed the lid, she took one last look at the bits and bobs that were *hers* – all the things that had been prized and cherished by *Dawn Buckle*. It felt almost as if she was packing herself away, too. She stowed the suitcase in the bottom of the wardrobe.

Dawn climbed into bed. Clop's little knitted body was sprawled on the pillow as if he was fast asleep. *Good idea*, thought Dawn. *It's going to be a big day tomorrow. You'll need as much rest as you can get.*

Dawn Buckle didn't care much for rag dolls and she decided that Kitty Wilson didn't either. She knew it wasn't allowed, but she didn't care. Even if she had to smuggle him in her knickers – Clop was coming with her to Cherry Bentley.

Chapter Eleven

A Couple of Problems

Dawn's wellington boots slapped against her calves as she traipsed along the corridor after Edith. If anyone had looked closely they would have noticed that one of the boots bulged slightly halfway down. As Dawn followed Edith into Red's office she glanced gratefully at the rain which was lashing against the windows.

She had woken up early and spent a good twenty minutes trying to think of a way to transport Clop without anyone detecting his presence. Balancing Clop on her head and trying to conceal him under a sun hat had not worked – his feet kept popping out below the brim. Wrapping him around her middle and knotting his legs together had proved just as ineffective for, although Clop's legs were very stretchy, they would not reach around her waist.

Then the rain had started and the solution had presented itself.

'Hurray for the British weather!' Dawn had said,

abandoning her sandals and tugging on her wellington boots. She had found that Clop fitted very snugly inside one.

'Goodness, what a downpour!' said Red, motioning for Edith and Dawn to take a seat in front of his desk. Trudy had arrived already. She was wearing a pair of jeans, a white polo shirt and a rather fed-up expression.

'Have you done a baggage check?' Red asked Edith.

'Yes,' she replied, setting down Dawn's sky-blue case beside her chair. 'I've had a thorough rummage. Everything is as it should be. There's nothing in there that belongs to Dawn.'

'Goody two-shoes,' said Trudy sourly.

'No name-calling, please,' said Red. He winked at Dawn. 'I'm afraid that Trudy didn't stick to the rules like you did, Dawn.' He pointed to a small pile of contraband on his desk, consisting of a silk scarf, a pot of nail varnish, a pair of high heels and seven different lipsticks. 'Emma found these in Trudy's suitcase,' said Red, shaking his head. 'Very disappointing.'

Dawn pretended to look shocked. Clop's woollen mane was making her leg itch. She tried to ignore it.

'Now,' said Red, 'before you set off, there are a few things I'd like to give you.' He tipped up an envelope, and a little collection of cards, certificates and documents fell out. He offered some to Trudy before turning to Dawn. Eagerly, she held out her hand. 'Here's your

164

library card,' said Red, placing it in her palm, 'and your junior bus pass.' Dawn examined them excitedly. Both had Kitty Wilson written on them, in different handwriting, and the bus pass included a head-and-shoulders shot of Dawn with her new haircut. He also gave her a school report, a sheaf of Brownie badge certificates, and a Young Ornithologists' membership card.

Dawn popped all the documents, each handcrafted expertly by Jagdish, into a beaded purse that she was wearing around her neck. Red produced a handful of notes and loose change from his pocket and Dawn added the money.

'Gosh, thanks,' said Dawn.

Red held up his hand. 'Haven't finished yet,' he said, lifting a small rucksack from the floor. He unbuckled its strap and delved inside.

Dawn watched with bated breath. It felt just like Christmas. 'A lunch box and a flask!' she said.

'They're not quite what they seem,' said Red, unscrewing the fat, plastic flask. Inside was a pair of binoculars. The contents of the lunch box were an even bigger surprise. Red opened its lid to reveal a radio set complete with headphones and a little instruction booklet.

'Wow!' said Dawn. She could not wait to try it out.

'Then, there's this,' said Red, taking a pack of playing cards from his pocket. 'Each card is perfectly ordinary ... except for the five of diamonds. P.U.F.F. have identified eleven men in Cherry Bentley who have lived in the village for ten years or less. If Murdo Meek survived the fall into the Thames, he would have turned up in Cherry Bentley sometime in the last decade. These eleven men are your main suspects, Dawn – and if you peel off the top layer of the five of diamonds you will find their names written beneath.'

Dawn popped the pack of cards into her suitcase.

'And something else ...' Red nodded to Emma who had been standing quietly behind him, watching the proceedings calmly. She crouched down to pick up a large cardboard box, brought it over to Dawn and placed it on her knee. Dawn began to lift up the four cardboard flaps which, to her bemusement, had been punched with holes.

'Eighty-eight per cent of children in Cherry Bentley have a pet,' explained Emma, 'so we thought you'd better have one, too. I wanted to get you a rabbit, but unfortunately, we didn't have the funds ...'

Dawn was a little disappointed. She had always wanted a rabbit – a big, fluffy, lop-eared one preferably. She peered into the box, not knowing what to expect, and was delighted to see the face of P.S.S.T.'s furriest member of staff looking up at her. 'Peebles!' she cried, and reached inside to stroke his head. 'Are you sure it's all right if he comes with me on the mission?'

166

'Ye-es,' said Emma, a touch reluctantly. 'But he'll have to go undercover, too. You must choose a new name for him, Dawn.' Emma unfolded a piece of paper and studied it. 'Now, according to the data provided by P.U.F.F., twenty-one per cent of cats in Cherry Bentley are named Tiger, nine per cent are called Smudge, eight per cent Cookie, six per cent Socks – and most of the others are named after fish or philosophers or jazz musicians. It's up to you …'

Dawn didn't know the names of any philosophers or jazz musicians and she found it quite difficult to think of more than three types of fish.

'How about Sardine?' she said eventually. 'I have those on toast sometimes with ketchup. They're delicious.'

'Sardine will be just fine,' said Emma, smiling at her.

Trudy cleared her throat. 'Is that it, then? Can we go now?'

'Actually, there's one final thing,' said Red. He held out his palm, upon which were two little white tablets.

Dawn and Trudy stared at them suspiciously.

'Mints for the journey,' explained Red. 'Could only afford one each, I'm afraid. Sorry.'

Dawn held the Good Luck card in her hands and read it through one last time. Then she tore it in half and began to eat it. She offered a piece to Trudy but the secretary declined with a shake of her head.

'It's chocolate-flavoured rice paper,' said Dawn. 'Tastes lovely.'

She had been really touched to find Socrates, Jagdish and Izzie waiting for her in the corridor to say goodbye. There had been hugs and handshakes all round and then Socrates had presented her with the card, signed (in cochineal) by everyone in P.S.S.T.

Loading the boot of the twelve-year-old white hatchback, which was parked outside the hotel, had not taken very long as Dawn and Trudy did not have much luggage. Their two suitcases, Dawn's rucksack, a crate filled with food and a few gardening tools were all that they were taking with them.

The Good Luck card was almost gone. Dawn folded up the last piece and slipped it into her mouth. It had been a clever idea to give her an edible message, so that, once eaten, nobody else would ever have the chance to read it. She made sure that the cardboard box containing Peebles was positioned stably on her knees before fastening her seatbelt.

Trudy switched on the engine.

Dawn found herself glancing up at the rain-splashed windows on the second floor of the hotel to see if any faces were looking out. She wasn't really very surprised to find that there weren't. The staff at P.S.S.T. were a highly disciplined bunch. They wouldn't risk being seen by a sharp-eyed passer-by who might wonder what was so fascinating about a girl and her mother setting off on a journey. Dawn took one last, lingering look at the grey-brick building. The flowers in its front yard were jewelled with raindrops and had never looked more beautiful.

Phhrrtt. The gear stick made a noise like someone blowing a raspberry.

'Pile of junk,' muttered Trudy under her breath as she struggled to find first gear. 'Probably won't get us to the end of the road, let alone the sixty-odd miles to Cherry Bentley ... Ah, that's got it.'

The car began to edge forward and Dawn's heart gave a little leap of excitement.

BANG!

Trudy hit the steering wheel with the heel of her hand and said something rude.

'What's happened?' said Dawn, clutching the cardboard box. There was a scrabbling sound coming from within it. She lifted up a flap and told Peebles calmly that everything was going to be all right.

'I'm no mechanic,' grumbled Trudy, turning off the engine, 'but that sounded like a burst tyre to me.' She got out of the car and Dawn did likewise, leaving the cardboard box on her seat.

They crouched down by the two front wheels and prodded the tyres with their fingers. 'Hmm ... nothing seems to be amiss,' said Trudy, scratching her head.

'Perhaps I should take a look under the bonnet.'

'What's this?' said Dawn, spying something trapped underneath one of the tyres. It was flat, orange, and crackled when she touched it. 'Bit of litter, I guess.'

'Can't see anything wrong in here,' said Trudy, propping the bonnet open. She let it slam shut. 'Jump in, Dawn, and I'll start up the engine again.'

'I'm *Kitty*,' Dawn whispered.

'Oh, stop being such a smart alec, and get in the car!'

Dawn and Trudy settled back into their seats. This time, the car moved away smoothly without being accompanied by any strange noises.

'It's a pity Red couldn't have managed to borrow a snazzier model,' moaned Trudy as they reached the junction at the end of the road. 'No sun roof, no CD player ... and,' she said, winding down her window, 'it smells of wet dog.'

Peebles did not take to travelling by car. Throughout the journey, he wriggled about in his box so that Dawn had to hold on to it quite tightly, and he would not stop miaowing. Whenever she opened the flaps a fraction, a paw shot out and tried to hook its claws into her dress.

Apart from worrying about her anguished pet, Dawn found the journey very pleasant. The streets of London were lined with interesting buildings and their pavements were teeming with people. Satisfyingly, her mint lasted almost to the outskirts of London, dissolving to nothing as they went through Wanstead.

On leaving the capital, Trudy joined a long, wide road with hardly any twists and turns. There were high banks on either side and, despite craning her neck, Dawn could not see what lay beyond them. With so little to look at, she decided to run through Red's instructions in her mind. Consequently, they seemed to reach Cherry Bentley in no time at all.

Dawn was familiar with the layout of the village, having studied the map and aerial photographs, but the real thing was far more impressive. The roads were narrow without any markings, trees were plentiful, and the grass was so shiny and lush that it almost looked good enough to eat. Cherry Bentley's buildings were all different shapes and sizes. There were cottages with tiny, latticed windows, lime-washed walls and thatched roofs; imposing houses made from dull orange brick with half a dozen chimneys; a slate-roofed pub called The One-eyed Stoat, and a big church, built from stone, with a tower on one end that put Dawn in mind of a castle.

Trudy drove slowly when they reached the Green and told Dawn to keep her eyes peeled for a road called Cow Parsley Lane. Dawn tried her best but found herself being distracted by the vast, grass-covered spread of land to her right. Towering lime and oak trees were scattered all around the border of the Green and at its lower end was a duck pond surrounded by weeping willows. The pond was literally swimming in feathered creatures.

'There it is!' said Dawn, having managed to tear her eyes away from a little brood of ducklings who appeared to be playing follow-my-leader. 'Cow Parsley Lane.'

Trudy flicked on the indicator and turned the wheel sharply. Dawn heard their suitcases clunking in the boot.

Daffodil Cottage was a sweet little place about halfway down Cow Parsley Lane, on the left. Its walls were the colour of vanilla ice cream and it had a white front door with three steps leading up to it. The front lawn was freckled with daisies, and dandelions sprouted in the cracks in its flagstoned path. Dawn fell in love with it instantly.

'Where do you think *you're* going?' said Trudy. As soon as the car had stopped outside, Dawn had thrown open her door and, carrying the cardboard box in her arms, had begun to walk up the garden path.

'How about some help with the cases?' said Trudy.

'Oh ... sorry.' Dawn put Peebles down and joined Trudy at the boot of the car.

'It's a lovely place, Cherry Bentley, isn't it?' said Dawn. 'Don't you think the air smells all clean and fresh? And aren't the houses pretty? I never realised the sky was so big – I suppose that's because I've spent my whole life in a city full of high-rise blocks.'

'Mmm,' said Trudy vaguely, unlocking the boot.

What happened next was so surprising that Dawn was rendered speechless. Trudy, on the other hand, had no problem expressing her shock. She screamed at the top of her lungs and fell backwards into the road. A grubby hearthrug seemed to tumble out of the boot and land on top of her.

'Thank goodness for that!' said a boy's voice, and a red-faced Felix sat up between two suitcases. He squinted and shaded his eyes. 'It was getting a little bit stuffy in here,' he said as he clambered over the crate of food, clutching a holdall. 'Hello,' he said to Dawn, as if emerging from the boot of a car was the most natural thing in the world. 'So, where are we, then?'

'Get this hairy animal off me!' said Trudy, giving Haltwhistle a shove. The dog licked her cheek and showed no signs of shifting.

'Haltwhistle! Off!' commanded Felix. He got hold of his dog's collar, and tugged. 'Come on, boy. Let's have a look around, shall we?'

'You'll do no such thing,' said Trudy, as Haltwhistle sprang off her and ambled into the front garden. 'Ugh … smelly brute,' said Trudy, brushing dog hairs from her clothes.

'What are you doing here, Felix?' said Dawn, finding

her voice at last. 'I ... I thought Red said that you couldn't come.'

'Huh!' said Felix. 'As if I was going to take any notice of what *he* said! Red was dim enough to tell me that you were leaving on your mission today – so my dog and I got up extra early and hid round the corner from your hotel until you came out. Then I thought up a really superb ruse to keep you busy while we sneaked into the boot of your car. I blew into a crisp packet and then slid the open end under the wheel of your car, trapping the air inside. When the tyre rolled on top of it – it popped.'

'Ah,' said Dawn. She remembered noticing a piece of litter underneath one of the front tyres. If only she had realised its significance at the time.

'You were meant to think that the tyre had been punctured,' said Felix.

'We did,' said Dawn.

'I know.' Felix looked very smug. 'You fell for it hook, line and sinker.'

'Wipe that smirk off your face,' said Trudy, giving Felix an icy stare, 'and get yourself and your odious hound into the car right now. I'm taking you back to London.'

'No, you're not!'

'Don't argue with me.'

'Shh,' said Dawn urgently. She had noticed an elderly

lady walking lopsidedly in their direction. Although it was no longer raining, the little plump woman was wearing a mackintosh, a rain hood and rubber boots. She held a walking stick in one hand and a bunch of keys in the other. Two small, wiry-haired dogs were trotting at her heels, tussling with each other over a piece of soggy material.

'Hello there, my dears,' she said, waving her stick. 'I saw you arriving from my kitchen window!' The old lady's face was soft, pink and powdered and reminded Dawn of a marshmallow. 'I live just up the road at Bluebell Villa,' she said. 'I'm Mrs Cuddy, your landlady, and these are my little dumplings: Honeybunch and Lambkin.' The old lady gazed with affection at her dogs. Dawn stretched out a hand to pat them, then changed her mind when she heard one growl. There was a ripping noise as the rag they were fighting over split in two. 'Dumplings!' said Mrs Cuddy warningly. 'Play *nicely*.'

'Pleased to meet you,' said Trudy, holding out her hand. 'I'm Sandra Wilson and this is my daughter, Kitty.'

Dawn stepped forward.

'Kitty, is it?' said the old lady. 'I see … yes. I believe you mentioned your daughter when you wrote and asked to rent my cottage.' Mrs Cuddy dropped the keys into Trudy's palm before shaking her hand. 'But tell me, Sandra … who is this handsome young man?'

'I'm her son,' said Felix, quick as a flash.

'Wayne,' added Trudy.

Wayne? mouthed Felix. He rolled his eyes.

'And your dog?' said Mrs Cuddy. 'Er … it is a dog, isn't it?'

'Yes,' said Dawn swiftly, before Felix could launch into his anecdote about Haltwhistle's grandfather almost winning Crufts. 'His name's … um … Fred.'

Mrs Cuddy nodded. 'Charming.'

'I'm sorry I didn't mention that we were bringing Wayne and Fred with us,' said Trudy smoothly. 'It was a last-minute decision.'

'That's all right, my dear. I quite understand. You just make yourself at home and if there's anything you need – just give me a tinkle. Tutty-bye, now!' Mrs Cuddy turned round and set off up the road, with her dogs close behind her.

'Ha ha,' said Felix, swinging his holdall on to his back. 'You're stuck with me now.'

'Don't bet on it,' snarled Trudy.

'Yes, you are. Mrs Cuddy is bound to notice if I suddenly disappear. How would you explain it? She might think you'd murdered me or something.'

'Don't tempt me,' said Trudy.

'Wayne!' said Felix in disgust. He pulled a face. 'Why'd you have to come up with a dreadful name like that?'

Trudy smiled thinly. 'It just seemed to fit,' she said.

Dawn wasn't paying much attention to their bickering. She had noticed that Haltwhistle was getting a bit too close to the cardboard box which she had left on the path. He sniffed one corner and made a whining sound.

'Get away from there!' shouted Dawn. Angry spitting noises came from inside the box and Haltwhistle wagged his tail. 'Leave ... er ... Sardine alone!' said Dawn, striding over to the dog. She attempted to push him aside but she might as well have tried to move a block of granite. 'Call your dog, please,' said Dawn, glaring at Felix. She wrapped her arms protectively around the cardboard box.

'Haltwhistle! Here, boy!'

'You have to call him Fred,' hissed Trudy.

'I will not!' said Felix. 'He'll never answer to that.'

Trudy gave a spluttering laugh. 'He doesn't seem to answer to his *real* name. I don't see that it matters *what* you call him! Brainless lump that he is.'

Felix was enraged. 'Take that back!' he snapped. 'My dog is remarkably intelligent. He knows seventy-three different commands –'

'For goodness sake, keep your voice down!' hissed Trudy. After she had slammed the boot, she walked up the garden path, a suitcase in each hand. 'So much for keeping a low profile,' she said, throwing Felix an evil look. 'Let's hurry up and get inside.'

Dawn glanced uneasily over her shoulder as Trudy opened the front door. Was anybody watching them? Had they been overheard? Her heart felt very heavy all of a sudden. She had known that Operation Question Mark was going to be a difficult challenge. Now, with the arrival of the insufferable Felix Pomeroy-Pitt, it looked almost impossible.

Chapter Twelve

Slow Progress

'Why aren't there any daffodils?' said Felix in the same snooty tones that he had used when commenting on the 'prehistoric kettle', the 'funny knick-knacks' and the 'cabbagey smell' inside Daffodil Cottage. He put his hands in the pockets of his shorts and strolled around the small patch of lawn in the back garden with the air of a lord inspecting his estate. 'There isn't a single daffodil anywhere,' he noted with scorn. 'Rather a lot of weeds, though. Perhaps I'll rename the place "Weed Cottage".'

'They're not weeds, they're wildflowers,' said Trudy casually. 'And it's the wrong season for daffodils. They bloom in the spring.'

Dawn stopped what she was doing to stare in awe at Trudy, who had obviously been swotting up on gardening, and was surprised to receive a smile and a wink.

Felix mumbled something about getting a glass of water and disappeared indoors.

A lusty miaow reminded Dawn that she was in the middle of something. Having set down the cardboard box on the grass, she began to open the flaps one by one.

'Out you come,' she said to Peebles.

The cat's head rose out of the box and swivelled from side to side like a periscope. Dawn made an attempt to pick him up but he was obviously not in the mood for being cuddled. Springing through her arms, he streaked across the lawn and hid himself under a hydrangea bush. Luckily, Haltwhistle had followed his master inside so there was no danger of Peebles being hotly pursued.

'Don't worry ... er ... Kitty,' said Trudy. 'He's probably a little bit out of sorts after the car journey.'

'Yes,' said Dawn, 'and I get the feeling that he's not too thrilled about meeting Halt— I mean ... Fred again.'

Trudy nodded. 'Poor old Peebles.'

'*Sardine*,' hissed Dawn.

'No wonder he was making such a fuss in the car,' continued Trudy, as she headed inside. 'He was probably trying to warn us about our two extra passengers. If only cats could talk, eh?'

'Mmm,' agreed Dawn. It had been a humbling experience to have to phone P.S.S.T. and tell them that Felix and his dog had tagged along on the mission. Red had been very disappointed when Dawn explained how they had stowed away in the boot of the car. She felt particularly upset that she had let Socrates down after all the training he had given her. 'Distracted by a crisp packet!' she had heard him mutter. 'I can't believe you let them smuggle themselves right under your nose. A good spy is always on the alert, Dawn. Remember what I taught you!'

Red had been in favour of concocting a story which would allow Trudy to bring Felix and his dog straight back to London. He was afraid that Felix's parents would think that their son had run away or been abducted. If they contacted the police, Operation Question Mark would effectively be over, and the mysterious disappearance of Angela Bradshaw would never be solved. However, Felix insisted that no one would have any idea that he was missing. His parents were halfway up a mountain in New Zealand on a hiking holiday and Felix had told his au pair that he was staying with his best friend Josh for a couple of weeks. Therefore, it was decided that Felix should remain where he was.

Sounding angrier than Dawn had ever heard him, Red had insisted that Felix should stay inside Daffodil Cottage until a parcel of suitably inconspicuous clothing could be delivered. Thereafter Felix should only be allowed outside occasionally, during which time he was absolutely forbidden to interfere in the mission. Dawn had passed on these instructions to Felix, but she wasn't entirely confident that he would stick to them. He did not seem like the type of boy who did what he was told.

'Kitty!' called Trudy, reappearing in the garden. She was holding a shopping bag and an umbrella. 'I'm just popping out to the post office. Would you like to come?'

'Yes, please … Mum,' said Dawn loudly, for the benefit of anyone who might be listening on the other side of the garden fence. It was the first time that she had referred to Trudy as her mother. It felt very weird.

Dawn kept her wellington boots on but remembered to remove Clop before they set out for the post office. She sat her donkey on the windowsill in her new bedroom so that he could survey the street outside. With the keenness of one who had been forced to stare at the inside of a boot for most of the morning, Clop pressed his nose against the windowpane.

They left Felix and Haltwhistle lying on their stomachs on the living room floor with a chessboard between them. A cupboard next to the television set was bursting with board games. According to Felix, Haltwhistle was already able to play draughts and ludo, and would probably pick up the rules of chess in no time at all. Dawn had her doubts – and she wasn't alone.

'That boy is crackers,' said Trudy as they closed the front door behind them. 'It's perfectly clear to the rest of us that his dog is as daft as a brush, yet Felix continues to treat him like some kind of canine genius. I doubt that Haltwhistle could fetch a stick, let alone play *chess*.'

'Fred,' whispered Dawn.

'Oh, yes,' said Trudy. 'Sorry.'

Dawn gave Trudy a curious sideways glance. Ever since the unexpected arrival of Felix and Haltwhistle, her behaviour towards Dawn seemed to have changed. Her biting comments had ceased, her voice had softened and she had even made the odd attempt to be quite chummy. Dawn found Trudy's sudden friendliness a little unsettling. *Maybe she's realised that I'm not quite so bad after all*, thought Dawn. *Compared to Felix, that is.*

'Deadheading?' The woman behind the counter at the post office glanced up from the piece of card which Trudy had pressed into her hand. 'What kind of business did you say you were in?'

'I'm a gardener,' said Trudy.

'Oh, *that* sort of deadheading,' said the postmistress. 'Thought for a minute you might be scouting for work up at the abattoir.'

'No,' said Trudy firmly.

Thankfully not, thought Dawn.

'So, you do weeding, digging, pruning and mowing, too, do you?' said the postmistress, her eyes roaming over the card upon which Trudy had written a few lines advertising her services. 'How very physical.' She stared hard at Trudy as if she was sizing her up. 'Sure you can manage all that, my love? You're a bit on the skinny side. Don't look as if you could *lift* a spade – never mind dig a hole.'

'I'm tougher than I look,' insisted Trudy, her fingers tightening around her umbrella. Dawn hoped that Trudy wouldn't lose her cool and hit the postmistress over the head with it.

'Well ...' The postmistress seemed to deliberate for a moment. She stroked her brassy hair. 'I suppose I could put your card in my window ... for a small fee.'

Trudy parted with a five-pound note. Then she seized Dawn's hand and pulled her across the chequered floor into a corner of the post office, muttering 'the nerve of some people' under her breath. Hearing the tinkle of the bell above the door, Dawn slipped away from her to see who had just come in, leaving Trudy to seethe quietly behind a spinner full of greetings cards.

Apart from a gaunt young man in a khaki boiler suit who had been examining the same packet of envelopes for several minutes, and another, older man with a neat white beard who was tying up a parcel with string, there was now a new customer in the post office. She was a middle-aged lady with rouged cheekbones and a beaky nose. The drooping brim of a straw hat hid her eyes from view. She wore a loose-fitting lavender sundress, and carried a wicker shopping basket over one arm.

'Good morning, Mrs Arbuthnot,' said the postmistress.

Dawn's ears pricked up immediately. *Mrs Arbuthnot!* When Angela Bradshaw had recognised the voice of Murdo Meek, he had been commenting upon the prizewinning cucumber of the very woman who had just walked through the door! Dawn grabbed a colouring book from a shelf and casually leafed through it, intending to listen, with every fibre of her being, to the ensuing conversation.

'A good morning it is, indeed, Miss Flinch,' said Mrs Arbuthnot, the brim of her hat undulating as she spoke. 'We've had a nice drop of rain. I don't think I'll need to use my watering can today.'

'You're one person who won't be needing much help from our newest resident,' said the postmistress. Dawn thought that she sounded quite smug.

'I beg your pardon, Miss Flinch?' said Mrs Arbuthnot.

'Sandra Wilson,' said Miss Flinch, her square jaw working up and down at speed. 'Recently arrived in Cherry Bentley. She's a gardener, don't you know. I've just this minute put her card in my window. Let's hope she hasn't got green fingers when it comes to cucumbers, eh, Mrs Arbuthnot? How many years on the trot have you won that trophy?'

'Nine,' said the man with the white beard, perching his parcel on the counter. 'Isn't that right, Bess?'

'Er … actually, it's ten,' said Mrs Arbuthnot modestly.

'A grand achievement,' said the man, 'and, if I may say so, Bess, you looked quite splendid in your photograph.'

'So did you, Larry,' said Mrs Arbuthnot. 'I've always wanted to enter the funny-shaped vegetable category, but I can't seem to get my cucumbers to grow imperfectly. It must have taken considerable skill to grow a beetroot in the shape of a steamroller.'

'It was a fluke, I assure you,' said Larry.

'How I wish I hadn't had to miss the show this year,' said Miss Flinch. 'I do so enjoy spending a summer's afternoon looking at a load of plants and vegetables. The show fell on my birthday, you see, and Neville had promised to take me on a romantic outing. A visit to a tank museum wasn't quite what I'd been expecting, but we had a nice picnic afterwards.'

'It's a shame you couldn't come to the show,' said Larry, 'but there's a very nice display of photographs in the village hall. Perhaps you'd care to take a look at them when you have a moment to spare.'

'Those photographs still up?' said Miss Flinch, stifling a yawn. 'It's about time they were taken down, don't you think? *Everyone* must have seen them by now.'

There was an awkward silence.

'Well, I must be off,' said Larry, shaking the contents of a paper bag in his hand. 'Time to feed the ducks! I'd be obliged if my parcel could catch the midday post, Diana.' He dipped his head politely. 'Goodbye, ladies.'

'Wasn't it a dreadful shame?' said Diana Flinch, once the bell above the door had finished jingling.

'You've lost me, I'm afraid,' said Bess Arbuthnot.

Diana Flinch gestured towards the door through which the man with the white beard had just departed. 'Mr Grahams was awfully upset when that duck went missing from the pond.'

'I don't expect they ever caught the culprit ...'

'No,' said Diana Flinch, 'but there have been rumours.' She leaned over the counter towards Bess Arbuthnot and cupped her hand around her mouth in a secretive manner (quite pointlessly, as it turned out, because she did not even attempt to lower her voice). 'I've heard talk that roast duck sandwiches suddenly appeared on the menu at *a certain pub* not long after that old mallard vanished.'

'Poppycock!' said Bess Arbuthnot. Plainly, she was shocked. 'I refuse to believe that the landlord of The One-eyed Stoat would be involved in something like that.' She delved in her basket and drew out a purse. 'I'll have five second-class stamps, if you don't mind, Miss Flinch,' she said in clipped tones.

'Right you are,' said the postmistress sulkily. She

produced a sheet of stamps and began to tear off a corner. Without looking up, she bellowed, 'Seth Lightfoot! Are you still dithering over those envelopes? Make up your mind. Do you want them or not?'

The man in the boiler suit gulped, and threw down the packet he was holding. In his haste to reach the door, he tripped over his own shoelaces and crashed into some pots of glue which had been displayed attractively in a pyramid. Without pausing to pick them up, he yanked open the door and ran off.

'Well, thank you *very* much!' called Diana Flinch in the manner of someone who wasn't grateful at all. She began to grumble about mucky fingerprints on her envelopes and the heartless destruction of a work of art.

Bess Arbuthnot paid for her stamps and left almost as swiftly as Seth Lightfoot.

'Let's go, too,' said Trudy, nudging Dawn's elbow. 'If I have to listen to that busybody for one more minute I might feel obliged to tell her exactly what I think of her.'

Wow! What luck! It's open, thought Dawn as they approached the village hall. It was an old, red-brick building with arched windows and two solid oak doors. Sitting on a chair outside, with a plastic bucket in his lap, was an elderly man. A toothpick was jutting from a corner of his mouth. Dawn stopped and read a poster which had been stuck to one of the doors.

'Please can we have a look at the art exhibition?' she said to Trudy.

'You can, if you like,' she replied, 'but potato prints aren't really my thing. Why don't I have a sit-down over there, on that bench by the pond, while you check out the paintings.'

'OK, Mum.'

Trudy smiled weakly and released Dawn's hand. She looked pale, tense and exhausted. Dawn knew precisely how she felt. Pretending to be a different person was immensely draining. She wished that she could switch off her brain for a while and relax in the sunshine with Trudy – but she couldn't. She had work to do.

'I'd like to see the exhibition, please,' said Dawn, dropping the twenty pence entry fee into the man's bucket.

He chewed on his toothpick, nodded vaguely and waved her inside.

Dawn spent a couple of minutes wandering up and down admiring the artwork of Cherry Bentley Primary School. Out of the corner of her eye, she saw some photographs pinned to a large sheet of yellow sugar paper in one corner of the hall and, reaching into her pocket for her miniature camera, she casually ambled towards them.

Somebody had taken great pains to write the words

'Garden and Allotment Show' as fancily as they could, with the result that they were almost impossible to read. The photographs had been arranged in a circle around the words which meant that Dawn had to tilt her head to get a proper look at them. They all seemed to feature a person showing rather a lot of teeth with a trophy or rosette in one hand and a particularly fine example of a marrow or a bunch of sweet peas or a pot of jam in the other.

Dawn found the photograph of Bess Arbuthnot. She was wearing a hat with a narrow, stiff brim, a dress with a lace collar, and a pair of white gloves. In the crook of her arm she held a magnificent cucumber, the size and lustrous colour of which Dawn had never seen in any supermarket.

Flicking open one end of the box of chocolate raisins with her finger, Dawn lifted it until it was level with the photograph of Bess Arbuthnot and pressed the shutter release button. She then proceeded to do the same with the other photographs. In one, she saw Larry Grahams holding up an unusually shaped beetroot, his face glowing with pride. Seth Lightfoot, the man whom Dawn had seen leaving the post office in great haste, was in five different photographs. He was dressed quite scruffily and appeared to be looking at something on the ground in each picture.

When she had finished, Dawn tucked the miniature camera back into her pocket and sauntered out of the hall. So far, so good, she thought, delighted that her photographing session had gone so smoothly.

Dawn had presumed that she would find Trudy alone on the bench, having a quick snooze or watching the ducks rush across the pond to snap up breadcrumbs thrown by Larry Grahams. She was surprised to catch her 'mother' chatting amiably with Seth Lightfoot. Trudy and Seth were sitting on opposite ends of the bench with Trudy's shopping bag between them.

Seth was resting one of his hands on a street-cleaner's barrow. There was a dustpan and brush tied to one of its handles, and a filthy toy panda had been attached to the front of the barrow. The panda had a proud look about him, despite being rather tatty and minus one ear. He reminded Dawn of a figurehead on the prow of a ship.

'Chewing gum is the worst,' confided Seth with a grimace.

Trudy nodded sympathetically.

'Can't shift it when it's sticky, you see. Have to wait until it's good and solid. Best time to tackle gum is on a nice, frosty morning. The cold weather sets it rock hard on the pavement. Then I get out my scrapy-thing and give it a prod. Comes off lovely … like a crusty old scab.'

'Aha, that's how it's done,' said Trudy.

Seth coughed modestly. 'It's easy when you know how.'

'And how long have you been a litter collector?'

'Officially,' said Seth, 'I'm called a "refuse technician". Been doing the job for … well, it'll be nine years this Tuesday, as a matter of fact. Before that I was a cleaner on a cruise liner. Travelled all over the world.'

'How wonderful,' said Trudy. 'I bet you saw some sights.'

'More vomit than I knew what to do with,' said Seth, 'when the sea got all choppy, like.'

Trudy nodded and looked slightly anxious. Then she caught sight of Dawn approaching them.

'Ah, here's my daughter,' she said, not quite succeeding in hiding her relief. 'Did you enjoy the exhibition, Kitty? Well … Mr Lightfoot –'

'Call me Seth.'

'It's a pleasure to have met you … Seth … but I really must be going.'

'Oh, yes … me too,' he said hurriedly. 'There's a styrofoam cup on the ground over there that I'm just *itching* to pick up. Perhaps we can have another chat again some time.' He got to his feet and turned to face Dawn. 'Goodbye, little girl.'

Dawn didn't answer for a moment. She was taken aback. From a distance, Seth had seemed to be about twenty-five, but now that she was able to study him up close, she could see the creases around his eyes and the corners of his mouth – which meant that he was at least ten years older than she had first presumed. As soon as she got back to Daffodil Cottage she decided that she would take a look at the five of diamonds and see if his name was listed as a suspect.

Trudy's voice floated up the stairs. 'What was that you said, Dawn? *Nathan?* On a *moped?* Are you *sure?*'

Dawn planted her elbows on the windowsill of her bedroom and gave Clop an enquiring look. Her donkey gazed at her steadfastly, which was enough to convince Dawn that her assumption was correct.

'Yep,' responded Dawn. 'It's definitely him.'

When she had heard the low whine of a motorcycle stop abruptly outside Daffodil Cottage, she had stopped reading the booklet of instructions on how to use the radio set, jumped off her bed, and joined Clop at the window. Outside, she had seen a gangly young man astride a moped with panniers on each side. He had been in the process of removing a motorcycle helmet which had a telephone number printed on the back. She had suspected straight away that the moped rider was Nathan, even though he was wearing an unfamiliar outfit: trousers with red-and-white stripes and a T-shirt emblazoned with the words: 'Nice Slice Pizza Company'.

'Heavens. I think you're right,' said Trudy, appearing beside Dawn. 'What an earth is he doing here?'

'Making a delivery, I think,' said Dawn, watching

carefully as Nathan opened one of the panniers and slid out three flat, square boxes. Whistling cheerfully, he wedged them under his arm and unlatched the front gate.

There was a noise downstairs. It was the sort of sound that suggested movement at great speed through a house filled with furniture and ornaments.

'Felix!' said Dawn and Trudy, their faces frozen in panic.

By the time they reached the front door, Felix had already flung it open. He was standing on the doorstep, his eyes boring into the boxes that Nathan was carrying. 'One of those had better be pepperoni,' said Felix, licking his lips.

'I think you might be disappointed,' replied Nathan as he placed the boxes in Felix's outstretched arms.

'Thanks. Goodbye,' said Trudy brusquely, pulling Felix indoors.

Dawn lingered on the doorstep. Back at P.S.S.T. headquarters, Red had mentioned that he was going to use Nathan as a messenger.

'Have you got something to tell me?' she whispered.

'Not this time,' he replied. Just before he turned away he added mysteriously, 'Izzie's been working like a Trojan. Make sure he wears them.'

Dawn was puzzled. She smiled at Nathan, then closed the front door.

'Smart idea to order supper,' said Felix, grinning.

'I'm absolutely starving.' He began to unfasten one of the boxes. 'I wonder what kind of topping this one's got … Pepperoni's my favourite, but I wouldn't turn my nose up at spicy chicken or …' His face crumpled in disappointment. 'It's a T-shirt!' he said.

'And a pair of jeans and a tracksuit,' said Dawn, rifling through the contents of the box. She realised what Nathan had been hinting at. 'They're your new clothes from P.S.S.T.!'

Felix looked totally unimpressed. 'You mean that guy *wasn't* a pizza delivery man?'

'Right,' said Dawn. 'He wasn't. Didn't you recognise him? That was Nathan!'

'What's in this one?' said Trudy, tugging at the box underneath. She prised open its lid. 'Oh, socks and underwear.'

'Get off!' said Felix crossly, snatching it back.

'Izzie must have sewed like stink to produce this little lot,' said Trudy. 'You'd better go and get changed right away.'

'Maybe later,' said Felix, glowering at her. He dumped the boxes on a table in the hall. 'After I've had something to eat.'

'Suit yourself,' said Trudy, 'but you won't be showing your face in the village until you do.'

Dawn rested her lunch box on a tree stump and had a

furtive look around. She was in the midst of a dense thicket of young birch trees. Ahead of her, through the mesh of thin branches and gauzy leaves, she could just glimpse Felix at the edge of a field, earnestly poking about in a bed of nettles with a stick. She suspected that he was looking for clues *again*, even though he had been reminded, no less than five times during their evening walk, that he must leave all the spying and sleuthing to Dawn.

Trudy moved into Dawn's line of vision, jogging purposefully towards Felix. Even at a distance, Dawn could hear her give him a short, sharp command. He stopped what he was doing and threw the stick on the ground; then wiped his hands down the front of a faded blue T-shirt which he had eventually donned after several hours of protest.

Dawn looked away, determined not to waste any more time. Dusk would be settling shortly – and there was something that needed to be done.

Kneeling on the ground, she carefully opened her lunch box, into which the radio set had been ingeniously crammed. She stared at the little clusters of dials and switches for a moment; then slipped her hand inside the box and unravelled a length of wire attached to a small aerial. The instructions had said that she would need to position this as high as possible – so she balanced it in the forking branch of a nearby tree. Next she fitted on a pair of headphones and twiddled a large black dial to find the correct radio frequency. She checked her watch. It was nine fifteen. The P.S.S.T. team would be standing by, waiting for her transmission.

'Shrimp calling Barnacle,' said Dawn softly into the microphone, using the code words that Red had instructed her to use. 'Barnacle … come in, please.'

There was a crackling noise. Dawn twisted the big black dial slightly to the left. 'Shrimp,' said someone through her earphones. The voice sounded a little fuzzy but Dawn recognised it as Red's. 'This is Barnacle,' he said. 'What do you have to report? Over.'

Not a lot, thought Dawn guiltily. However, she was not prepared to admit that. Desperate to make up for her earlier blunder, which had resulted in Felix gate-crashing the mission, she tried to make her first day's findings sound as impressive as possible.

'Have crossed two suspects off my list,' said Dawn. 'Neither of them were at the Garden and Allotment Show so they can't be Murdo Meek.' She heard Red clear his throat. 'Oh … er … Over,' she added, cursing herself for forgetting to say the word which signified that she had finished speaking and was awaiting a response.

'Could you please identify them. Over,' said Red.

'Their names are Neville Shaw and Martin Gough. Neville was at a tank museum with his girlfriend Diana

Flinch, and Martin was on a weekend fishing trip. His wife says he's married to his fishing rod,' said Dawn. 'I had a little chat with her this evening, while she was cleaning her doorstep. I've … er … made contact with two other suspects but haven't been able to eliminate them yet. One's Seth Lightfoot and the other's Larry Grahams. Over.'

'Anything else?' said Red. 'Over.'

'Not really,' she said feebly. Before she could say 'Over' she happened to look round and saw leaves quivering violently behind her. She knew, instantly, that their movement was being caused by something more than a mild evening breeze. Hastily, she removed her headphones and, in doing so, she heard the unmistakable sound of somebody approaching.

'Shrimp!' said Red's voice faintly from the headphones which Dawn had tossed into the lunch box. 'Shrimp! Please come in!'

'Over and out,' whispered Dawn into the microphone before flicking a switch and ending the transmission. As she snatched the aerial from its position in the nearest tree, she caught sight of a pencil-sized Trudy striding across the field with Felix in her wake. Dawn's heart thumped wildly. The other person in the thicket must be a total stranger and, if she didn't shut her lunch box in the next two seconds, her undercover career would be very short-lived indeed.

Chapter Thirteen

A Clue or Two

Felix threw his arms around his dog. 'Haltwhistle must have picked up Granny's scent,' he said, glowering at Dawn. 'He was doing his best to follow her trail and you got in his way.'

Dawn was lying on the ground like an upturned tortoise, as if she had just been winded by some rampaging animal and was too shocked to get up (which, in actual fact, was exactly what had happened). Her body didn't seem to be able to move but her eyes were lively enough. They were darting from Felix to Haltwhistle and then back to Felix again. She was trying to decide which, out of the two of them, she hated the most.

'Don't … you … go … blaming … Dawn,' said Trudy, who was still breathless, having sprinted the entire length of the field. Although she could not remember, Dawn supposed that she must have made some kind of alarmed noise just before Haltwhistle blundered into her with the force of a battering ram. She could not recall if it had been a scream or a shout or a mixture of both, but it had certainly caused Felix and Trudy to arrive pretty fast.

'Is my radio OK?' asked Dawn, twisting her neck to see where it had landed after suddenly parting company with her hands.

Luckily, the lunch box seemed to have been cushioned by a bed of moss and looked surprisingly dent-free when Trudy lifted it in the air to show her.

Phew, thought Dawn as she rolled over on to her side. *Thank goodness for that! I think Red may well have booted me off the mission if anything else had gone wrong.*

'Does it hurt anywhere?' demanded Trudy, kneeling beside Dawn. Her tone was stern but Dawn appreciated that she was trying to be kind. 'Is there anything broken?' she persisted.

'Don't think so,' said Dawn. She sat up and examined a graze on her elbow. It stung a little and prompted her to say, 'Ouch!'

'Haltwhistle's all right, too,' said Felix in a loud, out-raged voice. 'Thank you very much for asking!'

The withering stare that Trudy gave him was impressively Edith-like in its intensity. 'Get out of my sight!' she commanded, getting to her feet.

'Can't,' said Felix insolently. 'I'm not allowed. *You* said that I wasn't to wander off. *You* said that you wanted to keep your beady eye on me at all times ...'

Trudy made a menacing growling noise, which was

enough to make Haltwhistle put his tail between his legs and cause Felix to look slightly worried.

'Just sit down and don't move,' she snapped.

Surprisingly, Felix did as he was told, although he grumbled about the dampness of the ground and the unfairness of Haltwhistle being blamed for something that wasn't his fault.

'He was tracking my granny,' said Felix. 'She must have come through this wood at some stage. If you'd only let him sniff around for a bit he might be able to pick up her trail again ...'

Dawn didn't take much notice of his ramblings. She stood beside Trudy and dusted herself down.

'What was that?' she said as a large bird with out-stretched wings swooped silently over her head.

'An owl,' said Trudy, 'out hunting. It'll be pitch dark in half an hour or so. We should get back. All right, you,' she said rudely to Felix, 'up you get. Now, where's that stupid dog of yours?'

'He's not stupid!' said Felix. 'He's found Granny's scent! Look!'

Dawn glanced around the thicket and saw Haltwhistle with his nose buried in leaf litter. He lifted up his muzzle and his jaw began to move as if he were chewing something. When he had finished, his tongue flopped out on to the ground and scooped up what looked like a black liquorice allsort.

Trudy turned to Felix with a disdainful look on her face. 'The only thing your dog has found is a heap of rabbit pellets.'

'Yuk!' said Dawn as she realised what Haltwhistle was doing. 'He's eating poo.'

She turned away in disgust, and caught sight of the owl which had flown overhead a few moments earlier. It had cleared the thicket of birch trees and was drifting elegantly over the fields towards a steep slope. Dawn stood on tiptoe and tilted her head so that she had a clear view through the branches. She saw the owl, which was now the size of a five pence piece, hovering in the sky. Then she noticed something else behind it: a flickering light moving up the slope. The light seemed to be approaching a lone building which was silhouetted against the skyline. Dawn remembered the tip of Red's ruler touching upon a black drawing pin on the map of the village. The house on the hill was a derelict mansion called Palethorpe Manor.

Dawn had never been to church before. On Sunday morning, she went to St Elmo's by herself, in her Brownie uniform. She mingled with all the other girls her age who were dressed in brown and yellow as they lined up outside the west door at the side of the tower. Along with the Guides, Scouts and Cubs, they were waiting to participate in Church Parade, which happened once every month.

Ignoring the sound of the church bells tolling, Dawn listened to the conversation of the two Guides nearest to her to see if she could find out anything useful, but, to her disappointment, they talked incessantly about a couple of Scouts called Ed and Jay (teenage boys with winsome smiles who were doing their best to forge their way towards the Guides through the crowd). The Cubs, on the other hand, were boys of Dawn's own age, and they couldn't have been less interested in gaining the attention of their female counterparts, the Brownies. All they seemed to want to do was pull stupid faces and knock each other's caps on to the ground.

Dawn felt comfortingly anonymous in the crowd of chattering children. No one enquired as to her name or to which Brownie pack she belonged. She was just another Imp in a brown and yellow mass of Imps, Gnomes, Pixies, Sprites and Elves, and she was free to eavesdrop to her heart's content.

Led by a few serious-looking children who were carrying flags far taller than themselves, the Brownies, Guides, Cubs and Scouts began to march through the west door. Their chatter died away as they entered the church. Dawn watched with interest as they passed by several dangling ropes and the bell-ringers who had just finished pulling them. Most were youths with their sleeves rolled up; there was one woman wearing a tartan cape and a pork-pie hat, and a distinguished-looking gentleman with a Roman nose and jet-black hair.

Dawn found the church service a little bit dull. The vicar was a young woman with the worst pudding-bowl haircut that Dawn had ever seen, which was the only part of her that was visible when she stood in the pulpit because she was remarkably short. Despite her diminutive stature, the vicar had a powerful voice that seemed to fill every crevice and corner in the vast, draughty old church. Not that Dawn was paying much attention to what the vicar was saying. She was rather more intent on checking out the congregation. Having managed to secure a seat on the end of a pew, she had a clear view up and down the nave and she spent most of the service trying to establish if any of the men in her field of vision were on the shortlist provided by P.U.F.F.

As luck would have it, Dawn had chosen to sit next to a Brownie called Jessica Kingsley, who, it transpired, was a know-it-all Gnome with fifteen badges – and an impressive depth of knowledge when it came to naming members of the congregation. Dawn thought it best to question her unwitting informant during the singing of hymns when the two Brownies' whispers were drowned out by the warbling voices of those around them.

In an hour the service was over, and Dawn was feeling much more positive about her mission. Jessica had pointed out several men whose names were written on the five of diamonds. She had also been good enough to eliminate two of them from Dawn's investigation. Clive de Moyne and Winston Edge, both of whom were choristers, had been playing in a tennis tournament on the first of July, which was the day of the Garden and Allotment Show. Jessica had been a spectator at the tournament and was even able to tell Dawn that neither man had a very good serve.

As the vicar and other members of the clergy began to file out of the church, Dawn dug Jessica in the ribs for the final time.

'That man with the black hair and the big nose – he's a bell-ringer, isn't he?'

'Yes,' said Jessica. 'That's Mr Noble, that is. The Right Honourable Charles Noble. He's the Tower Captain – that means he's the head bell-ringer ... and he also gives out the prizes at the Garden and Allotment Show.'

'Noble ... ah,' said Dawn. Certain that his name was written on the five of diamonds, she sneaked a specially long look at him as he walked past.

'Not *again*.' Trudy groaned as the telephone started to ring. She put down her cup of tea, rose out of an armchair and headed into the hallway to answer the phone. She reappeared a few minutes later, waving a pad of paper and frowning. 'That's the fourth one this afternoon,' she said to Dawn.

205

'Is it?' said Dawn, looking up from the coded letter she was writing to Red. She sucked the end of her gold-plated fountain pen. 'Was that another booking?'

'Yes,' said Trudy, glancing at the notepad. 'Mrs Gee of nine, Mildew Mead wants me to clear some rhododendrons from the bottom of her garden. Her husband's on that shortlist of yours, isn't he?'

Dawn nodded. 'Yes. His name's Brian.'

'Good. Well, I told her the earliest I could fit her in would be Thursday afternoon.' Trudy sank into her armchair and blew out her cheeks. 'Hurry up and find Angela, would you, Dawn? I'll be exhausted by the end of this week if I have to sort out all these people's gardens.' She tossed the notepad on to a footstool and took a greedy gulp of tea.

Dawn shrugged. 'I'll do my best,' she said. Then she continued with her letter to Red. She was writing on a sheet of cream paper from the writing set that P.S.S.T. had provided. She had already written the address and date, and below her alias's initials (K.A.W.) she had written the first paragraph.

The code that Dawn had chosen to use was called 'Noah's Ark'. It meant that she had to conceal her message by writing the letters two by two in each consecutive word. This required a lot of concentration and so Felix and his dog had been sent into the garden with a cricket bat and a tennis ball, and strict instructions not to annoy

Peebles, who was halfway up a rowan tree, basking in the sun.

After five minutes had passed by, Dawn put down her pen.

'Finished?' said Trudy.

'Not even nearly,' said Dawn with a sigh. 'I've asked Red for some more information about the suspects, and now I'm trying to put together a progress report.'

'Surely that shouldn't take long,' said Trudy dismissively. 'It's not as if you've got very far with your investigations.' She drained her teacup and looked enquiringly at Dawn. 'Well … have you made any breakthroughs that I don't know about?'

'I've managed to cross off two more suspects from my list,' said Dawn, referring to the tennis-playing members of the choir whom she had mentioned to Trudy over lunch.

'Three,' corrected Trudy. 'You're forgetting Mr Zuckerman.'

'Oh, yes.' Dawn made an amendment to her letter. Harold Zuckerman had telephoned that morning while she had been at church. He had asked if Trudy could choose a few tasteful statues for his garden – and he had spoken in a distinctive American drawl. Angela Bradshaw had never said that Murdo Meek had an accent, and Dawn had been content to put a line through Harold's name.

'What else are you going to put in your progress

report?' asked Trudy. 'The fact that you've found no clues at all in your hunt for our missing colleague?'

Trying her best to ignore her, Dawn picked up her fountain pen. 'I'm going to tell Red about the light I saw on the hill last night. I think it was someone with a torch and they were heading for Palethorpe Manor.'

'That tumbledown old ruin?' said Trudy. 'Why would anyone want to poke around up there?'

'I don't know,' said Dawn, 'but I intend to find out.'

'Tonight?' said Trudy, gripping the arms of her chair. She seemed a tiny bit concerned. 'All by yourself?'

'I thought I might wait until tomorrow,' said Dawn, surprised by how confident she sounded. 'There's a full moon then, you see. Socrates says that torches are far too noticeable. He says it's always best to find your way by moonlight when you're snooping about in the dark.'

'Gone to rack and ruin, that place has. Been derelict for donkey's years. I wouldn't go near it if I were you, unless you want half a ton of bricks and masonry falling on your head.' Seth Lightfoot waved his dustpan and brush warningly at Felix before sweeping up some dusty old chips that someone had dropped in the gutter. 'Palethorpe's not for playing in,' said Seth grimly. 'You kids had better stay away.'

'Yes, good idea,' said Dawn. Then, as discreetly as she could, she kicked Felix in the ankle. 'Come on, Wayne.

We can't stand here chatting all morning.' She seized his hand and managed to drag him past the duck pond and halfway up the Green before he squirmed out of her grasp.

'You're awfully violent for a girl,' said Felix, massaging his wrist. He leaned against a telephone box and examined his ankle. 'What d'you have to go and kick me for? I'm in excruciating agony here.'

'Oh, shut up,' said Dawn. She was very angry indeed. 'I'm wearing *sandals* so it can't have hurt that much. Anyway, you deserved it.'

'You're jolly lucky that Halt— I mean, Fred, was looking the other way,' said Felix, ruffling his dog's fur, 'otherwise he would have gone for you.'

'Hmm,' said Dawn, casting a doubtful glance at Haltwhistle, who had just started to lick her toes. He was such a placid dog that she could not imagine him taking a bite out of anybody. Although he seemed rather fond of barking, his woofs were always accompanied by a happily wagging tail. How, thought Dawn, could someone be so mistaken about his own dog?

'Ooh,' said Felix, wincing with pain as he put weight on his ankle.

Dawn began to feel slightly guilty. 'I wouldn't have had to kick you,' she hissed, 'if you hadn't struck up a conversation with that man. What in the world made you ask about Palethorpe Manor?'

'I was curious,' said Felix. 'What's the big deal? I was

only making small talk. The chap looked harmless enough.'

'That was Seth Lightfoot,' said Dawn. 'He's a suspect! And now you've put it into his head that we're interested in Palethorpe.'

'Well, what's wrong with that?' grumbled Felix. 'How am I supposed to know what not to mention if you never tell me anything?'

Dawn didn't bother to respond. The last thing she wanted was for Felix to find out about the escapade she had planned for that evening. She did not want to be followed by a meddlesome boy and his idiotic dog when she went on her moonlit walk to Palethorpe Manor. Ignoring his questioning stare, Dawn began to examine the side of the telephone box.

'Look!' she said, putting her arm through a small rectangular gap. 'There's a pane of glass missing.'

'So what?' said Felix grouchily.

'This is the place where Bob ended up. He was the second agent to come looking for your granny. The missing piece of glass might be a clue to what happened to him. He was found in a bit of a state,' explained Dawn, 'and he hasn't spoken a word since.'

'Poor guy,' said Felix. He hobbled into the telephone box and looked around eagerly. 'I know – let's see if we can find some more clues.'

'Wait!' said Dawn, following him inside. She opened

her purse, which was hanging round her neck, and took out several coins. 'People might wonder what we're doing in here. Put a coin in the slot and act like you're talking on the phone. Then drop some money on the floor and I'll pretend to be looking for it.'

'Do I *have* to?' said Felix.

'Yes!' Dawn told him. 'Don't make a fuss – just do it.'

'Crikey,' he said, lifting the receiver. He chuckled to himself. 'When I first met you I thought you were a bit of a wimp – but I'm beginning to change my mind!

'Where have you been?' said Trudy, giving Dawn a sour look. She stopped leaning against a moss-covered brick wall and grasped the handles of a wheelbarrow. 'I told Mr Grahams that we'd be starting work at nine thirty. You're a quarter of an hour late!'

'I'm really sorry,' said Dawn.

'Well, that's all right,' said Trudy, her tone mellowing a little. 'I expect it was *his* fault anyway.' She glared reproachfully at Felix, who had paused at a lamppost a few paces away for Haltwhistle to relieve himself.

'No,' said Dawn. 'Actually, Wayne wasn't to blame.' Her voice dropped to a whisper. 'I chanced upon a clue – that's what held me up.'

'Great,' said Trudy softly. 'What did you find?'

'A missing pane of glass,' said Dawn. She decided not to mention the other thing that she had found. The grey feather that had been lying on the floor of the telephone box had not looked important enough to be a clue. She had pocketed it, nevertheless, having decided that it would make a pretty bookmark.

'What's so special about a missing piece of glass?' said Trudy.

Dawn hesitated. She had spied somebody walking towards them. 'Gosh, Mum, what lovely plants,' she said loudly, turning her attention to the wheelbarrow. It contained several flowering shrubs in brown plastic pots as well as an assortment of gardening tools and a small sack of peat. 'I bet Mr Grahams will be pleased with these beauties.'

'Er … yes,' said Trudy, looking somewhat tense as a man approached with a newspaper tucked under his arm. 'I picked them up at Scattergood's Nursery this morning,' she said to Dawn. 'Couldn't decide between the pansies and the chrysanthemums – so I got both.'

'Nice day for it,' said the man, smiling pleasantly as he passed. His shoes made crunching sounds with every step as he turned into the gravel drive of the house next door. Dawn recognised his sleek black hair and aquiline nose. It was the bell-ringer whom she had seen at church the day before. She had checked to see if his name was definitely on her list of suspects – and it was. His name was Charles Noble.

'Where did you find it?' said Trudy, once Charles

Noble's footsteps could no longer be heard. She nudged Dawn's elbow. 'The missing pane of glass!'

'Telephone box,' said Felix before Dawn could reply. Haltwhistle had finished with the lamppost and was now sniffing the wheelbarrow's plump black tyre.

'The one where Bob was found,' said Dawn. 'I'm certain the missing pane of glass must be a clue. I just don't know exactly what it *means* yet.'

'Oh,' said Trudy. She seemed disappointed. Lifting the handles of the wheelbarrow, she propelled it alongside a wall and stopped when she reached a narrow wooden gate. Beyond the gate was the home of Larry Grahams: a red-brick house called 'Rustlings'.

Obeying a nod from Trudy, Dawn opened the gate to allow her 'mother' to pass through with the wheelbarrow. Felix lingered in the road with a hopeful look on his face. He appeared to be waiting for an invitation to join them. Trudy cocked an eyebrow at him.

'Go home, Wayne,' she said firmly.

His face fell.

'And I don't mean, "Take the most roundabout route possible and get into heaps of trouble on the way,"' she said. 'Straight home – and no chatting to *anyone*.'

Felix adopted a sulky expression, tugged on Haltwhistle's lead and began to trudge towards the Green.

'Come on, Fred,' he mumbled. 'We know when we're not wanted.'

Chapter Fourteen
The Sandal Snatcher

To Dawn's eyes, the back garden at Rustlings resembled a wildlife haven. Everywhere she looked there were fluttering wings, darting insects and glimpses of furry creatures in the trees. She counted three bird feeders which swayed and shook as they were visited by little birds with short, slim beaks. Dozens of boisterous starlings with greasy-looking black feathers descended on the stone birdbath in the centre of the lawn. They dipped their heads under the water and wiggled their bodies, surrounding themselves with plumes of sparkling droplets.

Larry Grahams was proud of his garden. Dawn could tell by the way his eyes gleamed when he talked about it. He was particularly pleased with his vegetable plot. However, as he explained to Trudy, he wasn't as young as he used to be. His knees were inclined to seize up if he knelt on the hard ground for too long, which meant that he had neglected to do any weeding in recent months. When he had seen her notice in the post office window, he had finally admitted to himself that it was time to ask for a helping hand.

While Trudy set to work pulling up weeds and dropping them in a tin pail, Dawn flitted about the garden with a trowel, prodding the soil for appearances' sake, keeping an eye open for Larry.

Their employer seemed to be a kind, if rather dreamy, man. Dawn guessed that he was a year or two younger than her grandfather. He was a lithe fellow who chose to dress in rich, earthy colours. His white beard was neatly trimmed and he wore a tweed cap and a neckerchief. Once Trudy and Dawn had started to busy themselves in the garden, Larry disappeared inside his house.

An abundance of trees and mature shrubs meant that Dawn could easily slip out of sight and have a jolly good snoop. She found a compost heap that reeked of rotting vegetables and a dark shed full of cobwebs. Her most interesting discovery was a tortoise, which she found dozing under a clump of lavender. As she stretched out a finger to stroke its rough, bumpy shell, she saw Larry coming towards her. He was holding a tray.

'Ah, *there* you are! I see you've found Pilliwinks,' he said, smiling at his sleeping pet. 'Isn't she a treasure? She's a Greek tortoise, you know. I had half a mind to let my friend Rex Hutton take her with him when he emigrated out there. Thought it might be nice to return the old girl to her homeland. When it came to the crunch I couldn't part with her, though. She's far too dear to me.'

'Your friend has moved to Greece?' said Dawn, trying not to appear too curious. Rex Hutton's name was on the five of diamonds.

'Yes,' said Larry. 'Upped sticks and left a month and a half ago. Said he wanted to spend his twilight years in a place with a nice, hot climate.'

'I see,' said Dawn, managing to stay perfectly calm. If Rex had relocated to Greece in June that meant that he could not be Murdo Meek. So far, she had eliminated six out of the eleven suspects on her list.

Only a few more names to cross off, thought Dawn as she accepted the glass of lime cordial and the custard cream that Larry offered her.

'Do you think you and your mum will be all right if I pop down to the pond and feed the ducks?' asked Larry. 'It's part of my morning routine. I know it's a bit silly at my age, but I'm very fond of my feathered friends.'

'Did they ever find the one that went missing?' said Dawn, remembering the conversation that she'd overheard between Diana Flinch and Bess Arbuthnot in the post office.

'Sadly, no,' said Larry, and Dawn was dismayed to see a tear slip down his cheek. 'Poor old Bernard.'

'Bernard?' said Dawn.

'That's the name I gave him. He was the pond's most senior resident; feathers were starting to lose their sheen and he was getting a bit doddery. It's a shame that he's gone. I do miss the old boy.' Another tear began to well in Larry's eye, and Dawn changed the subject hurriedly.

'Where would you like your pansies planted?' she asked. 'Mum and I were wondering.'

'Oh, anywhere,' said Larry in a faraway voice. He gave the tray to Dawn. 'Would you oblige me by handing out the rest of the refreshments? I really must shoot off. My ducks will be wondering where I've got to.'

'Sure, Mr Grahams. No problem,' she said, smiling to herself.

With Larry Grahams safely out of the way, Dawn seized her opportunity to explore inside his home. Conveniently, he had left the back door unlocked. Dawn removed her sandals before entering the house so that she did not leave any tell-tale traces of mud on the carpets within. Clutching the tray (which she planned to set down in the kitchen, giving herself a reason to be indoors should Larry return to find her there), Dawn stepped over the threshold.

She moved carefully through each room, her eyes goggling at the paintings on the walls, the overcrowded bookshelves, the outmoded furniture and the numerous porcelain animals which seemed to be displayed everywhere. It was obvious to Dawn that Larry was a tidy person. All his possessions were neatly arranged and there wasn't a speck of dust to be seen. Taking great care not to disturb anything, she lifted lids, opened drawers and peered into cupboards but, to her disappointment, she did not find a scrap of evidence to suggest that Larry Grahams was anything other than a harmless old man.

Sensing that Larry could be back at any moment, Dawn trod softly through the house and opened the back door, intending to put on her sandals as quickly as possible.

'Oh, flip,' said Dawn. Her forehead wrinkled in bewilderment.

Where there had been two sandals sitting on a flagstone outside the door – now there was only one.

Dawn's heart fluttered like a moth's wings against a light bulb. Although she was finding it awkward to walk around the garden wearing only one sandal, that wasn't what was bothering her. Neither was she fussed about the grass stains or lumps of dirt on the underside of her left foot. It was the identity of the person who had taken her sandal which was making her worry.

Trudy wasn't responsible. Dawn had asked her straight away.

'In case you hadn't noticed,' Trudy had said, wiping a gloved hand across her sweating brow, 'I happen to be quite busy *working*. Anyway, what on earth would I want with one of your smelly sandals?'

When Dawn had asked her if she had seen anyone else in the garden, she had shaken her head and hurled a handful of dandelions into her pail.

Ignoring the scowl on Trudy's face, Dawn had pressed on with another question. 'What about Larry?' she'd said. 'Has he come back yet?'

'Not to my knowledge,' Trudy had muttered acidly, 'but I wasn't aware that it was my job to keep watch. I'm just the gardener. You're the one who's supposed to be the *spy*.'

Dawn had searched the lawn and flowerbeds. She had poked about in the compost heap, scoured the vegetable plot and even had another peek in the spider-infested shed. Her sandal was nowhere to be found. She stood in a secluded corner of the garden and glanced edgily around her. Was it possible that Larry had returned, unseen, and witnessed Dawn searching through his belongings? But, if so, why hadn't he confronted her? What reason could he have had for stealing her sandal? And if Larry hadn't been the culprit, then who had? Sandals didn't walk off by themselves.

Dawn's eyes stopped darting about, and fixed upon a broken twig in the hedge next to her. She examined it earnestly. At the breakage, the wood was pale and moist as if it had been snapped in two a matter of moments ago. Then something else caught her attention. Lying on the ground were three or four tiny sprigs of hawthorn leaves and, as Dawn crouched beside them, she spotted a strand of blackish hair tangled around a slender stem. She remembered reading in *Keeping to the Shadows* that tiny signs like these could turn out to be big clues when a spy was attempting to follow the tracks of his quarry.

Somebody's been through here, thought Dawn. *I'm certain of it.* Glancing over her shoulder to check that she wasn't being observed, she squeezed through the hedge by wriggling on her stomach and emerged in the garden next door.

The lawn was as spick and span as a recently vacuumed carpet. Its grass had been mown in such a way that stripes of light green alternated with those of a slightly darker hue. There was a rockery, and a pond with an ornamental stone fish in its centre, spewing a long stream of water from its mouth. Dawn took refuge behind a tall conifer tree and peered cautiously around it.

The house at the end of the garden seemed to be a strange sort of hybrid. The lower half looked ordinary enough – if rather ancient. It was made of flame-coloured bricks and had small, latticed windows. The roof, however, was an unusual conical shape with an octagonal window at the top, which reminded Dawn of the highest storey of a lighthouse. Crowning this was a weather vane with a jade-green dragon twisting and turning in the wind. Despite its freakish appearance, she had a hunch that only a very wealthy person would be able to afford to live in it.

Dawn saw Charles Noble's face at one of the ground-floor windows and swiftly flattened herself against the tree. Could *he* have stolen her sandal? The colour of his hair certainly matched the strand that she had found on the hawthorn sprig. She started to entertain the possibility that Charles Noble could be Murdo Meek. What would he do to her if he found her in his garden? She hurriedly dreamt up a story about a wild rabbit with a distressing limp, and practised her most anguished facial expression. This changed to a look of open-mouthed horror when she happened to glance at the fountain.

There he was! The sandal thief! With the pilfered item lying at his feet. He was standing in full view of the house with his head hanging down. She couldn't see his face but she could hear the slap of his tongue against the water as he took a lengthy drink from the pond.

'*Haltwhistle*,' said Dawn. She was livid. 'Youuuuu ...' She stopped herself from calling him something rude and, instead, peeked around the conifer tree to see if Charles was watching. Fortunately, he was no longer at the window. Dawn tried to attract Haltwhistle's attention by clicking her fingers. 'Fred!' she whispered urgently. 'Oi, Fred! Come here, you *monster*.'

The dog stopped drinking. He raised his head and looked directly at Dawn, water dribbling down his hairy chin. Patting her thighs, Dawn gave him an encouraging smile.

'Come on, boy,' she said, and then had a moment of inspiration. 'Biscuits!' she added enticingly, although she did not have so much as a crumb in her pockets.

Haltwhistle hesitated. Then he seized her sandal in his mouth and gambolled off in the direction of a small outbuilding close to the house. Dawn ground her teeth together in fury before taking a deep breath and haring after him.

'Ha! Got you cornered,' said Dawn, closing the door of the outbuilding behind her. She took a couple of paces into the musty-smelling interior. Judging by the tools hanging from nails on the walls, the dining chairs stacked up in a corner and three bikes chained together, Dawn guessed that the building was being used as a workshop-cum-storeroom. Feeble rays of light filtered in through two high windows, leaving much of the room smothered in shadow. She saw a movement underneath a bench on top of which a ladder rested, broken into several pieces.

Haltwhistle crawled out from under the bench and ventured into a shaft of sunlight, meekly wagging his tail at Dawn. He dropped her sandal and it made a hollow tap as it landed on the concrete floor. Dawn lunged at her sandal and put it on. Then she grabbed Haltwhistle's shaggy neck and felt around it for his collar. It wasn't there.

The dog almost knocked her over as he jumped up, put his paws on the bench, and sniffed the ladder. She shook her head in wonderment as he started to lick one of the rungs.

'You are one dozy dog,' said Dawn, and she allowed herself to smile. Now that she had retrieved her sandal and managed to entrap Haltwhistle, she felt too thankful to be angry. Her moment of relief proved to be all too temporary, however.

'Crikey! Someone's coming!' said Dawn, hearing a noise outside. She threw her arms around Haltwhistle's body and, mustering all her strength, bundled him into a shadowy corner. Then she pinned him to the ground behind the stack of dining chairs and gave him a really stern look. 'Shh,' she said, putting her finger to her lips as the door creaked open.

Dawn heard two sets of footsteps enter the outbuilding. She sneaked a look through the chair legs and saw Charles Noble standing in the doorway with the old man who had been sitting outside the village hall collecting entrance fees for the art exhibition in his bucket.

'You sure 'bout this, Mr Noble?' she heard the old man say.

'Yes, Reg. I couldn't be more positive,' replied Charles.

The old man scratched his head. 'Don't seem right, somehow. Sawin' a perfickly good ladder into bits.'

'It's broken, Reg,' explained Charles patiently, 'in several places.'

They moved closer to the bench where the ladder was resting. Dawn tightened her grip around Haltwhistle's muzzle.

'Nice bit of wood, that,' said Reg. 'You wouldn't like me to see if I can fix it?'

'No,' said Charles. 'It's kind of you to offer, but I'd rather it was chopped up for firewood. Since that unlucky chap's accident, I've barely been able to bring myself to look at it. Broke both his legs, poor devil.'

'Oh, that's right,' said Reg slowly, as if he were willing his brain to remember. 'Window cleaner, weren't he?'

'Mmm,' said Charles, retreating towards the door. 'Well, I'll leave you to it – and afterwards, if you wouldn't mind seeing to that other little job I mentioned ...'

'Right-o,' said Reg, lifting down a large saw from a hook above his head. 'Will do.'

'Excellent. I'll be in my study if you need me,' said Charles, his hand on the doorknob, 'finishing off today's cryptic crossword. Cup of tea at eleven, as usual? Three sugars, isn't it?'

'Four,' said Reg, and sniffed. Then he gripped the ladder with one hand and began to make a groove in the wood with the saw's toothed blade.

Dawn's eyes were as round as marbles. She sat, as motionless as she was able with a headstrong dog squirming in her arms, and gave herself a good talking to in her head: *You ninny, Dawn. Fancy not realising that Charles Noble's house was the scene of Miles's accident. Red pointed it out to you on the map of the village and you weren't paying proper attention. What did he say its name was? The Old Toast House or something …*

She watched Reg's elbow swing back and forth as he sawed the ladder into segments. Dawn shared the old man's opinion that it was rather wasteful to reduce the ladder to a stack of firewood. It was also a blow to her investigation. If she had realised the ladder's importance when she first set eyes on it, she could have examined it to check for any signs of foul play. Now she would never know if Miles's fall had been engineered or if he had merely lost his balance.

Like most dogs, Haltwhistle did not have very good manners – and neither did he have very clean teeth. Unfortunately, Dawn learnt both these facts in quick succession when he opened his cavernous mouth and yawned right in her face. With no prior warning, Dawn did not have a chance to turn her head away before the blast of doggy breath hit. Instinctively, Dawn's fingers flew to her nostrils to block out the smell.

If Dawn had credited Haltwhistle with having the tiniest scrap of intelligence (which she didn't), she might have thought that he had yawned on purpose. To fend off his unpleasant breath, she was compelled to release him with one hand. This gave him a distinct advantage and he wasn't slow to act upon it. One moment Dawn was pressed up against him, eyeball to eyeball, and the next she was watching helplessly as his feathery tail disappeared through the door. Fortunately, Reg seemed to be far too engrossed in his task to notice a dog slipping past him, followed by a vexed eleven-year-old girl with a very light tread.

Once she was out in the open air, Dawn could hear a distant voice calling the same name over and over again.

'Fre … ed! Fre … ed! Fr … ed!'

She looked desperately about her but Haltwhistle was nowhere in sight. Bracing herself to bump into Charles at any moment, she dashed over to the strangely shaped house and, pressing her back against it, moved crabwise along its wall until she reached a corner. Just as she peered round it, Dawn heard a noisy scampering sound and saw Haltwhistle bolting down the gravel driveway towards a scrawny boy with his arms outstretched.

'What do you think you're doing?' she hissed at

Felix, as soon as she had joined them outside the front gate of the house.

'Don't glare at me like that,' he said, frowning at her. He stroked Haltwhistle's head, and the dog gave a contented sigh.

'You're supposed to be at home!' fumed Dawn. She stole a quick look at the house behind them, and noticed a porcelain tablet beside the front door which confirmed that she had misremembered its name. It was called 'The Old Oast House'. 'Of course…that was it,' she said under her breath.

'He slipped out of his collar, didn't he,' said Felix, producing a choke chain from his pocket and dropping it over the dog's head. 'Wily old thing,' he added as he clipped on a lead.

Dawn narrowed her eyes. She had a sneaking suspicion that Felix wasn't being truthful, but she didn't want to argue with him in such a public place. Instead, she suggested that they should move a little further up the road: she was worried that Charles Noble might glance out of a window and wonder what they were doing skulking about outside his house.

'Cracked the case yet?' said Felix cheekily.

'Funnily enough … no,' said Dawn. 'I've been too busy chasing your dog all over the place. He could ruin this whole mission if you don't keep him under control.' She glared at Felix. 'Now, go back to the cottage, please.

You know you shouldn't be here.'

'Neither should you,' responded Felix with a smirk. 'That fellow whose garden you're working in is going to be mightily puzzled by now. Let's hope Trudy could come up with a story to explain where you'd disappeared to.'

'What?' said Dawn, her eyes widening. 'Has Larry come back? How long ago did you see him? You'd better not be pulling my leg ...'

'Old bloke?' said Felix glibly. 'Bandy legs ... beard ... brown paper bag?'

Dawn nodded, her heart sinking.

'Sure I saw him ... He walked in through his front gate about five minutes ago.'

Chapter Fifteen

The Third Moon

'**D**id you get fish and chips?' said Felix, hurtling down the stairs of Daffodil Cottage three at a time. By some miracle, he managed to avoid tripping over Haltwhistle, who seemed to be determined to beat his master to the bottom step. 'Well?' said Felix eagerly, as he landed in the hallway. His restless eyes settled on Dawn's rucksack and, before she could protest, he had snatched it out of her hand and unfastened it. 'I'm absolutely starving,' he said, rummaging inside the bag. 'I hope you got an extra-big portion for me.'

'You've got no manners,' said Dawn feebly. She didn't have the energy to give him a proper lambasting: her muscles ached, her feet were all grimy and the tip of her nose was tender to the touch.

Felix groaned and let the rucksack sag in his arms. 'You didn't get my message, did you. Oh, by the way,' he said, 'have you looked in a mirror? Your nose is sunburned right on the end. Either that or you've got a very big spot.'

Dawn sighed. She had worn a sun hat dutifully for the entire day but its brim had obviously not been wide enough.

'What message?' she said.

'The one I sent you by telepathy. I asked you to stop at the chip shop on your way home.'

'No, I didn't get your message,' said Dawn wearily, resisting the temptation to add, 'you nutcase.'

'Don't know what Trudy's going to make us for supper,' said Felix. 'There's hardly any decent grub in the kitchen. Bit of bread, some funny-looking cheese, a jar of plum jam and an egg. Where is our lovely mother, anyway?'

Dawn put her head around the living-room door. Still wearing her muddy shoes, gardening gloves and baseball cap, Trudy had collapsed untidily on to the sofa.

'She's fast asleep,' said Dawn, succumbing to a little yawn herself. 'I'm not surprised. We've worked in four different gardens today. Weeded at "Rustlings", watered at "Fledglings", mowed the lawn at "Ogle Lodge" and dug a deep pit at "The Eerie Eyrie". Well, *I* hardly lifted a finger. Trudy did all the backbreaking stuff …'

'"The Eerie Eyrie", did you say?' Felix sniggered. 'What kind of weirdo would choose a name like that?'

'Seth Lightfoot lives there,' said Dawn a little defensively. 'He is a bit odd, but he's very kind. He chatted to

Trudy for ages, and kept us well supplied with iced tea and arrowroot biscuits.'

'Isn't he the man who warned us not to go near Palethorpe Manor? I thought he was a suspect,' said Felix.

'He is,' said Dawn, 'but I managed to search every room in his house and I didn't find anything suspicious.'

'So, what was the pit for?'

'To anchor his totem pole.'

'W-e-i-r-d-o,' said Felix, looking smug.

'Seth made it himself, out of bits and pieces that people had thrown away,' explained Dawn with a touch of awe in her voice. 'He recycles the litter he collects and makes sculptures out of it. He even gave me one of his creations as a present.'

'I wondered what that junk was at the bottom of your bag,' said Felix, delving into her rucksack and lifting out a strange object. It consisted of several spheres attached to part of an umbrella frame by thin strands of wire. The spheres smelled of wallpaper paste and had been covered with scraps of newspaper. 'What's it supposed to be?'

'It's a mobile,' said Dawn. 'That big ball in the middle is meant to be the planet Neptune and the others are its moons.'

'Want me to bin it?' said Felix.

'No!' Dawn wrested it from his grasp. 'I'm going to

hang it in my bedroom.'

'Suit yourself,' said Felix. 'Hey, how d'you explain yourself to that chap Larry today? Was he cross that you'd slunk off when you were supposed to be tending his garden?'

'I told him that I'd gone to fetch ice creams for me and Trudy but that they'd melted on the way back and I'd had to eat them both. He believed every word,' said Dawn.

'Ice cream!' said Felix, rubbing his stomach and groaning. 'I could eat a whole tubful!'

'You'd be sick afterwards if you did,' said Dawn. She relieved him of her rucksack and began to climb the stairs. Unlike Felix, she wasn't at all ravenous. Courtesy of her four employers, she had eaten a dozen assorted biscuits, a chapatti, two jam tarts and a big hunk of pumpernickel over the course of the day. Supper was the last thing on her mind.

What she really needed was a good, long soak in a bathtub and a couple of hours' kip. The gardening chores had tired her, but it was the constant fear of discovery as she went about her spying tasks that had sapped her strength the most. By nine o'clock that night it was crucial that she should feel spry, alert and ready for anything, because that was when she planned to set off on her moonlit walk to Palethorpe Manor.

Removing her sandals first, Dawn clambered on to

her bed. The mattress was firm and noiseless – so different from her lumpy one at home that creaked reassur-
ingly whenever she sat on it. She stretched both arms
above her head and managed to attach Seth's sculpture
to a little hook in the ceiling. It dangled lopsidedly, the
balls knocking against each other.

'What do you think of it, Clop?' she asked brightly.

Dawn had always considered her donkey to be a con-
noisseur of all things artistic. Whenever she brought
home polystyrene space ships or dumpy clay monsters
or eggshell mosaics that she had made at school, he had
seemed to marvel at their exquisiteness. However, just
one glance at Clop's appalled expression was enough to
tell her that he thought Seth's handiwork was shoddy in
the extreme.

'It's not as bad as all that!' said Dawn, prodding the
largest sphere with her finger. 'Imagine that my bedroom is the solar system, right? Well, this ball's
supposed to be the planet Neptune and ... Seth did tell
me the names of all its moons ... um ...' She thought
hard for a moment, then began to point at the other
balls individually. 'Here's Triton ... and this one's Naiad,
and ... OH, MY GOSH!' Dawn seized the third moon
in the palm of her hand and breathed in sharply. Her
cheeks turned as pink as the tip of her nose.

In the midst of all the shreds and scraps of newspaper
which had been pasted on to the moon's surface, there

was a small mauve triangle. The colourful piece of paper was edged with gold, and upon it had been typed the words:

```
except pteronophobia.
```

* * *

Dawn reclined in a bathtub filled with steaming, scented water. She had found a bottle of frangipani bath essence in the cabinet above the sink and had tipped a generous amount into the bath while the taps were running. It had turned the water milky lilac: a colour strikingly similar to that of the fragment which had been torn from a sheet of P.S.S.T.'s distinctive notepaper. What were the chances, marvelled Dawn, of the missing scrap of paper from Bob Chalk's file turning up pasted to a replica of Neptune's third moon?

She had recognised the stiff mauve paper as being the property of P.S.S.T. in less than a second. It had taken a fraction longer to realise that she was staring at the corner of a sheet from Bob's file. Someone must have torn off the triangle of paper on purpose – and used the information against the P.S.S.T. agent.

How it had come to be in Seth's possession, Dawn could only guess. Had he found it on the street and innocently brushed it into his dustpan? Or had *he* been the one to steal it from the filing cabinet in the head-quarters of P.S.S.T.?

Dawn's brain tried to unscramble all the information that was massing in her head.

Pteronophobia. Thanks to her grandfather, who had heard its definition on a quiz show, she knew exactly what it meant. Pteronophobia was the fear of being tickled with feathers. When Gramps had introduced her to the word on the morning that she had set out for P.S.S.T., she hadn't really believed that knowing its meaning would come in useful. But it had! Dawn reminded herself how lucky she was to have a slightly mad grandfather who, instead of giving her boring advice, told her weird and wonderful facts in the hope that they just *might* come in handy one day.

As far as dislikes, allergies and phobias went, it was now evident that Bob had none ... except pteronopho-bia. Fearless in every other respect, he was a man who was frightened of feathers.

Feathers. There had been a feather in the telephone box where Bob was discovered in an hysterical state: a large, pale grey one. Its tip was currently poking out of the pocket of her shorts which she had tossed on to a chair when she'd undressed. Regrettably, Dawn had not realised the feather's significance when she had first set eyes on it – but she did now, of course. Someone had gained access to Bob's personal file and had learned his only weakness.

They could have lured him into the telephone box – and then what? Dawn remembered the missing pane of glass. Perhaps the villain in question had inserted some sort of tickling device through the hole and barricaded the door to prevent Bob's escape. But surely, thought Dawn, shaking her head, a *single* feather could not have reduced a tough P.S.S.T. spy to a gibbering wreck.

Still puzzling over these recent developments in Operation Question Mark, Dawn leaned forward to pick up a bar of soap and a flannel from the tray in front of her. As she took the flannel in her hand, something else fell out of the tray and dropped into the water. Instead of sinking into the milky lilac depths, it bobbed about on the surface, a painted smile on its orange beak. Dawn grinned. A little rubber duck had jumped in to share the bath with her.

A duck.

Dawn gave a shiver, and the soap slipped out of her hands.

'Bernard!' she said out loud. 'The duck that went missing!' He was a mallard, reasoned Dawn, which meant that his head was green, *but the rest of his body was mostly grey* – just like the feather she had found! She jumped out of the bath and left a trail of damp foot-prints on the floor. On reaching the chair, she slid the feather from her shorts pocket and stroked it gently.

She could barely bring herself to imagine what had happened.

Somebody must have snatched Bernard, thought Dawn sadly – *and then silenced his quack*. Having done the dreadful deed, she realised that the mystery person must have plucked the poor old duck and used his feathers to torture Bob.

As she returned to the bathtub, all sorts of questions began to besiege her brain. How had someone managed to sneak into the offices of P.S.S.T. and steal information? Was Murdo Meek the man behind the theft, and if so, was he also responsible for doing away with the duck? Could Seth Lightfoot be the heartless rogue she was looking for, or was another of her suspects the guilty one?

Deciding that she did not have time to consider these possibilities, Dawn began to lather her shoulders. She mustn't lose sight of her immediate priority, which was to check out Palethorpe Manor.

She had worked out that Bob Chalk's debilitation had not been an accident. The chances were that Miles Evergreen had also been a victim of the unknown villain – but, as yet, she had found no proof. Whether the perpetrator was Murdo Meek or not, Dawn figured that she would have to be extra vigilant when she embarked on her night-time mission in a few hours' time.

Dressed in her darkest clothes (navy trainers, a pair of

jeans and a slate-grey hooded top) Dawn crept down the stairs. She checked her appearance in the hall mirror and was disappointed to see that the end of her nose was still pinker than normal, despite having smeared it with several fingerfuls of Trudy's moisturising cream. She shrugged at her reflection. It wouldn't matter in the dark.

Dawn trod softly into the kitchen. She could tell by the debris on the work surface that Felix had taken on the role of chef that evening. Beside an empty jam jar, a broken eggshell and a discarded wrapper she saw two brown sandwiches on a plate. Neither sandwich looked very appetising, but she reminded herself that a spy must carry a snack at all times – and also, that beggars couldn't be choosers. She wrapped the sandwiches in a paper bag and slid the package into her rucksack, which also contained her torch (to be used sparingly because its light would instantly give away her location), her radio set and binoculars. Inside the pouch in her top she had tucked her shell phone (in case of emergency) and her miniature camera.

Trudy was still recumbent on the sofa, but she had taken off her shoes and placed a couple of cushions behind her head to make herself more comfortable. Dawn found that she had to shake her quite vigorously to get her to open her eyes.

'Don't shut me in the potting shed!' said Trudy in the manner of someone who had just awoken from a nightmare. 'Oh,' she said, blinking at Dawn. 'It's you.'

'Just thought I'd tell you that it's nine o'clock and I'm off,' said Dawn. 'Tonight's the night I explore Palethorpe Manor.'

'Would you like me to come with you?' said Trudy, struggling into a sitting position. She gave a massive yawn.

'No, that's OK,' said Dawn. 'You're worn out. Besides,' she said, thinking of something that Socrates had told her, 'a spy is at her most cunning when she's on a solo mission.'

'Well … if you're sure,' said Trudy reluctantly. 'Don't take any unnecessary risks, though, Dawn … and if you're not back by midnight, I'm coming to find you.'

'Thanks.' Dawn was quite touched, though she half-suspected that Trudy's offer was prompted by her belief that a child could never be as capable as a grown-up.

'Where's Felix?' asked Trudy suddenly.

'Don't worry. He's upstairs,' said Dawn. 'I listened at his bedroom door and heard all these little beeps and explosions coming from inside. I think he must be busy vaporising aliens on his Game Boy.'

'Either that or Wonder Dog has learned another skill,' said Trudy with unconcealed sarcasm. 'Good luck, then, Dawn.' She leaned back against the cushions and, in a matter of seconds, had fallen asleep again.

The setting sun looked like a giant piece of barley sugar melting slowly in the sky. Twilight was mere minutes away. Dawn stood on the doorstep of Daffodil

Cottage, her rucksack strapped tightly to her back. She glanced quickly up and down the street to check who was about.

Sailing past the garden gate on an ancient bicycle, with the air of someone who longed to be in the Famous Five, was the vicar of St Elmo's church. For a moment, Dawn thought that the vicar had updated her image by dyeing her hair a violent green, but when she looked harder she realised that it was, in fact, a rather garish bicycle helmet.

On the other side of Cow Parsley Lane, sitting on a bench with his nose in a book, was a spiky-haired teenager who kept dipping his hand into a bag of crisps. Behind him, and to the right, was Mrs Cuddy, wobbling on a stool as she watered a hanging basket in her porch. Not one of them seemed to be aware that a young girl was standing, observing them all, from her doorstep.

Satisfied that she had managed to emerge from Daffodil Cottage without being noticed, Dawn set off. She moved a little more purposefully than her normal unhurried amble. Remembering not to let the front gate clang behind her, she stepped out on to the street.

Dawn could tell that Peebles was up to mischief by the skittish way in which he crossed the road. He pounced on the shoelaces of the boy reading his book before taking a perfectly judged leap on to a low brick wall. Running lightly along it, the cat chose to stop directly in front of Bluebell Villa, where Mrs Cuddy had finished her watering and disappeared inside. Almost instantly, two little white heads appeared at a window and began to yap non-stop. Peebles did not seem to be in the least bit bothered. Ignoring the dogs, he tucked his paws underneath him, as if he were settling down for a snooze. The barking became even more impassioned and Dawn heard a thud, and then another, as Honeybunch and Lambkin threw themselves against the pane of glass in front of them.

Predictably, the incessant barking began to attract quite a lot of attention. The vicar, who had almost reached the end of the lane, looked over her shoulder to see what all the fuss was about and nearly came off her bike. A woman in a dressing gown opened her front door, and craned her neck to see what was going on. Curtains shifted and faces appeared, the reddest of which was Mrs Cuddy's. The old lady rapped on the window with her walking stick and waved her arms in an attempt to frighten the cat away (a tactic which had absolutely no effect). Only the boy on the bench seemed oblivious to the commotion caused by Peebles. Dawn figured that the book he was reading must be awfully good.

Preferring not to be spotted by any of the villagers, Dawn put her head down and increased her pace. She was fairly sure that everyone's eyes were focused on

Bluebell Villa, but she didn't like to take any chances.

Dawn had planned her route carefully. As she walked through the village, she used a few techniques that Socrates had taught her to check if she was being followed: taking long looks over her shoulder whenever she crossed a road, and suddenly turning to put litter in a bin or to pick up something that she'd dropped on purpose. She was rather suspicious of a couple walking their basset hound, who seemed to be behind her for about half a mile, but eventually the couple stopped to chat to the post mistress, Diana Flinch, and she did not bump into them again.

As she turned down a footpath, leading to a wood called Craddock Clump, Dawn felt confident that nobody was on her tail. The sun had sunk below the horizon and the light was fading fast but, just as she had anticipated, the moon was in its fullest phase. She looked up at it gratefully, and continued on the path as it dipped downhill towards the wood.

Nipping in between the trees, Dawn slipped her rucksack from her shoulder and took out her lunch box, intending to make contact with P.S.S.T. before it got too dark to see the knobs and switches on the radio set. She seized the aerial and cast about her for a suitably high nook in which to wedge it. However, Dawn was distressed to find that all the trees in Craddock Clump were Scots pines with tall, straight trunks and, try as she might, she could not reach even their lowest branches. She wished that she had been able to transmit from the birch thicket, as she had done before, but she knew that this was against the advice of Socrates. It was recommended that every radio transmission should be made from a different spot in order to stay one step ahead of the enemy. Dawn decided that she would just have to hold the aerial in the air and hope for the best.

'Shrimp calling Barnacle,' said Dawn. 'Come in. Over.'

There was a noise like someone squeezing a packet of crisps and an unpleasant tinny humming. Dawn checked that she was tuned into the correct frequency and twiddled the aerial in her fingers.

'Shrimp calling Barnacle,' she said more urgently, pressing her free hand against an earphone.

Red's voice was barely audible. He sounded as if he were trying to speak with a harmonica in his mouth. Fortunately, Dawn managed to catch the gist of what he was saying.

'Yes, I have several things to report,' she said, her eyes darting about the wood to make sure that she was alone.

'I went to Ogle Lodge today and discovered that Edgar Palmer was doing a sponsored bike ride on the first of July, so I can cross him off my list of suspects ... oh, and I've found conclusive proof that Bob was tickled with feathers. Over.'

'One less suspect. Got that,' said Red's fuzzy voice, 'but can you repeat last sentence … mmphzzz … Over.'

'BOB,' said Dawn, enunciating each letter carefully, 'TICKLED. OVER.'

'Rrbblpfzz … say again,' came the reply.

Desperately, Dawn spun the aerial like a majorette's baton. 'Bungalow Onion Bungalow,' she said, resorting to the Cumberbatch Alphabet, 'was tickled using feathers from a Doodah Unicorn Chutney Key-ring. He's got a phobia, you see. I found the missing piece of Puddle Armpit Puddle Egghead Roundabout.'

'Bob … tickled by a duck? Jmmshzzz … what was that last bit? Over.' Red sounded perplexed.

Dawn rubbed her forehead anxiously. Socrates had instructed her to keep all radio messages as brief as possible. Perhaps she should abandon this transmission and try again tomorrow.

'Must wait until next broadcast,' said Dawn. 'Am on my way to Palethorpe Manor … you know … the Hurrah Onion Unicorn Sausage Egghead on the Hurrah Idiot Leotard Leotard. Over and out.'

Dawn stuffed her lunch box back into her rucksack and rejoined the footpath. It took her around the eastern boundary of the wood, then along the edge of a field and on to a grassy barrow from where she could see the hill with the dark uneven shape of Palethorpe Manor on its crest.

Chapter Sixteen

A Prowler at Palethorpe

The hill took longer to climb than Dawn had anticipated. Its angle was steep and, although the moon was shining brightly, she didn't find it easy to see where she was planting her feet. Dawn fell on her bottom twice. The first mishap occurred when she ricked her ankle in a rabbit hole and then, about ten minutes later, she slipped on something squidgy and landed, rather haplessly, on a thistle.

Exercising the self-control of a true professional, Dawn did not utter the slightest squeak on either occasion. She dusted herself down, glanced at the sprawling wreck of a building on the hilltop, and continued with her ascent.

To be certain that she was heading in the right direction, it was essential for Dawn to look up regularly at Palethorpe Manor, but every time her eyes fixed on the dilapidated stately home, she felt her scalp prickle. In the moonlight, all she could see was a bulky, black rectangle, and the harder she stared at the house, the more it seemed to swell and sway as if it were alive. It was the sort of house, thought Dawn, that might appear in people's nightmares – and she did not relish the prospect of venturing inside it.

Bravely, Dawn continued to climb higher until she was standing in front of a ragged wire fence which she supposed had been erected around the house to keep out any inquisitive villagers. She turned round and looked back down the slope to check that no one had been following her. The moon had draped a silvery film over the hillside, and as far as Dawn could see, she was quite alone.

After her exhausting climb, Dawn figured that it might be a good idea to have a moment's rest before exploring Palethorpe Manor. As she sat cross-legged on the ground, she wished that she had brought something sweet and comforting with her – like a bar of chocolate. Then, remembering the sandwiches which Felix had made, she rooted around for them in her rucksack.

She slid one out of a paper bag and stared at it. The sandwich was squashed and misshapen and, worst of all, it smelt *odd*. Dawn peeked at the filling and realised straight away that what Felix had taken to be 'funny-looking cheese' was, in fact, lard. No wonder the sandwiches had been left on the plate, untouched.

Felix might be a brainbox at school, thought Dawn as she dropped the sandwich back in the bag, *but he's a real dumbo in the kitchen.*

Even after she had pushed her unsavoury snack to the very bottom of her rucksack, the smell of lard lingered in her nostrils. It was a weird, faintly unpleasant sort of odour, which was strongly reminiscent of something else …

Haltwhistle's breath!

Dawn gaped as three static images fanned out in her mind like a hand of playing cards. The first was a block of lard; the second – a ladder; and the final one was Haltwhistle's tongue.

Earlier that day, when they had been trespassing on Charles Noble's property, Dawn had witnessed Haltwhistle doing something rather strange, and afterwards, his breath had whiffed of the very same substance which Felix had mistakenly used as a sandwich filling. At the time, it had occurred to her that licking the rung of a ladder was not a normal thing to do, even for a dog; but as Haltwhistle was rather inclined to do stupid things, she had not given it a great deal of thought.

Dawn looked at the facts. A seasoned cook such as herself knew a fair bit about lard. It was soft and greasy. It also tended to become transparent once it was rubbed on to something, leaving a gleam but nothing more. What if someone had deliberately smeared lard on to one of the rungs of the ladder? Whoever it was must have known that Miles would slip and lose his balance as soon as he put his weight on the rung and, very probably, plummet to the ground.

Charles Noble had been inordinately keen to get rid of the ladder after the 'accident'. His handyman, Reg, had considered its destruction to be a shameful waste. Had Charles been prompted to reduce the ladder to sticks and sawdust because he could not bear to be reminded of his window cleaner's nasty fall? Or was he just trying to cover his tracks?

A roving light on the upper floor of the manor house put all thoughts of Charles and the ladder out of Dawn's mind. Keeping low to the ground, she moved along the fence, pressing her shoulder against it every few yards to test for any areas of weakness.

After a couple of minutes, she found an unstable fence post and some sagging strands of wire which she was able to prise apart wide enough to wriggle through. She crouched very still for a moment, her heart thumping, and watched the light swing back and forth at a window underneath the eaves. Then she made a dash for the porch. As she did so, Dawn almost tripped over a fallen sign which said 'DANGER' and 'KEEP OUT'.

The house must once have been a splendid place to live. Its entrance was framed by four massive columns which were cold and smooth to the touch. Dawn slipped between them, trying to avoid the lumps of rubble which littered the floor of the porch. Now that she was no longer out in the open, and the moon was hidden from view, Dawn found it much more difficult to see.

The darkness became a deeper, treacly black as she twisted a doorknob the size of her father's fist, and stepped into the hallway.

From the outside the house had seemed frightening, but now that she was on the inside, Dawn found it even spookier. As she groped her way along a wall, she could feel her hair standing on end.

A series of muffled thumps coming from the floor above made her hold her breath. She lifted her chin and stared blindly in the direction of the upper level. Who was up there? And what were they doing, creeping about in a condemned house after dark? Three nights ago, she had spied someone on the hillside with a torch. Could that person be the very same one whose footfalls she could now hear through the ceiling?

Dawn's heart quickened as a thought occurred to her. Was this where Angela Bradshaw was being held prisoner? The idea seemed to make sense. No rational, law-abiding person would dare to set foot in a derelict building which was in danger of falling down. It would be the perfect place for a cunning kidnapper to keep his victim under lock and key.

Dawn stubbed her toe against something hard and wooden. She decided to risk turning on her torch and discovered that she had found the bottom step of a flight of stairs.

Climbing them did not prove to be a problem. The

steps were uncarpeted but Dawn was naturally stealthy, and her trainers had soft soles. When she arrived at the top of the staircase, she switched off her torch and listened. A rumbling droning noise reached her ears. It sounded as if someone were speaking behind a closed door. Immediately, Dawn realised the significance of this. *There's more than one person*, she told herself as she edged along the gloomy corridor towards the voice.

Dawn knew exactly where to stop. Torchlight seeped through the cracks in the door, giving it the appearance of a rectangle outlined in gold. As gently as she could, she turned the doorknob and gave a little push. Then she prepared to take a peek through the gap she had just created.

Feeling breathless with excitement, Dawn slowly reached into her pocket and withdrew her miniature camera. If her suspicions were correct, and Murdo Meek was in the room, she would be the first person ever to capture his likeness on film.

Initially, all she could see was the bright yellow glare of a torch. There was a man's face behind it but his features were shadowy and unrecognisable. Was it Charles Noble? She couldn't tell. The man altered his position and lowered his hand so that the torch's beam fell on bare floorboards. In that instant, Dawn saw his face clearly enough to be sure of his identity.

She pressed the camera to her eye, and clicked. So, it

was Seth. Seth Lightfoot. Hadn't he been the one who'd insisted that she and Felix should stay away from Palethorpe Manor? It appeared that his warning had not been prompted by any concern for their safety, but rather to keep them from stumbling upon whatever it was he was up to. Dawn felt a twinge of disappointment. Earlier that day, he had seemed so friendly and had even given her one of his precious sculptures. She had wanted to believe that Seth had chanced upon the piece of paper from Bob's file as he went about his litter-collecting duties. Now she was not so sure. With a shiver, she realised that she had started to warm to a man who could very well turn out to be Murdo Meek.

Seth began to mumble something. Unfortunately for Dawn, he had turned his back on her so she did not manage to catch a single word of what he said. She gripped her camera tightly, poised to take a picture of the other person in the room just as soon as she caught sight of them. Dawn's eyes darted into every corner. Where was Angela Bradshaw? What kind of shape would the poor woman be in, having been held captive for one whole month? Dawn began to feel frustrated. As far as she could see (and it wasn't easy, given the limited supply of light) there was no one in the room apart from Seth. But how could that be?

Seth turned suddenly, and raised his voice. His words rooted Dawn to the spot.

'I know you're there,' he said. 'Show yourself.'

Dawn figured that she had two choices. She could leg it down the stairs and hope that Seth was a useless runner, or she could keep to her cover story and try her hardest to bluff her way out of trouble. Deciding that the second option was marginally better than the first, she tucked her miniature camera into her pocket and, with some trepidation, pushed open the door.

'Aha!' said Seth with vigour. He shone the torch directly in Dawn's face and she squeezed her eyes shut instinctively.

'Would you mind not doing that, please?' she said, sounding mildly irritated. In actual fact, she was feeling jittery and scared, but was determined not to show it.

'Oh!' Seth breathed out the word in a sigh of disappointment. The inside of Dawn's eyelids darkened as he aimed the torch beam somewhere else. 'For a moment, there, I thought … Hey, aren't you the gardener's kid? Kitty, isn't it? What you doing here, huh?'

Dawn squinted at him, and nodded. 'Yes, I'm Kitty Wilson – and I'm looking,' she said solemnly, 'for barn owls.'

'Where's your mum?' said Seth, frowning, in what Dawn considered to be a most sinister manner.

'She isn't with me,' Dawn replied casually. 'My mum doesn't feel the same way about owls as I do. I saw one the other night, flying about on the hill, and I thought it might have made a nest in this old house. Barn owls like raising their chicks in ruined buildings.'

'Bit of an expert on birds, are you?' said Seth.

Dawn thought that he sounded suspicious. She decided to back up her story. Unfastening the popper on her purse, she drew out her Young Ornithologists' membership card and handed it to Seth. 'I'm not really an expert,' she explained, 'not yet, anyway … but I have read quite a lot about them.'

'Like what?' said Seth. If Dawn hadn't known better, she might have thought that he was genuinely interested.

'Oh … *I Spy Birds*,' said Dawn, which she knew existed because she had once got it out of the library, 'and … er … *Birds in Your Back Garden* and … *Wings and Things*,' she said, making up the other two titles on the spur of the moment.

'Really?' said Seth. 'That's impressive.' He seemed convinced that she was telling the truth. 'Past your bedtime, though, isn't it, Kitty? Does your mum know where you are?'

'Sure,' said Dawn, trying not to panic. 'She's cool about it. I can go to bed when I like. My mum doesn't believe in too many rules and regulations. She thinks that kids should be allowed their freedom.' Dawn tried very hard not to wince after she had uttered these words. Would Seth be gullible enough to believe her?

'That's funny,' said Seth, tapping the end of the torch against his jaw. 'I had quite a chinwag with your mum this afternoon. She didn't seem like that type to me. I can't think that she'd approve of you wandering around at night on your own.'

'Oh … um …' Dawn floundered. *He knows it's all a pack of lies*, she told herself. *He's rumbled me. I'm in hot water now.*

'She's not on her own,' said a voice from the doorway. 'She's with me.' This last sentence was followed by a whine and one short yelp. 'And him.'

'I see,' said Seth.

Dawn looked over her shoulder. She would never have imagined that she could actually feel *pleased* to see Felix. In fact, she was more than pleased: she was overjoyed. Haltwhistle's tail thumped against the doorframe, and Dawn had to stop herself from throwing her arms around the dog's neck.

'This is my brother, Wayne,' she said, giving Felix a grateful smile.

'And this is Fred,' said Felix, winning another smile from Dawn for remembering to use Haltwhistle's alias. 'We often accompany my sister on her birding expeditions. I'm a lepidopterist, myself. Butterflies, you know.'

'And moths,' said Seth. He seemed a little taken aback.

'Indeed,' said Felix rather pompously.

'Well, you won't find any fluttery bugs up here …

254

nor any owls, neither. Leastways, I can't remember seeing any nests.' Seth narrowed his eyes. 'So you kids had better shove off. I think I mentioned to you before that this place isn't for larking about in.'

Dawn decided that the best course of action would be to follow his advice – or at least to appear to. She began to sidle towards the door.

'OK,' she said, lightly, 'we're going. I must've been mistaken about that owl.'

'Hang on a moment, sis,' said Felix, as Dawn hinted heavily that it was time to go by tugging on his sleeve and looking plaintively at him. 'Excuse me, sir,' he said, turning to Seth. 'Would you mind if I asked you a question?'

'I s'pose not,' said Seth, folding his arms, 'as long as you make it quick.'

'What are you doing here?' asked Felix. 'It seems a bit strange to me that you should bang on about how this place could fall apart at any moment and yet … well, here you are. It strikes me as *odd*.'

Dawn pinched his arm gently. 'Come on,' she whispered in his ear. 'Don't blow it.'

'Nosey, aren't you?' said Seth, who was beginning to get a mite fractious. 'It just so happens that it isn't any of your business.'

'I wonder if the *police* would be interested to know that you'd been trespassing on private property …'

Felix shot him a haughty look.

'Your brother's a regular pain in the backside, isn't he?' Seth smiled wearily at Dawn (who was desperate to agree but didn't think she should). 'All right, I'll tell you, but you must promise to keep it under your hat. If it gets out, there'll be coach parties and all sorts up here – and that'll be sure to drive her away, as sure as eggs is eggs.'

'Drive who away?' said Felix.

'The ghostie, of course,' said Seth. He tucked his torch underneath his arm, and wiggled his fingers. 'I was trying to get her to reveal herself when your sister showed up – and scared her off, no doubt.'

'Ghost?' said Dawn, edging closer to Felix.

'Load of baloney,' said Felix, putting his arm around her. 'There's no such thing as ghosts.' He glared angrily at Seth. 'You should be ashamed of yourself, frightening my little sister like that.'

'Well, you did ask!' objected Seth. 'And they're real enough, all right … I saw one large as life, just the other week. A lady ghost with long white hair and a face so sad it fair broke my heart to look at it. Standing at one of these windows, she was. I often take a walk up here on a nice summer's evening. Always had a feeling this place might be haunted – and now I know it is.'

'Rubbish,' said Felix hotly. 'That's absolute nonsense. Right, Kitty. We're leaving.'

As Dawn followed behind Felix, who had taken

possession of her torch and was already halfway down the stairs, she kept her fingers entwined in Haltwhistle's collar. Dawn told herself that this was a sensible thing to do because dogs were bound to be better than humans at finding their way in the dark. The fact that she was nervous about bumping into a ghost, and the reassuring way in which Haltwhistle's warm, hairy body padded along beside her, of course, had nothing whatsoever to do with it.

'What I don't understand,' said Dawn, as she scurried down the moonlit hillside, 'is how you managed to follow me. I didn't catch a glimpse of either of you; not once!'

'Is that so?' said Felix, striding ahead of her at a brisk pace.

'Yes,' said Dawn, breaking into a run in order to catch up with him. She tapped him on the shoulder. 'Hey, would you mind not walking so fast? Socrates told me that a spy should always proceed with caution, especially when she's travelling on foot in the dark.'

'You've got a perfectly good torch. Seems silly not to use it. Then you might manage to go a tiny bit quicker than snail's pace.'

'I *told* you,' said Dawn tiredly, 'we'll be seen from miles away if we use my torch out in the open. Can't you just slow down a bit?'

'Oh, all *right*.' Felix gave Haltwhistle's lead a yank.

'Whoa, there, boy. Old slowcoach can't keep up.'

Dawn opened her mouth to protest, then closed it again. Embarrassingly, her lip began to tremble. She pulled her hood up over her head, balled her fists and shoved them deep into her pockets.

If she had been pressed to evaluate her performance that evening, Dawn would have given herself three-and-a-half out of ten. Her blunders hadn't been disastrous, but there *had* been rather too many of them. She'd picked the wrong place to send a radio message to P.S.S.T., revealed herself to Seth unnecessarily, not been able to lie convincingly enough, and – worst of all – she had been trailed by Felix and his highly conspicuous dog, and hadn't even noticed! She was supposed to have a natural affinity for spying. How could her skills have deserted her quite so spectacularly?

Felix nudged her elbow. 'What's up with you, sulky-chops?' He brushed his hand against Dawn's hood so that it fell back on to her shoulders. 'Not still worried about that spook that Seth invented, are you?'

'No,' said Dawn miserably.

'OK ... hmm ... I know! You're annoyed about us tagging along on your little night-time jaunt,' said Felix. 'Is that it?'

Dawn shook her head. She couldn't quite bring herself to tell him how relieved she'd been when he and Haltwhistle had turned up.

258

'You must have trailed me for at least a mile – and I didn't have a clue,' admitted Dawn in a small voice.

'Oh, you're fretting about *that*,' said Felix, half-laughing. He gave her shoulder a playful shove. 'Well, you needn't, you great ninny. The reason you didn't see us following you ... is because we *weren't*.'

'What?' said Dawn. She was stunned, not to mention confused.

'You're wondering how I knew where you were headed?' said Felix, sounding rather pleased with himself. 'Remember yesterday afternoon, when you *demanded* to be left in peace while you wrote your letter to P.S.S.T ...'

'I might have asked you *politely* to leave the room for a bit,' said Dawn, bristling at his suggestion that she was a bossy sort of person. 'You said you were going to play cricket in the garden with Haltwhistle.'

'And I did, *eventually*,' said Felix, 'but only after I'd had a jolly good eavesdrop. I heard you telling Trudy about your plan to have a snoop around Palethorpe Manor, and we thought we'd invite ourselves along, didn't we, boy?' Felix reached down and patted his dog. 'We came through that little copse of birch trees, where you collided with Haltwhistle the other day.'

Dawn felt impelled to correct him. 'It was *your dog* who bumped into *me*,' she said.

'So, you see ... you're not such a hopeless spy, after all,' said Felix, and his teeth glinted as he grinned at her.

Dawn was not amused.

'Actually,' he said, patting a stile to encourage Haltwhistle to climb on to it, 'I think you're doing a fair job ... for a beginner. You're especially good at making up stories. Your fib about the barn owl was inspired. I almost believed you for a second myself.'

'Oh ... er ... thanks,' said Dawn. She wasn't used to receiving compliments from Felix. 'It's important to have a reason ready to explain why you're hanging around ... in case anyone ever challenges you. Socrates taught me that.'

'Your reason was heaps better than the one that litter collector came up with. What a load of old bunkum,' said Felix, clambering over the stile. 'He must have thought we were stupid. As if we'd believe some ridiculous story about a ghost! I wonder what he was *really* up to.'

'You didn't believe him, then?' asked Dawn.

'Not likely.'

Dawn stepped on to the stile and looked over her shoulder at the moon, which was the colour of curdled milk, and the smear of black beneath it that was Palethorpe Manor. It did not seem nearly so forbidding from a distance.

'What about you?' said Felix. ' You reckon his story was genuine?'

Dawn shrugged her shoulders, and frowned. 'I don't know,' she said.

Chapter Seventeen
The Stake-out

The alarm that sounded in Dawn's ears the next morning was an unfamiliar one. Instead of the piercing tinkle of bells, she heard a harsh rattling noise. Bizarrely, it did not seem to be coming from the table next to her bed, where her clock usually resided, but from somewhere near the ceiling in the corner of the room.

Dawn opened her sleepy eyes and was most surprised to see a magpie with lustrous black and white plumage strutting up and down on top of her wardrobe. He was a handsome creature with a long, green-glossed tail and a metallic-blue gleam to his wings, and Dawn would have been thrilled to wake up to such a vision if he hadn't been making such a terrible racket.

Once she had untangled her legs from the polyester bed sheet, Dawn stumbled over to the window and opened it as wide as it would go.

'Would you mind leaving, please,' she said, covering

one of her ears in an attempt to block out the incessant chack-ack-ack noise that the bird was making. 'Mr Magpie!' she said, patting the window frame to remind him how he'd got into her room. 'The sky is just through here.'

Twitching on the floor, at the foot of her bed, Dawn caught sight of a fluffy black tail. She moved closer to it, and saw Peebles sitting very still with his eyes trained on the agitated bird.

So that's why the poor thing is so upset, thought Dawn.

'Get lost, you!' she said to Peebles, scooping up the cat and depositing him outside her door, from where he could be heard miaowing aggrievedly.

Once Peebles had been evicted, the bird became much calmer. He stopped making such a dreadful din, gripped the edge of the wardrobe with his talons and swooped down on to the bed. Exasperated at first, Dawn became concerned when she saw a slight swelling on one of the magpie's legs. She sat down beside the bird to get a better look, and was astounded when he jumped into her lap.

It wasn't a swelling at all; it was a tiny canister with a piece of rolled-up paper inside. Dawn had heard of messages conveyed by pigeons but she had never come across a carrier *magpie* before. Written on the small, square sheet was a coded message from P.S.S.T. She grabbed a pencil and prepared to decipher it.

Dawn had barely even started when the door was thrust open suddenly.

'Is everything all right in here?' said Trudy. 'I heard the most appalling noise …'

'No!' yelled Dawn, waving her hands frantically. 'Don't let Peebles in!'

The cat's claws missed the magpie's tail feathers by a fraction of an inch. In one bound, the bird reached the windowsill, and in another, he took to the air.

'Didn't you get any parsnip-flavoured crisps?' said Felix, emptying a string shopping bag with a disappointed look on his face.

'No, I most certainly did not,' said Trudy, heaving another bag on to the worktop. She began to unpack it at a swift rate. 'The village shop doesn't stock weird flavours.'

'You got ready salted!' said Felix, staring at a packet in his hands. He looked absolutely crushed. 'And …' He gasped in horror. 'It's past its sell-by date!'

'Only by a few days,' said Trudy briskly. 'It was dirt-cheap, which is good because I didn't have much to spend. Red only supplied me with enough cash to feed Dawn and myself. Stop making such a fuss, and put the kettle on, would you? I need caffeine.'

Dawn slipped into the kitchen without either of them noticing, and helped herself to a bowl of newly purchased Crunchy Bitz. She had so many things on her mind that she spooned the cereal into her mouth without even tasting it (which was just as well).

P.S.S.T.'s little note had been tricky to translate. The code they had chosen to use was called 'Tornado' which turned letters back to front and upside down. Dawn had puzzled over it for half an hour but the message turned out to be worth the effort. As she had requested in her letter to P.S.S.T. two days before, P.U.F.F. had dug a little deeper into the histories of the main suspects, and they had discovered something interesting about Charles Noble. He had swum the English Channel at the age of fourteen.

Which means he's a superb swimmer, thought Dawn as she gulped down the last little heap of Crunchy Bitz. *Which* means *that if anyone could have got himself to the riverbank after falling into the Thames in the middle of winter*, he could!

'I'll finish unpacking the shopping, if you like,' said Dawn sweetly, putting her bowl in the sink. She took a jar of peanut butter out of Trudy's hand and placed it on a shelf. 'Why don't you sit down and have some breakfast?'

'Thank you, Dawn,' said Trudy, making a beeline for the mug stand. She poured herself a black coffee and sighed with contentment as she took her first sip. 'So, tell me, have you managed to unscramble that message yet?'

'Yes.'

'Good.' Trudy looked at her watch, gasped, and took an enormous swig of coffee. Snatching up an apple she said, 'Leave the rest of that stuff, Dawn. Felix can do it. We need to be at the Bingham house in fifteen minutes – and put your wellies on. From what Bill Bingham said on the phone, we're going to be knee-deep in pond slime for most of the morning.'

Felix didn't seem too thrilled to be left in charge of kitchen duties. 'S'pose I'll have to do the washing up as well,' he grumbled. He buttered a piece of toast and crunched it crossly. 'So, Kitty Tight-lips,' he said, addressing Dawn, 'how about telling us what was in that message? We're dying to know, aren't we, Trudes?'

Trudy glared at him. 'Yes,' she said. 'I'll admit I'm curious, but I'm more concerned with getting to the Binghams' on time. We've got to finish that job by mid-day because then we're due at the Masons' in Chickweed Close.' She beckoned to Dawn impatiently. 'Get your skates on, miss.'

'I'm afraid,' said Dawn, cringing behind a large bag of long-grained rice, 'I shan't be able to come with you today.'

'WHAT?' Trudy's face changed colour quicker than a traffic light. 'WHY NOT?'

'I need to … um … mount a surveillance operation on my chief suspect,' said Dawn, using some of the lingo she'd learned in her training sessions with Socrates. She thought it made her sound as if she knew what she was doing.

Trudy's eyes widened in astonishment. '*You've got a chief suspect?*' she said.

'Wow!' said Felix. 'Who is it? The weasel-faced chap who told us that fib about seeing a ghost?'

Dawn shook her head. 'It's Charles Noble. He lives in The Old Oast House at the top end of the Green.'

'Hallelujah!' said Trudy, who seemed quite overcome. She pressed her hands against her face (nearly poking herself in the eye with the apple) and beamed so widely that Dawn was concerned her face might split. 'Oh, that's *brilliant*,' said Trudy. 'That's marvellous.'

'Don't get too excited,' said Dawn. 'Charles is only my *chief* suspect. I've got another three that I haven't eliminated yet. I don't know that Charles is Meek, for *sure*.'

'It'll turn out to be him, you'll see,' said Trudy happily. Throwing down the apple, she picked up a frying pan and set it on the cooker. 'I'll make us all a slap-up breakfast to celebrate! Who's for some eggy bread and some hash browns?'

'What are you doing?' asked Dawn in astonishment. 'I thought you were due at the Binghams' house in a few minutes.'

'Well, I don't have to go now, do I?' said Trudy cheerfully. She poured some oil into the pan and

266

started to hum a tune.

'Why not?' said Dawn.

Playfully, Trudy patted Dawn on the head with a spatula. 'Because, you *clever* little spy, you've found your man … which means you won't need to snoop around people's houses any more … and I won't have to toil away in their stupid gardens.' She laughed at Dawn's anxious expression. 'Don't look so worried! I'll ring the Binghams and the Masons in a minute and tell them I've had to cancel.'

Dawn wrinkled her forehead. 'That doesn't sound like a very good idea,' she said. 'It's bound to make them annoyed if you pull out at the last minute … not to mention suspicious. And what about all the other appointments you've got? It'll look awfully fishy if you cancel those as well. I think it would be best if you carried on as normal.'

Trudy shrieked, and looked as if she were about to burst into tears. 'You're heartless … absolutely heartless!' she said, throwing down the spatula and glowering at Dawn. 'Give me one good reason why I should do what *you* say!'

'I'll supply you with three,' said Felix swiftly. 'Dawn's argument makes perfect sense; Dawn's in charge of the mission; and I don't think either of us fancy your idea of a slap-up breakfast. What on earth is "eggy bread"? It sounds gross.'

'Two against one, then, is it?' said Trudy bitterly. 'I see. Well, I'd better be off to the Binghams', then, hadn't I? What a fun-filled day I'll be having.' She stuck her sizeable nose in the air and stalked out of the kitchen.

'Oh dear,' said Dawn. 'She seemed quite upset.'

Felix shrugged, and dipped a knife into a pot of marmalade.

'Thanks for sticking up for me,' said Dawn. 'That was nice of you.'

''S all right,' said Felix. He spread marmalade lavishly on a slice of toast and took a bite. 'So,' he said, 'what time are we starting this stake-out?'

'We?' said Dawn. 'Oh, no, no, no. *You* can't come. It's strictly a one-woman job.'

'Rotten old spoilsport,' mumbled Felix. 'I would have thought you'd be glad of our help.' He tossed a piece of toast at Haltwhistle, who lunged at it and missed.

'Actually,' said Dawn slyly, 'there *is* something I was going to ask you to do for me ... if it's not too much trouble.'

Instantly, Felix snapped out of his bad mood. 'Is it to do with the mission?'

'Yes,' said Dawn.

'Is it ever so difficult and ... and fraught with danger?'

'Of course!' Dawn bent close to his ear. 'Now, listen very carefully ...'

***

Pretending to read a comic called *Nutty* which she had picked up for ten pence at a second-hand book fair in the village hall, Dawn watched The Old Oast House. She had chosen to sit on a bench beside an enormous lime tree, and reckoned that she could not have found a more perfect spot from which to observe Charles Noble's movements. The bench was just the right distance from Charles's front gate: close enough to catch sight of him should he show his face at a window but not so near that he might suspect he was being spied upon. The lime tree was a bonus. It threw a shadow over the bench and rendered Dawn almost invisible.

For the first two hours, Dawn hardly stirred. She blinked every now and then, and occasionally turned a page of her comic – but that was all. Her eyes were trained on The Old Oast House and her mind was focused on the task in hand. Halfway through the third hour, however, she began to experience little lapses in concentration and by the fourth she found herself fighting the urge to read about the adventures of Bananaman (the superhero who featured in a cartoon strip on *Nutty*'s front page). When Dawn realised what was happening to her, she was stunned. For perhaps the first time in her life, she was actually on the verge of being *bored*.

'Get a shift on, Charles,' murmured Dawn, willing

him to emerge from his front door. One of her toes began to wriggle impatiently. 'Oh, how I wish that something would happen!'

Two minutes later she cursed herself for opening her big mouth. In desperation, Dawn raised her comic a couple of inches and tried to hide behind it; but despite her best efforts to escape detection, she was spotted.

A nose shoved itself underneath her copy of *Nutty*. A big black wet nose attached to a hairy muzzle.

'Go away, Fred,' hissed Dawn anxiously. As usual, the dog did the exact opposite of what he'd been told to do: jumped up on to the bench and gave her ear a clumsy lick.

'Hi, Kitty!'

Dawn grimaced at the sight of Felix running towards her. She folded the comic in two and dropped it into her lap.

'Thought you'd be lurking around here somewhere. Bet you're surprised to see us so soon,' said Felix, plonking himself down on the bench. 'Mission accomplished!' he declared, and dropped a large stone into her hand.

'This isn't –' began Dawn.

'I know!' Felix laughed and nudged her in the ribs. 'That's my little idea of a joke.' He delved into a pocket of his shorts. 'Here's your precious thingumajig,' he said, producing Dawn's shell phone. 'We stumbled across it on the hillside. Well, Fred's the one who found it, really. It had rolled down a rabbit hole.'

'Thanks,' said Dawn, stuffing the phone into her rucksack.

'You don't seem very pleased!' Felix sounded rather put out. 'Aren't you going to give Fred a pat?'

'If I must,' said Dawn. She glanced at The Old Oast House to make sure that Charles had not made an appearance; then touched Haltwhistle lightly between his ears. 'Clever dog,' she said.

In truth, she was tremendously relieved that the phone was in her possession again. Earlier that morning, when she'd discovered that it was missing, Dawn had felt angst-ridden. Losing a gadget counted as a very grave error. If a villager had found it – and if Murdo Meek had got to hear of its existence, Operation Question Mark might have had to be abandoned. Dawn had asked Felix to look for it to keep him occupied so that he and his boneheaded dog would not be able to mess up the surveillance operation. Unfortunately, they had found the phone much quicker than she had expected. Dawn guessed that she must have dropped it when she got her foot stuck in a rabbit hole the night before.

'I'm really grateful to you both,' said Dawn in a slightly strained voice, 'but I'm in the middle of something important ...'

Felix did not seem to take the hint. 'I'm parched,' he said. 'Got anything to drink?'

'I might have a drop of water,' said Dawn, with a sigh. 'If I give it to you, will you promise to go away?'

Felix ignored her offer. He tilted his head as if he were trying to hear a faraway sound. Dawn listened, too – and heard the tinkling warble of an ice-cream van. It grew louder and louder.

'How about treating me and Fred to a couple of ice lollies … as a reward for finding your dumb old phone?' said Felix.

'All right,' said Dawn, wearily. She was prepared to agree to anything if only Felix would make himself scarce. Fumbling in her purse, she drew out a five-pound note.

'Thanks,' said Felix, snatching it out of her hand. He started to walk towards the ice-cream van, which had parked a little way down the street. Haltwhistle leaped off the bench and bounded after him. 'Oh,' said Felix. He stopped, and looked over his shoulder at Dawn. 'Suppose you'd like one, too?'

Why do I bother? thought Dawn resentfully. *I try my utmost not to draw attention to myself and then Felix turns up and ruins everything.* She gave a frustrated moan.

'Was that a "yes"?' yelled Felix. 'What sort do you want?'

Dawn decided that there was no longer any point in attempting to be discreet. 'A Blackcurrant Tongue-tingler, please,' she answered.

Felix gave her the thumbs-up, and sauntered over to the white-and-yellow van with pictures of ice creams and brightly coloured lollies pasted around its serving hatch. She watched as Felix pressed his finger against three of the pictures and spoke to the ice-cream man who was wearing a white cap and apron. The man rubbed his chin thoughtfully and said something back. Felix nodded; the man handed over three lollies and took the money that he was offered. He seemed a pleasant type of person with a shock of red hair and an engaging smile.

'It can't be!' said Dawn, and she scrambled to find the pair of binoculars in her rucksack. She took less than thirty seconds to press them to her eyes and adjust the focus, but in that short space of time the ice-cream man had driven off.

Sucking a green ice-lolly in the shape of a racing car, Felix returned to the bench beside the lime tree. He made his dog sit (on the seventh attempt) and ripped off the wrapper of a rabbit-shaped lolly with hundreds and thousands stuck to it. Haltwhistle took the whole lolly in his mouth and crunched it as if it were a dog biscuit, his tail sweeping the ground.

'He'd run out of Blackcurrant Tongue-tinglers,' said Felix, handing Dawn an unfamiliar lolly, 'but the chap said that this one is just as mouth-watering. It's called a Chilblain.'

Dawn undid the wrapper and was very disappointed to find a plain red ice-lolly underneath. She gave it a half-hearted lick. It tasted vaguely of rhubarb.

'Tell me about the ice-cream man,' said Dawn. 'Did you get a good look at him? Could you have met him before, do you think?'

Felix shrugged, and made an unattractive slurping noise. 'I don't know,' he said, removing his lolly from his mouth and smacking his lips, which had turned faintly green. 'He was just an ordinary bloke.'

'I thought … he looked … a bit like Nathan,' said Dawn hesitantly.

'No,' said Felix, but he didn't sound completely sure.

'So, he didn't give you a message … ' Dawn's mouth dropped open. All thoughts of finishing her sentence went out of her head when she caught sight of Charles Noble walking down his driveway.

'What's the matter?' asked Felix. He followed Dawn's gaze. 'Oh. Is that your chief suspect? Are we going to follow him now?'

'Yes,' said Dawn, tucking her belongings into her rucksack. 'I'd rather trail him on my own, but if you insist on coming too – you'll have to promise to keep a low profile and do exactly as I say.'

'Of course!' said Felix. 'No problem.'

Chapter Eighteen

At The One-eyed Stoat

They pursued Charles at a safe distance, stopping whenever he knelt to tie a shoelace or paused to look in a shop window. Dawn did not take her eyes off him for a moment.

Could he be on his way to meet someone? she wondered. In her opinion, Charles was dressed quite smartly for a stroll about the village. His trousers seemed to have been freshly ironed and his shoes fairly gleamed. Every so often he glanced at his watch and lengthened his stride as if he were anxious not to be late for an appointment.

'Want to hear a joke?' said Felix cheerfully. He held his lolly stick lengthways and read the words that had been etched on to it: '"Why did the ball of wool go on holiday?"'

'Don't know,' said Dawn. She licked her Chilblain, and watched Charles closely as he crossed a road.

'"To unwind!"' said Felix.

Dawn groaned.

'I agree,' said Felix, tossing the stick into the nearest litter bin. 'Not exactly side-splitting, is it.'

The joke had nothing whatever to do with Dawn's anguished utterance. 'He's heading for the pub,' she said despondently, 'and if The One-eyed Stoat is anything like our local in Hackney, children won't be allowed inside.'

'We'll have to creep in on all fours and hide under a table,' said Felix, 'when we're sure that nobody's looking.'

Dawn wasn't at all confident that his idea would work. If she concentrated extremely hard, it might be possible for *her* to sidle into the pub unseen, but if Felix and Haltwhistle accompanied her, she was certain that they would all be spotted in five seconds flat. Persuading Felix to wait outside while she ventured in alone was *not* going to be easy, though.

Charles had already passed through the pub's doorway by the time Dawn and her hangers-on made it to the other side of the road. Not allowing herself to panic, Dawn ambled along at the same pace until she reached The One-eyed Stoat. It was a quaint little place with a red front door, mullioned windows and Virginia creeper wrapped around its brickwork like a leafy shawl.

'What do we do now?' whispered Felix as they stopped underneath a hanging basket.

Dawn swallowed. 'Don't get all huffy – but I've come to the decision that it might be best if I ...' She lost her thread completely as her eyes settled on an easel standing by the door. Written upon it in chalk were the words: GLORIOUS GARDEN ROUND THE BACK – FAMILIES WELCOME. 'Problem solved!' she said gleefully, grabbing Felix by the arm. 'With any luck Charles will choose to take his pint outside. I can't believe he'd want to sit in a dingy corner of the pub on such a beautiful day! Come on!'

They unlatched a gate at the side of the building. A paved path led into a small, grassy garden which contained several picnic tables, and wooden tubs crowned with flowers. There was no sign of Charles, but at least a dozen people were sitting at the tables, lazily sipping their drinks or munching on doorstep sandwiches.

Dawn and Felix bagged a table close to the back door of the pub through which they could see bodies milling in a darkened room. Dawn noticed that their table's previous occupants had left behind their unfinished drinks and a half-eaten ploughman's lunch. She cupped her hand around a glass with orange liquid at the bottom and pretended it was her own. Felix did likewise, and Haltwhistle whined until he was slipped a crust of bread.

'*Uh*,' said Felix with relief, 'it's nice to sit down for a bit. Fred and I must've walked for miles this morning.

We searched every inch of that hillside, not to mention Palethorpe Manor ...'

'What?' said Dawn, tearing her eyes away from the pub's gloomy interior. 'You went back to Palethorpe? Did you find anything?'

'No,' hissed Felix impatiently. 'I already told you that we found your phone down a rabbit hole.'

'I know that!' Dawn leaned closer to him. 'I was wondering if you'd come across anything unusual that might lead you to believe that someone had been living there.'

'Are you deranged, or what?' said Felix, and he snorted. 'Of course I didn't. There was just loads of dust and cobwebs and big lumps of rubble ... and before you ask – I didn't see any spook, either.'

'Ah ... Seth's ghost,' said Dawn. She sucked her Chilblain thoughtfully. Little rivulets of red juice streaked past her knuckles as the lolly started to melt. 'I've been thinking about her.'

'Why waste your time doing that?' scoffed Felix.

'Because I don't doubt that she was real.'

'Have you lost your marbles?' he said rudely. 'Ghosts don't exist – and anyone who says they do is talking utter rot.'

Dawn sighed. 'I didn't mean that I thought she was a real *ghost*.' She looked Felix straight in the eye. 'I'm certain that she was real ... as in ... *human*.'

He turned ashen as the penny dropped. 'Granny! You

think that Seth saw Granny and mistook her for a ghost …'

'That's right,' said Dawn. 'Her kidnapper must have kept her imprisoned in the manor for a while before he decided to … um …'

'… move her somewhere else,' finished Felix. He stared at the slice of lemon at the bottom of his glass, and his lower lip began to wobble.

'Here,' said Dawn, pushing her lolly into his hand. 'You can finish my Chilblain if you like. I'm going to sneak into the pub to see if I can find Charles.' She rose to her feet, but before she turned to go, she patted Felix on the shoulder. 'Try not to think the worst,' she murmured, hoping against hope that, wherever she was, Angela Bradshaw was still alive.

Inside The One-eyed Stoat it was hot and murky, and crowded with people. Dawn squeezed past a group of guffawing men with large bellies, a woman in dungarees who was sipping a lurid cocktail and two old ladies playing a rather aggressive game of beggar-my-neighbour. Planning to give the excuse that she was looking for the loo should anyone ask her what she was doing, Dawn hunted everywhere for Charles. She saw three other men who were listed on the five of diamonds before she discovered Charles, at last, propping up the bar, with a wine glass in his hand. He was holding a conversation with a fellow bell-ringer. It was noisy in the pub but

Dawn thought she heard them mention somebody called 'Little Bob'. Could the Bob they were discussing be Bob Chalk, the P.S.S.T. secret agent? She crept closer.

'Kitty!' Dawn felt someone prod her in between her shoulder blades.

She turned round. 'Hello, big brother,' said Dawn wearily. Felix had a maddening habit of showing up at the worst possible moment. 'What are you doing in here?' she whispered.

Felix grinned, and jigged up and down, brandishing a lolly stick. 'I've come to show you this!'

'I'm really not interested in hearing another joke right now,' said Dawn.

Felix remained unfazed. 'At first I thought there'd been a mistake,' he said, breathless with excitement, 'and it had been printed in a foreign language or something – but then I realised it was in some kind of code!'

'What?' said Dawn. In the midst of a room of chattering people, she wasn't quite sure that she had heard him correctly. 'Code, did you say? Can I have a look?'

There wasn't enough natural light in the pub to read the words properly so Dawn was forced to return to the garden, where she found Haltwhistle guiltily wagging his tail as he bolted down the rest of the ploughman's lunch which, presumably, he had stolen from the plate. Frustrated at having to miss Charles's conversation with his bell-ringing friend, Dawn was nevertheless intrigued to discover what had been written on the lolly stick. She sat down at the picnic table and held the stick in her lap.

Unless it was a joke that had been atrociously mis-spelled, Dawn decided that Felix was right. To an untrained eye, the words printed at one end of the stick would have proved unfathomable, but Dawn was an agent of P.S.S.T. and – what was more – she was getting rather good at decoding messages. In less than two minutes she had managed to identify the particular code which had been used, and in another seven, without the aid of pen or paper, she had succeeded in working out what the message said.

The first word was URGENT, which explained why P.S.S.T. had elected to send the message with Nathan rather than wait to pass on the information over the radio waves at the scheduled hour. It was, now, no longer in doubt that the ice-cream man had been Nathan Slipper. Dawn realised that he must have been instructed to sell her the Chilblain, no matter what she asked for.

The message was a short one – but devastating nonetheless:

URGENT. S.H.H. CHIEF KNOWS ALL. ABORT MISSION AND RETURN TO BASE TOMORROW.

Felix was distraught when Dawn broke the news to him.

'They can't do *that*!' he said. 'I won't go back to London without my granny … I *won't*. Who does this high-handed S.H.H. big shot think he is? I'll jolly well knock his block off.'

'*Her* block,' said Dawn. 'She's called Philippa Killingback, and from what the others have said about her, she's *super*-scary. Somehow, she must have heard about Operation Question Mark. Red tried to keep it a secret from her. He was sure that she wouldn't let him go ahead with the mission so he didn't bother telling her about it.'

'The Chief of S.H.H. sounds like a silly old moo,' said Felix. 'Why would she object to Operation Question Mark? Doesn't she care what's happened to my granny?'

'Apparently,' said Dawn, 'Philippa thinks that P.S.S.T. is making a great big fuss over nothing. She won't believe that Murdo Meek can still be alive … and she'd never agree to someone as young as me being sent on a mission.'

'What a rotter,' said Felix. 'I know! Let's pretend we didn't see the message!'

Dawn shook her head. 'It wouldn't do any good. They'd only send another.'

'It's not *fair*,' protested Felix, and he stared vacantly into the middle distance. He looked so miserable that, for a fleeting moment, Dawn thought about giving him a hug – but before she could, she happened to glance at a nearby picnic table, and noticed something odd.

'That wasn't there before,' she said. 'Was it?'

'Huh?' said Felix blearily.

'The chalk mark on that table leg.' Dawn's heartrate doubled as she recalled Socrates lecturing her on the subject of dead letter boxes. 'I'm *sure* it wasn't there when we arrived. Don't you remember?'

Felix shrugged unhelpfully. 'Haven't got the foggiest.'

'Wait here,' said Dawn, slipping the lolly stick into her pocket and standing up. Her eyes roamed about the garden. She saw Diana Flinch sitting with a whey-faced girl, a basket of chips between them; a man folding a crisp packet into a neat triangle; an old couple bickering; and a group of youths talking animatedly with the vicar. As far as she could tell, not one of the people in the garden was looking in Dawn's direction. Furtively, she moved towards the empty table which had been marked with white chalk.

A few days ago, in the Codes and Devices room, Socrates had told her all about dead letter boxes (most commonly known as 'drops'). They were a means of communicating secretly. A spy would pop a message for another spy in a particular hiding place and would then make it known that he had done so by leaving a signal. This signal was – more often than not – a chalk mark somewhere close by.

Just as Dawn was about to pass behind the table she pretended to stumble and fell to her knees. This gave her the perfect opportunity to check if there was a message taped to the underside of the tabletop. There wasn't. Getting to her feet slowly, Dawn glanced around. She was looking for a crevice or some sort of container where a piece of folded paper could be squirrelled away. The tub of flowers next to the table caught her eye. She inspected it closely under the guise of smelling a cluster of geraniums and her heart flipped over when she found what she was looking for. Tucked between the wood and the metal band surrounding the tub was a small slip of paper. Dawn eased it out carefully and unfolded it. She had expected the message to be written in code and was pleasantly surprised to find that she was wrong. It read, simply:

Meet me by the duck pond.
Ten pm. Tonight. M. M.

Fearing that the spy for whom the message was intended could make an appearance at any minute, Dawn swiftly returned the piece of paper to its hiding place. Then she went back to the table where Felix was waiting for her with a bemused frown on his face.

'What were you doing?' he asked.

Dawn was so excited she could barely speak. 'It's him,' she said. 'Murdo Meek. He's definitely here, in this village – and he isn't working alone, either.'

'How do you know that?' said Felix in sullen tones. 'You're not making any sense.'

Dawn took a few deep breaths to calm herself down. 'Meek left a message for someone and I've just intercepted it,' she said. 'He's going to meet this other spy at the duck pond after dark –'

'Big wow,' said Felix, who seemed to be having an attack of the glums. 'In case you'd forgotten – Operation Question Mark has just been cancelled by Philippa Pain-in-the-neck ... or whatever her name is ...'

'Killingback,' said Dawn.

'And we've got to pack our bags and leave Cherry Bentley in the next twenty-four hours.' Felix gave Dawn a puzzled stare. 'Correct me if I'm wrong,' he said, 'but that *is* the meaning of "Abort mission and return to base tomorrow", isn't it?'

'Mmm,' said Dawn, thoughtfully, 'but when *exactly* are we meant to abort the mission? Right *now* – or tomorrow? It isn't very clear.' An idea suddenly popped into her head. 'Perhaps Red worded the message like that *on purpose* ... to give us a bit more time.'

'Brilliant!' said Felix, shrugging off his bad mood. He looked at Dawn with shining eyes. 'If we don't have to chuck in the mission until tomorrow, we've still got a few hours left to save my granny!'

'Oi! You kids!' A burly man in a tight-fitting shirt appeared at the back door of the pub, and wagged his finger at them. He had been serving behind the bar a few minutes ago, and Dawn had supposed him to be the landlord of The One-eyed Stoat. 'Get yer 'orrible dog out me garden. Go on ....'op it!' He gestured with his thumb towards the garden gate.

'Gosh,' said Felix, scowling at the man, 'how awfully rude you are.'

'Whatchoo say?' thundered the landlord. He began to lumber towards them.

'Time to go,' said Dawn, seizing Felix by the arm.

'I don't know why you're making such a fuss,' said Felix brazenly as the landlord drew closer. 'My dog has been perfectly well behaved – and he's *certainly* not horrible. By the way, I think you'll find that "horrible" begins with an "H"– not an "O".'

'Everybody's looking at us,' whispered Dawn in a panic, 'and the landlord's turned a funny colour. I really think we should leave, now.'

'Oh, all right,' said Felix. He glared at Dawn until she released her hold on his arm; then, calling Haltwhistle to heel, he stormed out of the garden.

Dawn's exit was a lot less theatrical. As she slipped quietly away, she glanced over her shoulder to see if the chalk mark was still on the table leg. It wasn't.

While Felix had been cheeking the landlord someone had sneakily rubbed it out – and picked up Murdo Meek's message.

Sitting cross-legged on a cushion with a ginger nut in one hand and the five of diamonds in the other, Dawn frowned hard. She dipped the biscuit into a mug of steaming cocoa. It was sheer luck that she didn't dunk the playing card into the cocoa instead. She was thinking so deeply about Operation Question Mark that she probably would not have noticed her mistake until her teeth clamped down on a slippery piece of card.

So far, Dawn had managed to rule out more than half of the eleven suspects. Six names had been scribbled through when she discovered that they had been nowhere near the Garden and Allotment Show on the first of July, which was the day that Angela disappeared. The seventh man had been discounted because of his foreign accent.

That left four suspects. Of these, three had definitely been at the show: the Right Honourable Charles Noble had presented the prizes, Larry Grahams had won a trophy and Seth Lightfoot had been there in his capacity as 'refuse technician'. Whether the remaining man, Brian Gee, had attended the function on the village green, Dawn had not found out yet.

'Explain to me again why Charles is your number

one suspect,' said Trudy from an armchair. As she bit into a Bourbon, a few crumbs landed on Peebles's fur. The cat gave a little shiver and curled into an even tighter ball. There was no room to spread himself out on Trudy's lap because her legs were so very slender.

'Lots of reasons,' said Dawn. 'Miles was cleaning *Charles's* windows when he had his accident; Charles was very keen to get rid of the ladder afterwards; he seems quite wealthy; I heard him say that he does cryptic crosswords – so he must be quite brainy; he was in The One-eyed Stoat when Murdo Meek left his message … *and* he's a really good swimmer …'

Trudy looked blankly at her. 'Swimmer?' she said. 'Oh, I see. Yes. Murdo Meek is supposed to have jumped into the Thames. Potty thing to do, if you ask me. Well, Dawn … I suppose you could be right. Charles does seem to be a likely candidate. It's a shame that our glorious leader has pulled the plug on Operation Question Mark when you're so close to getting to the bottom of things.'

'A *shame*?' said Felix indignantly. He stopped peering through Dawn's microdot viewer and shot Trudy a look of pure venom. 'It's an *outrage*, that's what it is.'

There was an awkward silence during which Dawn nibbled her soggy biscuit and avoided catching anyone's eye. Trudy was making a valiant effort to seem disappointed about being recalled to London before the completion of the mission – but Dawn could tell that she was hugely relieved to be going home. Felix, on the other hand, was furious about it.

'I'm going to kick up an almighty stink when I get back to P.S.S.T.,' he growled, seizing a strip of tiny microdots and holding it underneath the viewer.

'I know it's hard to accept,' said Trudy in a kindly voice, 'but things don't always turn out exactly how we'd like them to.' She stroked Peebles's head. 'You win some; you lose some.'

'Hey!' objected Dawn. 'If you don't mind, this mission isn't over yet … although you're both talking about it as if it were. When Meek shows up at the duck pond tonight, I'll be waiting for him – and, with any luck, he'll lead me straight to Angela.'

'That's the spirit!' said Trudy.

'I wish you'd let *me* come,' grumbled Felix, moving the viewer on to another microdot. 'It's a daft idea to go on your own. I'd promise to be quiet. Please change your mind.'

'No,' said Dawn firmly. 'You're not coming.'

An uncomplimentary stream of words poured forth from his mouth but Dawn didn't take any notice. She knew that he was just upset about his granny. Over the course of the evening, Felix had been getting more and more on edge and Dawn had tried to think of ways to placate him. She had given him the last two chocolate biscuits in the cookie jar, made him a hot milky drink, and even allowed him to look through her microdot viewer – but nothing had seemed to improve his mood.

'Why do you keep staring at the names on that silly old playing card?' he said to Dawn. 'I thought you'd made up your mind that Charles Noble is the man you're looking for.'

'I'm almost sure,' said Dawn, raising her mug of cocoa to her lips, 'but Socrates said that a spy should never be overconfident. Hmm … Larry Grahams,' she murmured, her eyes travelling down the list of suspects. As Charles's next-door neighbour, Larry would have had plenty of opportunity to slip into the garden of The Old Oast House and smear lard on the ladder. He had also put together a huge collection of porcelain animals which must have cost him a fortune. She remembered how traumatised he had been at the mention of Bernard's disappearance. *No*, she told herself firmly. *He wouldn't have been capable of killing that duck.*

'I don't suppose you'd be interested in my opinion,' piped up Felix. Without waiting for Dawn to respond, he ploughed on. 'I'm still suspicious of that Seth chap. Remember when we found him poking around up at Palethorpe Manor? If he was the kidnapper, he could have returned for something he'd left behind when he moved Granny to a different hiding place … like a length of rope or handcuffs or something – and we caught him in the act.'

'That's possible,' said Dawn, uncertainly. Her brain began to unscramble all the information she'd found out in the past few days. 'I'd certainly like to know how he got his hands on that scrap of paper from Bob's file.'

'WHAT?' Trudy's yell was followed by an even louder exclamation when Peebles showed his displeasure at having been rudely awoken and sank his claws into her thighs.

Dawn smiled meekly. 'I ... er ... forgot to mention that I found the missing corner from that sheet of paper in Bob's folder. It was stuck to the sculpture of Neptune and its moons that Seth gave to me. Bob had pteronophobia,' she explained.

Trudy looked extremely upset. 'Do you have any idea what this means?' she said.

'Um ... pteronophobia is the fear of being tickled with feathers, I think ...'

'No, you silly girl,' snapped Trudy. 'It *means* that somebody stole that information from my filing cabinet and passed it on to Meek. It *means* that P.S.S.T. has been infiltrated.'

'Huh?' said Dawn. She wasn't quite sure what Trudy was getting at.

'One of our colleagues,' said Trudy grimly, 'is a traitor.'

Chapter Nineteen

Murdo Meek is Revealed

Evidently, Clop was made of stern stuff (as well as wool and snipped-up stockings). Despite being informed by Dawn that the night-time excursion to the duck pond might be dangerous, he practically begged to be allowed to go, and even seemed to give a carefree wriggle of his tail as she slipped him into her rucksack.

She had already put on her warmest, darkest clothing, and pocketed her shell phone. Now that Dawn had thought of a feasible reason to be lurking at the edge of the duck pond (she was going to pretend to search for Clop whom she had 'mislaid' earlier in the day), everything was set. She was ready.

Before swinging the rucksack on to her back, Dawn unfastened it to check that Clop was comfortable. He seemed to imply that it was a bit dark and that the packet of sandwiches he was sitting on (which had peanut butter as their filling and, thankfully, not lard) was less comfy than a pillow, but it'd do.

Dawn turned out the light in her bedroom, pulled back the curtains and looked out on to Cow Parsley Lane. She saw yellow strips and squares gleaming from the neighbouring houses, which otherwise had been blackened by nightfall. There were no streetlamps so she wasn't able to see clearly enough to be sure that the road was empty.

In the living room, she received two frosty stares from Trudy and Felix and several thwacks on the leg from Haltwhistle's tail. Peebles had decided to drape himself over the ancient television set in the corner. He observed Dawn with his green, glassy eyes.

Dawn smiled timidly. 'Aren't you going to wish me luck?' she said.

No one did.

'I think it's a really stupid idea for you to go by yourself,' said Felix, who had cast the microdots aside and was positioning pieces on a chessboard. He glanced at Dawn and gave her a worried sort of frown. 'At least take Haltwhistle with you.'

'It's best if I don't,' said Dawn, choosing not to mention that his dog was a colossal nuisance and would probably ruin any chance she had of following Meek, 'but thanks for the offer,' she added politely.

'*I* think it's insane for you to go *at all*,' said Trudy. She was clearly agitated and could not seem to keep her hands still. Snatching up the microdot viewer, she twiddled it in her fingers. 'How does this thing work, then?'

'It's simple,' said Dawn. 'The viewer magnifies those tiny little photographs called microdots. You just place one of the microdots under one end of the viewer and look through the other end.'

Trudy followed Dawn's instructions. 'The thought of a traitor at P.S.S.T. makes me feel quite faint,' she said, one eye pressed to the viewer. 'I'd willingly pack my bags, right this minute, and leave Cherry Bentley, *tonight*.'

'I don't believe that anyone at P.S.S.T. could be mixed up in all this,' said Dawn. She had been giving the matter some thought. 'Isn't it possible that Murdo Meek or a really crafty burglar friend of his could have pinched the information from Bob's file?'

Trudy snorted. 'If you went on tiptoe, held your breath and happened to know a spell that would make you invisible you still wouldn't have a hope of making it past Edith. She's got eyes in the back of her head, that woman.'

'It's no good, Trudy,' said Dawn in heartfelt tones. 'You won't change my mind. This is my last chance to find Angela Bradshaw and I'm not going to pass it up.'

'I never realised what a stubborn little madam you are,' said Trudy resignedly. 'Have it your own way, then – but don't blame me if it all goes wrong.' She examined a microdot under the viewer. 'What's this supposed to be a picture of? It looks a bit like a beetroot, but it's lumpy in all the wrong places. What on earth possessed you to take a photo of this?'

'That'll be Larry Grahams winning the funny-shaped vegetable category at the Garden and Allotment Show,' said Dawn, 'on the day Angela vanished. I took photos of the pictures on display in the village hall.' She glanced at her watch. 'I really should be going, now.'

'Oh. Bye, then.' Trudy studied another microdot. Her hands were shaking and she looked quite teary-eyed.

'Don't worry,' said Dawn. 'I'll be all right. I got eighty-one-and-a-half per cent on my spying test, remember.' She turned towards the door and found Felix barring her way, his arms firmly folded.

'I've decided,' he said. 'You're not going anywhere without Haltwhistle. He's loyal, he's fearless – and if anyone sees you walking a dog, they won't wonder what you're up to, whereas if you lurk around the duck pond on your own ...'

'I don't need him,' insisted Dawn.

'Yes, you do! You're forever harping on about that old fellow, Socrates, and how he advised you that spies always need an excuse to be where they are.'

'I've already got an excuse,' she said, and – to prove it – Dawn opened her rucksack and lifted out her toy donkey. 'This is Clop,' she said. 'I dropped him this afternoon when I was feeding the ducks – at least that's what I intend to say if anybody challenges me.'

Trudy lowered the microdot viewer and gave Clop the once-over. 'What a drab little bundle!' she said. 'He looks as if he's been around for years. No one would ever guess that Izzie threw him together less than a week ago.'

'She didn't!' said Dawn, hugging her donkey tightly. (She was afraid that Trudy might have hurt his feelings.) 'He's mine. My very own.'

'You smuggled him to Cherry Bentley?' said Trudy, looking somewhat impressed. 'You're a sneaky one, you are.'

Dawn checked her watch again and gaped in horror. 'Could you let me past, please,' she said to Felix. 'I've only got ten minutes to make it to the duck pond.'

Stepping aside grudgingly, he told her to be careful.

Trudy mumbled something similar but she couldn't seem to bring herself to look in Dawn's direction. Instead, she jammed her eye against the microdot viewer and began to pore over the rest of the pictures.

'I'll be extra careful, I promise!' said Dawn as she hurried into the hallway. 'And I've got my shell phone with me in case I have any problems. See you later, then!' She opened the front door and prepared to set foot outside.

'Wait!' yelled Trudy from the living room. 'There's someone in this shot who shouldn't be! It doesn't make sense for *her* to have been at the show. Dawn! Hold on!'

But Dawn didn't. She was already late and, if she delayed any longer, she might miss the rendezvous between Murdo Meek and his co-conspirator. Trudy's feeble, last-ditch attempt to stop her from getting to the duck pond on time was not going to cut any ice with Dawn.

'Nice try!' called Dawn over her shoulder. Then she pulled the front door closed behind her and hurried away into the night.

The duck pond was a very different place in the dark. By day, its waters were ruffled by webbed feet and pocked by breadcrumbs. At night, however, its surface was as smooth and shiny as a slick of oil, and there was not a quack to be heard. All the ducks, moorhens and coots had put their heads under their wings and were huddled together on the island in the middle of the pond, or hidden in the reeds and bushes surrounding it.

Dawn crept around the edge of the duck pond and took refuge under a weeping willow tree. Crouching beside its trunk, she watched and listened, expecting Meek or his fellow spy to appear at any moment. All was tranquil until the church clock struck the hour, sombrely informing the village that it was ten o'clock.

Any minute now, thought Dawn, her eyes straining to catch the slightest sign of movement in the darkness. She slipped a hand into her rucksack and drew out Clop with the idea of placing him somewhere nearby for her to 'discover' should the need arise. However, once she had tucked him under her arm, she found that she was loath to put him down: his little woollen body felt so warm and comforting. Dawn and her donkey sat together in companionable silence – and waited.

Apart from the toot of a car horn and the plopping sound of what Dawn supposed was an amphibious creature taking a dip in the pond, she heard nothing: no footsteps, no breaking twigs, no murmur of voices.

The first she knew about the person creeping up behind her was when a hand closed over her mouth.

Dawn didn't have a chance to squeal or struggle. She only just managed to shove Clop up her jumper before another hand gripped her face and pressed a strong-smelling cloth over her nose. Its odour was sweet and overpowering and, within seconds, Dawn felt herself slipping into unconsciousness.

The room had uneven, stony walls and no carpet. There wasn't a scrap of furniture, apart from the makeshift bed upon which Dawn had found herself when she came to. The bed was nothing more than a hard, wooden bench and a couple of itchy blankets.

Dawn had failed to find any windows in the room, but it hadn't been easy to search for them with her hands tied behind her back and a blindfold fastened tightly over her eyes. She hadn't come across a door, either.

There was no way of knowing to which location her kidnapper had brought her. Dawn could not imagine where she was, although she wouldn't have been surprised to learn that she was in some sort of medieval prison cell. She hoped that she was somewhere in Cherry Bentley but, having no idea how long she had been unconscious, Dawn had to face the possibility that she might be hundreds of miles away.

Feeling chilled, woozy and horribly alone, Dawn returned to the bench and attempted to snuggle underneath a blanket. Judging by the small mound in her jumper, Clop was still with her, and that thought lifted her spirits a little. Not wishing to lie on her stomach and flatten him, Dawn tried to find an alternative resting position, but her bound hands and a bulky object in her pocket made this very difficult.

Spies weren't supposed to cry. Socrates had told her that. If they were unfortunate enough to be captured, they kept a cool head and seized the first chance they could to escape. Dawn felt close to tears but she blinked them away. She was hugely disappointed to have been abducted, not to mention scared out of her wits, but she was also determined to act like a proper spy and to stay calm – no matter what.

She drifted in and out of sleep for the next quarter of an hour or so. Then her eyes flicked open when she heard a creaking sound followed by a loud crash. Wishing that she could see what was going on, Dawn sat up. She knew that a person had entered the room when she heard footsteps. Then somebody spoke to her. It sounded like a man's voice, but because he chose to communicate in a hoarse whisper she could not be sure.

'Hello, Dawn,' he said.

'My name's Kitty. Kitty Wilson ... and I'd very much like to go home, please. My mum will be wondering where I am.' The fear in her voice was real.

The man laughed unpleasantly. 'Don't bother lying to me, child. I know who you are ... and I rather think that you're familiar with my name, too, aren't you, Dawn?'

She shook her head.

'I'm Murdo Meek.'

Dawn tried her best not to tremble. So, Meek *hadn't* drowned in the Thames ten years ago.

'Murdo who?' she said. 'Haven't ever heard of you. Sorry.'

'Continue with your little charade for now, if you must,' whispered Meek amusedly. 'You've got pluck – I suppose that's why you were recruited by P.S.S.T. Yes, I know *everything*, Dawn. That conniving bunch thought they could outwit me, didn't they? It was quite a shrewd idea to send a spy young enough to be above suspicion. Not really playing fair, though, were they, Dawn?'

'My name's Kitty,' she said, 'and ... and I don't know

what you're talking about.'

'Yes, you do!' hissed Meek. 'Why else were you loitering about near the duck pond at such a late hour?'

'I dropped my toy there this afternoon,' insisted Dawn. 'I went back to look for him.'

'Nonsense!' said Meek savagely. 'You were skulking by the duck pond because you expected *me* to be meeting someone there. Poor, foolish girl! When you read my message, you had no idea that it was meant for *you*. "Meet me by the duck pond. Ten p.m. Tonight." It was good of you to be on time.'

Dawn was astonished and appalled in the same moment. Meek had set a trap and she had fallen straight into it! She had been so busy congratulating herself on finding the message in the garden of The One-eyed Stoat that she hadn't stopped to question why it had been written in plain English. The reason was all too obvious, now. Uncertain of Dawn's decoding abilities, Meek had opted to make things easy for her by neglecting to use any code whatsoever. He had lured her to the pond so that he could kidnap her under cover of darkness, with no one to witness his dastardly deed.

To be duped with such ease was mortifying but, somehow, Dawn managed to conceal her feelings. Keeping her face blank, she stuck steadfastly to her story.

'I went to the duck pond to look for my toy,' she said, 'and I don't understand why you won't believe me.'

'Confound it, girl!' Meek seemed to be losing his patience with her. She heard him pacing around the room, his shoes striking against the floorboards. 'Admit to me that your name is Dawn Buckle!'

'I'm Kitty Wilson,' said Dawn.

Meek's footsteps came towards her. She felt him tugging at the ropes which bound her wrists. Then her arms flopped forward. For the briefest of moments, Dawn dared to hope that she had proved convincing enough for him to free her – but she should have known better.

'Hold out one of your hands,' said Meek in his strange, husky voice.

Dawn was still none the wiser as to his true identity. Reluctantly, she obeyed his order.

'Tell me again who you are,' he said.

'I'm Kitty …' began Dawn. Then she gasped as something grabbed the tip of her forefinger and squeezed hard. 'Ouch!' she said, and bit her lip.

'Who are you?' said Meek again.

'Kitty Wilson,' said Dawn in a voice that was very high-pitched. 'I've got a mum called Sandra, a … a brother called Wayne and my pets' names are Fred and Sardine.' Whatever it was that had attached itself to her finger tightened its grip. The pain reminded her of the occasion when she had caught her finger in a letterbox. Her eyes moistened.

'If you tell me the truth, I'll make it stop,' said Meek in kindlier tones.

Dawn gritted her teeth and said nothing. *So this is how he wheedles his information out of people*, she thought. *He tortures them with some kind of finger-clamping device.* From the depths of her jumper, she felt Clop willing her to hold her nerve. *If Meek thinks he's going to make me crack*, she thought bravely, *he's sadly mistaken.*

'You're being very stubborn, Dawn ...' said Meek, but the rest of his sentence was drowned out by a deafening clang which resonated around the whole room. Dawn found herself wishing that she had brought her ear-muffs with her when eleven more thunderous booms rang out – but by the time the last note had died away, she could not have cared less about the throbbing sensation in her ears, or the pain in her finger, for that matter. A lifetime of living with her father and his large and varied clock collection had caused her to develop a particularly sensitive ear when it came to recognising chimes and other noises that clocks were inclined to make. The clock, which had just struck midnight, was familiar to her. She was one hundred per cent certain that it belonged to St Elmo's Church – which meant that she was still in Cherry Bentley!

Dawn pieced together all the clues she had amassed in an effort to pinpoint her whereabouts. The room had bare boards, rough lumpy walls, no windows, hardly any furniture to speak of *and* it was a stone's throw from the clock. A shiver ran through her when she realised where she was. *I'm in the church tower,* she thought.

Ignoring the burning pain in her fingertip, Dawn concentrated on listening to the hoarse whisper of her captor as he asked her repeatedly to admit her name was Dawn. Could the voice belong to Charles Noble? As the head bell-ringer it was likely that he would be able to visit the church whenever he pleased.

Heartened by the thought that Daffodil Cottage was less than a mile away, Dawn began to formulate an escape plan. With any luck, Meek would soon tire of her refusal to comply with his wishes, and remove the object that was pinching her finger. Once both her hands were free, Dawn intended to throw one of the blankets over him, rip off her blindfold and run as fast as she could to the exit. It would be her best chance to get away from him. If she allowed Meek to retie her hands, she would be just as helpless as she was before.

'What a tiresome girl you are,' said Meek when, for about the fiftieth time, Dawn declared that her name was Kitty Wilson. She felt relief as well as excitement when the pressure on her fingertip began to ease. Slowly and deliberately the fingers of her other hand closed around the blanket.

'Not everyone responds to that method of persuasion,' said Meek as the clamp finally released Dawn's finger, 'but there are other ways to extract the truth.'

Dawn braced herself. Then she moved like lightning – which was something of a new experience for her. Springing off the bed, she hurled the blanket at where she estimated Meek to be standing. From his roar of fury, she knew that she had aimed well.

The blindfold was bound tightly and Dawn had to paw at it to get it off. She stood, bewildered, for a second. Then she stared around the barren room, her eyes desperately searching for a way out. Just as she had surmised, there was no door! She glanced at Meek. The blanket had fallen over his head but he was struggling vigorously beneath it and was likely to be free of it in no time at all.

Dawn's panic-stricken gaze fell on an oil lamp which was resting on the floor. Then her heart lifted as she spied something behind it.

'A trapdoor!' exclaimed Dawn joyfully.

She raced over to the square hole in the centre of the floor and sank to her knees, but before she could place her foot on the first rung of the ladder below, her arm was seized roughly and she was dragged to her feet.

'It's you!' cried Dawn, goggling at the man beside her. Meek glared back at her, his mouth twisted into a livid scowl, and thrust his face into hers.

'YOU ... INFURIATING BRAT,' he said, the hairs in his beard scratching her skin.

Dawn tried to squirm away from him. '*Larry Grahams,*' she said in amazement. 'I … I never suspected *you.*'

Larry threw her a look of contempt. 'That's because you're just as thickheaded as all the rest,' he said, no longer needing to speak in an indistinct whisper. 'I gave those dimwits at S.H.H. the biggest clue they could wish for – and still they couldn't guess my real identity.' Keeping a tight hold on her arm, Larry reached into the pocket of his corduroy trousers and produced a crumpled piece of paper. He shoved it into Dawn's hand.

'Well?' said Larry.

'Um,' she said, staring at the message which she had stumbled across several hours before in the garden of The One-eyed Stoat.

Meet me by the duck pond.
Ten pm. Tonight. M. M.

'Study it, carefully,' said Larry.

Dawn scrutinised the note but she didn't have the first idea what she was supposed to be looking for. If the words had a hidden meaning, she was quite unable to deduce what it was.

'Amateurs … the lot of you!' said Larry in disgust. He prodded the final part of the message with his finger. 'Haven't you ever wondered why I always sign

306

my name in pencil like this?'

Dawn looked at the two Ms on the scrap of paper. 'No,' she said, truthfully.

'Grey Ms!' Larry stared expectantly at Dawn. Then he put the two words together. 'Grahams,' he said. 'You see – I handed S.H.H. my name on a plate.'

'Ohhhh!' said Dawn. 'Red and the others will *kick* themselves when they find out.' She gave a horrified gasp and pressed a hand over her mouth. The shock of discovering Meek's true persona had loosened her tongue.

'You might as well come clean,' he sneered. 'You *are* Dawn Buckle, aren't you?' Larry's smugness was unbearable.

Having already betrayed herself, Dawn did not think that there was any point in continuing to deny it.

'Yes,' she said wretchedly. 'I am.'

The triumphant look on Larry's face made her feel quite nauseous. Choosing to avert her eyes, she was astonished to see something resembling a four-legged Cornish pasty moving slowly across the floor. Dawn looked more closely and saw that the pasty was, in fact, a tortoise.

'Isn't that Pilliwinks?' she said in a puzzled voice. 'Why have you brought your pet along with you?'

Larry smiled. 'She was a *little* unwilling to leave her favourite flowerbed, but when I told her about the pressing engagement that she should attend ...'

'*Pressing* engagement?' said Dawn, glancing uneasily at her forefinger, which was strawberry-coloured and rather swollen. Casting another glance in Pilliwinks's direction, she realised that her finger was just the right size to fit inside the tortoise's mouth.

'Her skills can come in very handy in my line of work,' said Larry. 'Of course, she's a wonderful companion, too. Animals are so much nicer than people, don't you agree?'

'We ... ell,' said Dawn. She remembered that Larry's house had been chock-a-block with porcelain creatures and his garden had been teeming with wildlife. 'You like animals rather a lot, don't you?' she said.

'Oh, yes,' said Larry happily. 'They're superior to humans in every way. I adore them. They're my friends.'

'Then how *could* you have murdered *Bernard*?' said Dawn. 'The poor, defenceless duck!'

'Shut up!' said Larry, his voice beginning to tremble. 'I don't like to speak of it.'

'Animal lovers don't do horrible things like that!' persisted Dawn.

'I know!' wailed Larry. 'I didn't *want* to do it, but I needed rather a lot of feathers to make my tickling stick. I chose to bump off Bernard because he was the oldest, you see. He'd had a long, happy life. I even fed him some crumbs from a freshly made fruit scone before I ... er ... wrung his neck.'

'Well, *I* think it was a *despicable* thing to do,' said Dawn.

Larry stifled a sob. He gave Dawn a push, tucked Pilliwinks under his arm and snatched up the oil lamp before climbing down the stepladder at speed. There was a crash as he shut the trapdoor behind him.

Dawn was left in the dark. In his distress, Larry had neglected to bind her hands, so she felt around on the floor for the blanket. Once she had found it, she pressed a button on her watch, which lit up its face and helped her to find her way across the room to the bench. Stunned by the evening's revelations, she sank down on to it, reached inside her jumper and pulled out Clop, who seemed to be in quite a state of shock himself. She decided that the best thing for them both would be to get a few hours' sleep. Hugging her donkey to her chest, Dawn lay down under the blanket, but she soon sat up again when a hard object dug into her hip bone.

Larry must have confiscated her rucksack, because there had been no sign of it in the room, but he had forgotten to search her pockets.

'My phone!' exclaimed Dawn as she slipped a hand into her jeans and drew out the tiger cowrie shell. 'Don't worry, Clop,' she said, stroking her donkey's woolly mane. 'Help will soon be on the way.'

Chapter Twenty

Donkey Riding

'Well, so much for that,' said Dawn. She was bitterly disappointed. No matter how many times she had pressed the splodges on the shell (in the correct sequence, at first, and then, in every order she could think of) the phone had remained lifeless. She had shaken it, warmed it in her hands, and even knocked it against the leg of the bench – but nothing seemed to make any difference. Dawn was forced to accept the fact that it was broken.

She supposed that it must have got damaged the night before, when it had dropped out of her pocket – or perhaps Haltwhistle had pummelled it with his paws a little too zealously when he'd tried to retrieve it from the rabbit burrow.

'Bang goes Plan B,' said Dawn. (Plan A had been the failed attempt to hamper Larry with a blanket and bolt for the trapdoor.) She wondered if Larry had already discovered that the phone was useless, and for that reason had allowed Dawn to keep it in her possession.

Sighing heavily, she lifted Clop on to her lap. 'Your turn,' she said. 'I'm all out of ideas. *You* can come up with Plan C.' It might have been her imagination, but Dawn thought she felt the donkey sit up a little straighter as if he were applying his mind to the problem instantly. 'Tell you what, Clop,' she said, reclining on the bench and closing her eyes, 'why don't you sleep on it.'

Startled out of her dreams by a prolonged, mournful cry, Dawn's eyes flicked open. As the stifled wailing sound reached an even higher pitch, Dawn glanced around her to try to establish where it was coming from and realised that the room was far less dark than when she had fallen asleep. Scanning the walls, she saw that she had not been mistaken about the lack of windows in the tower room but she had missed a narrow slit which looked just like a white rod glowing in the wall. Through it, daylight was filtering in.

There was something otherworldly about the cry that suggested to Dawn that it might not be human. She was only too aware that the church was surrounded by a graveyard, and tried to put all thoughts of ghosts and vampires out of her mind. Deciding to investigate every corner of the room, Dawn got to her feet, almost stepping on her donkey in the process. Clop must have fallen off the bench in the night. He was lying on the floor with his head turned to one side, as if he were listening to something beneath the floorboards.

'I think you're right, Clop!' said Dawn, dropping to her knees. She crawled across the floor, guided by the caterwauling noise which seemed to have increased in volume. 'It's coming from round about here,' she said, pausing beside a floorboard with two screws missing. Something was knocking against its underside as if it were trying to force the board upwards.

Dawn dithered for a moment or two until her inquisitiveness finally overcame her fear. With her heart in her mouth, she attempted to lift up the board using the tips of her fingers. The wailing stopped.

Like a streak of black smoke, a cat slipped through the space that Dawn had created, and hightailed it over to a corner. Then, with great urgency, it began to wash itself all over.

Cobwebby and smeared with dust, its fur was in a sorry state. Dawn approached the cat cautiously.

'Peebles,' she said, screwing up her eyes, 'is that *you*?'

The cat paused in mid-lick and shot her a scathing look as if to say, *Yes, of course it's me ... who else were you expecting?* Dawn was overjoyed to see him, but she was polite enough to wait until he had finished his ablutions before attempting to give his head a stroke.

'How on earth did you get up here?' asked Dawn,

guessing the answer to her own question as soon as it had left her lips. She remembered being told by Red that Peebles was a first-rate climber and was able to squeeze himself through the slimmest of gaps.

She wondered if the cat had found her purely by chance, or whether somebody had sent him, suspecting that she was in the building. Dawn left Peebles purring in the corner and hastened over to the narrow slit in the wall. If she stood on tiptoe, she found that she could see rooftops and the uppermost branches of the yew trees in the graveyard. In an attempt to give herself a better view, Dawn dragged the bench over to the wall and stood on it. Her eyes searched the ground outside but, to her disappointment, there was no sign of Trudy or Felix, and the dog that she saw sniffing around a gravestone was far too small and neatly groomed to be Haltwhistle.

'If *only* I had a pen and paper,' said Dawn, 'I could slip a message through this crack. Someone would be bound to pick it up … or perhaps I could try waving to the people below.' She attempted to push her hand through the slender crevice but, although she managed to squeeze four fingers through, her hand was too plump – and got stuck. She told herself that her stubby little fingers were unlikely to be noticed by any passers-by, no matter how energetically she wiggled them. Unless one of the villagers happened to be looking through a pair of binoculars and had them trained on exactly the right spot, Dawn's chances of attracting anyone's attention were slight.

'I don't suppose you've had any thoughts about Plan C?' she said to Clop.

The donkey did not give her any indication to show that he had.

Dawn turned to Peebles, who had jumped up on to the bench and was sitting on the blanket, watching her.

'It's a shame you're not wearing your harness,' she said. 'I might've been able to wedge something into it that was recognisably mine. Then the others would have known that you'd found me.'

Peebles blinked.

'Perhaps I could make a harness out of that blanket,' she said, trying to decide if she was strong enough to tear it into strips. 'What do you reckon, huh?'

The cat fastened her with a flinty stare.

'Or the rope! I could use the rope!'

Peebles seemed to like that idea. He sprang off the bench and started to weave himself between Dawn's legs, purring like a little lawnmower.

'But what can I tie to your back?' she said, stooping to retrieve the piece of rope. Larry had tossed it on to the floor after he had freed her hands. It was very fortunate that he hadn't thought to take it with him.

Kneeling on the floorboards, Dawn did her best to

fashion the rope into a rudimentary harness and wrap it securely around Peebles's middle. Then she took out the only possession that Larry had left her with and tried to wedge it underneath the rope.

'It's no good,' she said, as the shell phone slipped out of place and clunked against the floor. 'I need something that can be *squashed*.'

Dawn thought about removing her jumper and jamming that under the harness, but she abandoned that idea swiftly when she realised that it was far too big and heavy.

'What else is there?' she said. 'I can't think of a single thing.'

Peebles's miaow sounded rather reproachful.

'Sorry,' said Dawn in a glum voice.

After a few minutes of sitting in doleful silence, she got the funniest feeling that someone was trying to catch her eye. Searchingly, she looked around the room.

Her throat tightened when she saw him. 'No, Clop! Oh, no ... not *you*.'

He was the perfect size, as squashable as it was possible to be and, of course, braver than a mountain lion, but Dawn was going to take some persuading before she would allow him to be strapped to Peebles's back.

'Look, here, Clop,' she said, balancing her donkey on her knee. 'I know I asked you to come up with Plan C but I didn't mean that you should take it upon yourself to go and fetch help. It's awfully heroic of you, but …'

Clop was sitting in a defiant pose with his chest pushed out and his ears erect. He looked more determined than Dawn had ever seen him.

'What happens if you fall off?' she said. 'I might never find you again.'

Her donkey's expression remained unchanged.

'Oh, all *right*,' said Dawn reluctantly. She lifted his chin and kissed him on the nose. 'But you'd better *promise* to be careful.'

Dawn took longer than was really necessary to fit Clop securely into the harness. She fussed over him, tucking in his hooves, and tying his pleated tail to the rope as a precautionary measure. Impatient to be off, Peebles twitched his ears and miaowed at regular intervals until Dawn was satisfied that he and his passenger were ready.

'Good luck, you two,' she said, lifting the loose floorboard. She reached out to stroke Clop's mane for a final time but Peebles was too quick for her. As agile as a weasel, he darted into the gap and was gone.

No sooner had they disappeared than Dawn heard muffled tapping sounds. Someone was coming up the stepladder. She got up from the floor and waited for the trapdoor to open, clinging to the vain hope that her visitor was someone other than Larry.

When a woman's head and shoulders appeared,

Dawn could not believe her luck.

She looked slightly younger than Trudy, and had dark, bouncy, shoulder-length hair which gleamed like the bottles of burgundy wine which stood on Dawn's sideboard at home. Her features were soft and pretty but, as the woman turned towards her, Dawn saw that her eyes had a shrewdness about them that did not seem to belong on such a gentle face.

'Thank goodness!' said Dawn, rushing forwards. 'I've been locked in …'

Saying nothing, the woman looked pityingly at her and shook her head as if she were shocked.

'I'm so pleased to see you,' said Dawn, even though she had never clapped eyes on the woman before. 'I'm sorry that I haven't got time to explain, but I really must get out of here.' She hurried over to the trapdoor and was about to descend through it when the woman put out her hand and grabbed Dawn's shoulder.

'Not yet,' she said.

Dawn heard the sound of someone else climbing up the rungs. She stepped back from the trapdoor and laughed.

'Good idea,' she said, appreciating that it would be an immensely tricky feat to pass another person on a ladder. She gave the woman a friendly grin, which, to her bewilderment, was not returned.

Feeling that something wasn't quite right, Dawn

managed to wriggle out of the woman's grasp. She retreated until she was standing beside the bench. Then she waited, with growing unease, for the second person to arrive at the top of the ladder.

'You see,' said a voice that chilled Dawn to the bone, 'I told you she was quite unscathed.'

Dawn watched, aghast, as her captor emerged through the hole in the floor. Larry was wearing a tweed cap, a tank top over a short-sleeved shirt and a pair of turn-ups. Dressed in the garb of an ordinary old man, the most cunning spy in England stepped into the room.

'Your assurances mean nothing, Meek,' said the woman coldly. 'I wanted to see the child for myself,'

'And now that you have, you can push off back to London.'

'As you wish,' conceded the woman, 'but Dawn is coming with me.'

Larry chuckled in a disquieting way. 'Over my dead body,' he snarled. 'The little brat has seen my face. She's not going anywhere.'

'Think logically,' said the woman. 'Dawn would be far more secure in my neck of the woods, amongst city-dwellers who mind their own business. Villagers are notoriously nosy. This tower isn't a safe place to keep her, and even if you moved the child to a different spot, someone would be bound to stumble across her sooner or later.'

'The vicar's got vertigo,' said Larry. 'No one ever comes up here – apart from a few mice, maybe. It's perfect.'

'You said the same about Palethorpe Manor. Do I have to remind you what happened there?'

'That was bad luck,' said Larry, agitatedly. 'Seth Lightfoot isn't normal.'

'Who?' asked the woman.

'That interfering pest who spotted Angela and thought she was some kind of spectral being. Regular folk don't hang around a building that's supposed to be dangerous. I spent a whole evening hammering those signs into the ground to warn people to keep away from the manor. Everyone else did as they were told – but not Seth Lightfoot … the obstinate little twerp.'

'Do the sensible thing,' said the woman, coaxingly. 'Dawn is an inconvenience you could do without. Looking after children isn't exactly your forte, is it? Let me take care of her for you.'

'No!' said Larry. 'You may have sweet-talked me into handing over the old woman but I shan't be making you a present of Dawn.'

'Please.'

Larry Grahams pursed his lips and shook his head fiercely.

Having had her spirits dampened by Larry's arrival, Dawn was feeling rather subdued. She was also very curious as to the identity of the woman with the bouncy hair. Larry had mentioned that she came from London and, indeed, she was dressed like a sophisticated city type in an elegant plum skirt, matching jacket and suede high heels.

Whoever she was, the woman seemed to be very strong-minded. She continued to argue with Larry about who should hold Dawn captive. It had occurred to Dawn that the woman might be Larry's helper, but it was obvious from the way she refused to kowtow to him that they were both on an equal footing.

Rather than listen to them wrangling over her (Dawn had never been so popular), she climbed stealthily on to the bench and endeavoured to have a look through the slit in the wall. She could hear some dogs barking below, and wondered what was going on. The short, high-pitched yaps were nothing like the booming woofs of Haltwhistle, which would have been music to her ears, but nevertheless she was curious to know what all the fuss was about. She almost lost her balance when she saw what the dogs were barking at.

Peebles and Clop.

The cat was perched precariously on a large, tilted gravestone while two hysterical Jack Russell terriers snarled and yipped at him, jumping into the air on their little hind legs. Peebles was making spitting noises and, even from her lofty vantage point, Dawn could see that his tail had swollen to the size of a small draught excluder.

'*Oh, no,*' hissed Dawn, as the dogs bounced higher, their jaws snapping together an inch away from Peebles's whiskers. Dawn glanced desperately around the graveyard. She was looking for Mrs Cuddy. If *only* the old lady would appear and call Honeybunch and Lambkin to heel.

By the look of him, Peebles was starting to panic, too. He was casting about him, no doubt searching for somewhere to spring to; but there were no other gravestones within leaping distance. Dawn suspected that Peebles was beginning to regret that he had teased the dogs by parading up and down outside Bluebell Villa. There was no pane of glass to shield him from them now.

The cat crouched and seemed to stiffen. Dawn guessed what he was going to do. 'He's decided to make a break for it,' she breathed, barely able to bring herself to look. 'Oh, Clop,' she said woefully. From such a distance she could not see the expression on her donkey's face, but she expected that it was as serious and resolute as ever.

'What's she doing? Make her get down from there!'

The woman responded to Larry's sharp command by seizing Dawn's wrist and pulling her from the bench.

'Nooo!' screamed Dawn, frantically trying to free her

hand. She heard a furore of yapping and growling, and concluded that Peebles had made his move. 'I must see … I have to find out …'

'What's she wittering on about?' snapped Larry. 'Do you think the little tyke's been signalling to someone?'

'No,' said the woman, peering through the slit whilst keeping a tight hold on Dawn. 'There's nothing going on down there – apart from two dogs having a fight.'

'A cat … can you see a cat?' muttered Dawn. She couldn't summon the energy to struggle any more. Leaning weakly against the woman, she remembered, just in time, that spies weren't supposed to cry, and bit her lip instead.

'There, there,' said the woman kindly. She seemed to understand that Dawn was upset. 'Don't distress yourself. You'll soon be out of this draughty old tower.'

'She will *not*,' said Larry, tramping towards them. 'When are you going to get it through your thick skull –'

'You owe me a favour, Meek,' said the woman tartly.

'We're quits,' he replied, 'and you know it.'

'If I hadn't rummaged about in those files at P.S.S.T., you'd never have been able to get rid of those spies so quickly. Evergreen and Chalk would have tracked you down if *I* hadn't stepped in to help you.'

Dawn gasped and stared up at the woman. *How could she have slipped past Edith and gained access to the upper*

322

floor of the Dampside Hotel? She must be an even better spy than Murdo Meek, reckoned Dawn. *Thank goodness that Trudy was wrong about there being a traitor at P.S.S.T.!* She looked a little harder at the woman. *At least, I think she was ...*

Trudy had been convinced that Emma had been responsible for raiding her files. Could it be possible that the woman whose fingers were still clasped around Dawn's wrist was wearing a disguise? Was her bouncy, shoulder-length hair really a wig? Had she altered her voice?

'I don't owe you anything,' said Larry, his face hardening. 'Don't pretend that you've done any of this for *my* sake. You've only ever been interested in looking after your precious career. You're a hypocrite, that's what you are.' He laughed at the woman's troubled expression. 'You may spend all your time bossing other people about but *I'm* not going to stand for it! Perhaps a few hours in these delightful surroundings will convince you that *I'm* the best person to watch over Dawn.' He rushed towards the middle of the room, disappeared through the trapdoor and slammed it shut. 'So long, Philippa!' came his muffled cry.

'Philippa!' said Dawn in astonishment. With wide eyes, she looked into the woman's face. 'You're ... you're Philippa Killingback ... aren't you?'

Chapter Twenty-one

Secrets and Lies

The Chief of S.H.H. did not bat an eyelid when Larry locked her in the tower room; and when Dawn asked her to confirm who she was, Philippa nodded mildly and sat down on the bench.

'Are you terribly shocked?' she said.

'Am I shocked that you're in cahoots with Murdo Meek?' said Dawn. 'Yes, of *course* I am!' She stared disappointedly at Philippa, her mouth opening and shutting. There were too many questions that she wanted to ask and she couldn't think where she should start.

'Angela Bradshaw almost keeled over when she found out that I was involved,' said the Chief. She gave Dawn a weak smile. 'I suppose you'd like to know why.'

'I would. Yes,' said Dawn, wondering how on earth Meek had persuaded the highest-ranking member of S.H.H. to betray her country.

'I was so naive,' said Philippa wryly. 'I thought that it would be easy. If I did Meek one little favour he would disappear from my life and he'd never be a bother to S.H.H. again. I should have known that things are never that simple.'

'I ... I don't understand,' said Dawn, seating herself next to Philippa.

'It was so irresponsible to send you here,' said Philippa. 'I gave Red the tongue-lashing of his life when I discovered that he'd sent a *child* into the field. I suppose Socrates trained you?'

'Yes,' agreed Dawn, 'and I learned a lot from a book called *Keeping to the Shadows.*'

'Still using that old tome, is he? There are more up-to-date spying textbooks nowadays, but Socrates is something of a traditionalist. *Keeping to the Shadows*, eh? I haven't flicked through that in years. My old copy must be collecting dust up in the attic. Wanda used to swear by it.'

'Who?' said Dawn.

'Wanda Longshanks. She was the spy who trained me. Wanda retired to the Costa Brava thirteen years ago.' Philippa sighed heavily. 'P.S.S.T. just isn't the same without her.'

'P.S.S.T?' said Dawn. *'You used to work for P.S.S.T.?'*

'Graduated from Clandestine College in the July ... and P.S.S.T. offered me a position one month later. I was over the moon. I'd longed to work for a spying organisation ever since I was a little girl. Started work on my twenty-first birthday.' Philippa smiled wistfully.

'That was the most wonderful day of my life.'

'How long did you work for P.S.S.T.?' Dawn asked.

'Nine years in all – and I enjoyed almost every minute.'

Dawn did some swift calculations in her head. 'Then you must have been at P.S.S.T. when Murdo Meek jumped into the Thames and got away.'

'Yes,' said Philippa. Her face clouded over. 'I was there.'

'But you weren't involved in the attempt to capture him.'

'What makes you think that?'

Dawn was puzzled. She remembered reading about the events on the night of December the ninth in the file labelled 'Murdo Meek' and there had been no eye-witness account signed by a Philippa Killingback.

'I was the second one to arrive at the old warehouse by the river,' said Philippa, closing her eyes as she tried to recall what had transpired on that notable winter's night a decade before. 'Red turned up a few minutes later and we waited a bit longer for Socrates, but then he phoned to tell us that his bike had got a puncture and he was going to be delayed. Red, Angela and I had a quick conference. Then I crept round to the rear entrance, Angela stayed at the front – and Red ventured inside ...'

'*Pip Johnson* kept watch at the back of the warehouse,' said Dawn. She was very confused. 'All the accounts in Meek's file say so.'

'That's right,' said Philippa. '*I'm* Pip Johnson – at least, I was ten years ago. I was known as "Pip" in those

326

days and Johnson was my maiden name. I became a Killingback when I got married a few years later.'

'That was the night that Meek disappeared,' said Dawn. 'Everybody thought he'd drowned. You helped him to escape, didn't you?'

'Yes,' said Philippa. Dawn noticed that she had the decency to look shame-faced about it.

'*Why?*'

'Why?' repeated Philippa as if she were in a daze. She laughed rather bitterly. 'Because I had no choice.'

Dawn was shocked. 'Was he blackmailing you?' she asked.

'In a manner of speaking. Yes, he was.'

The church clock gave the briefest of whirring sounds before launching into its first sonorous boom. This was followed by a further eight strikes. As she waited patiently for silence to be restored, Dawn gazed at the stoical woman sitting beside her. Outwardly, Philippa seemed calm and composed, but there was a sorrowful look in her eyes which suggested to Dawn that the Chief of S.H.H. was concealing a painful secret.

'There were five of us,' said Philippa reflectively, when the last clang had died away. 'Three of us little ones, my mother and my father. Not that we saw a great deal of *him.*'

Dawn was curious as to why the Chief of S.H.H. had begun to reminisce about her childhood, but she decided not to interrupt.

'My father was never very interested in us children. He was always staying late at work or walking on the moors with our spaniels, Mixer and Menace. We only ever saw him at suppertime, and then, one night, he left the table between courses – and never came back.'

'How awful,' said Dawn.

'I was only four at the time,' continued Philippa. 'George and Vicky were even younger. When my mother remarried, we took our stepfather's name and forgot all about our real dad. Then, twenty years later, he turned up again right out of the blue.' She smiled sadly at Dawn. 'It's funny how our brains hold on to certain things, isn't it? As far as I was concerned, the man standing on my doorstep was a complete stranger. I didn't have the vaguest recollection of what my father looked like, but as soon as I heard his voice, I knew it was him.'

'His voice …' said Dawn thoughtfully.

'I made him a cup of tea. I thought that he might want to apologise for deserting us all those years ago. Fat chance of that!' she said. 'His reasons for getting in touch again were soon made clear to me.' She frowned, and squeezed her hands together in her lap. 'Sat at my kitchen table, as bold as brass, and told me he was Murdo Meek.'

'He did what?' said Dawn. She was stupefied. 'You mean … Larry Grahams is your *father*?'

'Tragically, yes, that's the truth,' said Philippa.

'But why did he reveal to you that he was Murdo Meek?' asked Dawn. 'Didn't he know that you worked for P.S.S.T.?'

'Of course he knew!' Philippa's face was etched with rancour. 'Meek makes it his business to know everything about everybody. He'd really done his homework on me. Sat there smugly, sipping his tea, and told me all about myself ... how I'd come top of my class at Clandestine College, been snapped up by P.S.S.T., cruised through my training programme to become the best spy they'd ever had ...'

'Gosh,' said Dawn, regarding Philippa with awe.

'He even had the cheek to suggest that I'd inherited all my skills from *him*!'

Dawn remembered what Red had said about spying talent sometimes running in the family, but decided not to mention this to Philippa. The Chief of S.H.H. did not seem to want to acknowledge that Larry's genes could have had any bearing on her choice of career.

'Wasn't Meek afraid that you would turn him in?' asked Dawn.

'No,' said Philippa, shaking her head firmly. 'The cunning old devil knew that I'd have to keep his secret. I was twenty-four then, and filled with ambition. I had every intention of becoming the first female Chief of S.H.H. If it had come to light that my father was Murdo Meek, I would probably have been kicked out of S.H.H. altogether.'

'I see,' said Dawn. She didn't think that it sounded very fair to punish Philippa for her father's crimes. 'But I still don't understand why your father told you that he was really Murdo Meek.'

'He wanted a safeguard.'

'Huh?' said Dawn.

'Spying is a risky profession. If Meek ever got himself into a tight corner, he wanted to know that he could call on me to help him get out of it.'

'And you agreed,' said Dawn.

'Yes,' said Philippa. 'If Meek was ever caught, I would stand to lose *everything*.' Her fingers travelled to her earlobe and she unclipped a large gold earring. Holding it in her palm, she showed it to Dawn. 'This is the only present I've ever had from my father. It's a phone,' she said, 'so that he can contact me whenever he wants.'

'Meek called you that night in December, didn't he?' said Dawn.

'That's right,' said Philippa. 'He thought he'd send P.S.S.T. a spiteful Christmas card but the gesture back-fired on him when Angela happened to realise who he was. Meek tried to give her the slip but she tracked him tenaciously like a bloodhound.'

'Tell me,' pleaded Dawn. 'How did he do it? How did he survive the fall into the Thames and swim to the bank through that icy water without anyone seeing him?'

'He didn't,' said Philippa.

'Oh … you mean he swam to the *bridge* and managed to climb up it somehow. That can't have been easy …'

'Wrong again,' she said.

Dawn shot her a quizzical look, and Philippa finally relented.

'Very well. Pin back your ears,' she said. '*This* is what happened …'

'I've given you ample time to reconsider,' said Larry, reappearing through the trapdoor. He produced a revolver from his trouser pocket and flaunted it at his daughter. 'So, tell me, Philippa, are you prepared to return to London alone?'

'No,' she replied, looking him in the eye, 'and pointing that thing at me won't make me change my mind.'

Larry's mouth turned down at the corners. 'What a pity,' he said.

'It's … it's all right,' said Dawn from a corner of the room, into which she'd retreated when Larry had taken out his gun. 'I don't mind staying in Cherry Bentley … honestly.' She was lying, of course. Given the choice, Dawn would have preferred to be held captive by the treacherous but likeable Chief of S.H.H. than to be left in the care of her gun-toting father and his unusual instrument of torture. (Her finger still hurt quite a lot.)

'Don't worry, Dawn,' said Philippa with confidence. 'I shan't be leaving you behind – and you won't be a prisoner for much longer, either. I'm going to return you to your family.'

'Whaaaaat?' Larry was incensed. 'Have you gone stark staring mad?'

'Not at all,' said Philippa. 'In fact, I've never felt more clear-headed.'

'But if you let her go you'll be unmasked as a traitor. There'll be a huge scandal and you'll be dismissed from S.H.H.' said Larry. 'Think of the humiliation you'll suffer … not to mention the lengthy jail term …'

'I know,' said Philippa.

'You stupid fool! Don't you care?'

The Chief of S.H.H. took a while to answer.

'No. Not any more,' she said softly. 'I made a terrible error of judgement when I helped you to escape ten years ago. I should have guessed that the lying and deceit wouldn't end right there and then. Ever since that fateful night, I've lived in constant fear that someone in P.S.S.T. would figure out exactly what had happened.'

'Don't make me laugh!' scoffed Larry. 'We pulled the wool over their eyes, good and proper. Those dull-witted buffoons at P.S.S.T. wouldn't be capable of guessing the truth – and nor would anyone else for that matter.'

'My secretary Mavis Hughes nearly did,' said Philippa, giving him a steely stare. 'She was far too astute for her own good. She couldn't understand why I seemed to have it in for P.S.S.T. Accused me of being stingy with their budgets and belittling their efforts. I thought that if I made things tough for them, Red would be forced to say goodbye to some of his staff. It seemed the only way to oust Socrates and Angela. Retirement didn't interest them – and the longer they remained at P.S.S.T. the more likely it was that they would start to suspect my involvement in your disappearance.'

'They were clueless,' snapped Larry. 'You shouldn't have panicked.'

'My secretary began to act oddly,' continued Philippa. 'She kept staring at me, and if she was on the phone, she'd clam up as soon as I walked in the room. Then one day, I caught her looking through my personal file. Well, that was it! I knew I'd have to get rid of her – and fast. I found out that she was going away for the weekend to Prague, followed her to the airport and slipped some confidential documents in her hand luggage. Then tipped off P.S.S.T. When the papers were discovered, she protested her innocence and tried to put the blame on me – but no one believed her, of course.'

'How deliciously *ruthless*,' said Larry, grinning.

Dawn wasn't impressed at all. She remembered being told by Red that the Chief of S.H.H.'s secretary had been put in prison for a very long time.

'That was a mean thing to do to Mavis,' she said.

'I know,' said Philippa guiltily.

'Couldn't you just have found fault with her typing and given her the sack?' said Dawn.

'Too risky,' said Philippa. 'I couldn't be sure how much Mavis had found out or how deeply she was prepared to dig into my past. The best way to silence her was to destroy her reputation – and put her behind bars so she couldn't do any more snooping.'

'I bet Mavis really hates your guts,' said Dawn.

'Oh, undoubtedly,' said Philippa, 'but when I hand myself over to the authorities, her name will be cleared and she'll be released from prison.'

Philippa's face seemed to crumple and, for a moment, Dawn feared that the Chief might burst into tears; but, displaying a will of iron, she managed to pull herself together.

'It's been a strain,' she said. 'I've done some awful things, Dawn – and they haven't been easy to live with. I've incarcerated Mavis, I've put two P.S.S.T. agents in hospital, I've lied, I've passed on secret information …'

'Wait a minute,' said Dawn. 'You weren't responsible for what happened to Miles and Bob! It was Larry who smeared lard on the ladder and almost tickled Bob to death. Not *you*!'

'I might as well have done it,' said Philippa grimly. 'I was the one who warned Meek about them, knowing what he was capable of. When I heard that he'd captured Angela, I bombed down here and tried to persuade him to let me take charge of her. Then, when I found out about you ...'

'I'm getting quite bored standing here,' cut in Larry, 'listening to you two rabbiting on. It's rather fortunate that I won't have to put up with your dreary chatter for very much longer.'

'What do you mean?' said Philippa. 'Are you letting us go?'

Larry smiled unpleasantly, and brandished his revolver. '*You* might be ready to spend the rest of your life in jail but I am *not*.' He glanced at his watch. 'In sixteen minutes it'll be ten o'clock,' he said. 'The church clock will muffle the sound of my gunshots nicely.'

'You wouldn't *dare*,' said Philippa. 'Dawn's just a child, and I'm ... I'm your *daughter*. Doesn't that count for anything?'

'No,' answered Larry. 'My freedom is all that I care about.'

Dawn gulped. She pressed her back against the bumpy stone wall, and tried to stop herself from quaking with fear. Her eyes were glued to the revolver in Larry's hand. Gradually, she became aware of the distant hum of voices and the faint clatter of footsteps outside. She looked over to the window slit.

With the tip of his gun, Larry indicated to Philippa

that she should move into the corner with Dawn. Once Philippa had complied with his wish, he approached the slit in the wall and took a swift peek through it.

'Ah!' he said, turning towards his captives with a chilling smile. 'How convenient. It looks as if we shan't have to wait until ten o'clock after all. The bell-ringers have just arrived for their Wednesday morning practice. In a minute or two they'll start yanking on those ropes of theirs, and when they do ...'

Philippa seized Dawn's hand and began to squeeze it urgently – not once but several times. At first, Dawn thought that Philippa was trying to be of some comfort. Then she realised that the squeezes actually meant something. The long knuckle-crunching clenches were 'dahs' and the brief pinches were 'dits'. Philippa was sending Dawn a message in Morse code:

W-H-E-N–I–S–A–Y–N–O–W–R–U–N–F–O–R–I-T

As soon as Dawn had worked out what the Chief was trying to say, she answered her with three long 'dahs' and then a 'dah-dit-dah' to show that she had understood.

Philippa let Dawn's hand drop.

For three seconds nothing happened. Then Philippa made her move.

In Dawn's experience, rugby tackles were usually

carried out by big, burly, muddy-kneed men on the television. She had never seen a young woman in a tailored suit and high heels launch herself at someone in such an aggressive manner. Larry was totally taken by surprise. When the Chief lunged at him and wrapped her arms around his knees he toppled over with a roar of rage.

'NOW!' yelled Philippa.

Dawn ran.

She hared over to the trapdoor, pausing briefly on the top rung of the ladder to glance at the Chief and her father grappling with each other on the floor. Then she climbed downwards as quickly as she dared. Her hands gripped the wooden ladder tightly and her eyes followed her fast-moving feet as they stepped on to each smooth rung.

Dawn had to pass through several levels and numerous trapdoors on her route to the bottom of the tower. She hardly noticed the beads of sweat gathering on her hairline or the rapid thump-thump-thump of her heart. All she could think about was reaching the bell-ringers before they had a chance to begin their recital. If just one toll rang out it would be enough to cover the sound of a single gunshot and that would be all Larry needed to put Philippa out of action.

'Stop!' shouted Dawn as her trainers made contact with a solid stone floor. Without pausing to catch her breath, she darted towards the nearest bell-ringer, who happened to be the lady in the pork-pie hat. 'You mustn't ring them!' she said desperately, grabbing the woman's sleeve.

The bell-ringer turned round and put a finger to her lips, and Dawn's mouth dropped open in shock. She had been expecting to see the wrinkled face of an elderly lady – not the youthful countenance of Emma Cambridge! P.S.S.T.'s recruitment officer put an arm around Dawn's shoulders and ushered her over to a corner.

'Are you all right?' whispered Emma.

'Yes,' said Dawn anxiously, 'but Philippa's not. She's up in the tower with Murdo Meek – and he's got a gun. He's going to shoot her as soon as somebody rings one of those bells. You can't let it happen!'

'Don't worry,' said Emma. 'There won't be any pealing of bells today.' She nodded towards the other bell-ringers. They were all members of P.S.S.T.!

'We persuaded the real bell-ringers to let us take their places,' said Red.

'And to borrow a few of their clothes,' said Socrates, winking at Dawn from beneath a peaked cap.

'I'm so pleased to see you!' said Dawn. She beamed at Jagdish, Socrates and Red.

'Likewise,' said Red. He beckoned to the others. 'Right, let's give this Meek fellow the shock of his life.' Treading softly across the floor, he stopped in front of the ladder and gripped it with his freckled hands. Before climbing upwards, he glanced over his shoulder at Dawn. 'You're absolutely sure that this chap really *is* Murdo Meek?'

Dawn nodded fervently.

'Well,' said Red, frowning, 'you can be sure that the cunning old rascal won't get away from us *this* time.'

With Red leading the way, the three P.S.S.T. members ascended the ladder. Each man had a grim, determined look on his face.

'Aren't we going, too?' asked Dawn, and Emma shook her head firmly.

'You've been put in quite enough danger already,' she said, steering Dawn through the doors which led into the nave of the church, 'and although I wouldn't mind helping to capture Murdo Meek – I don't think I'd better leave you on your own.'

'I can look after her,' said a voice, and Dawn grinned as Trudy rose from one of the pews. She was cradling something in her arms.

'Peebles!' said Dawn, rushing forwards. 'You made it!' To her delight, Trudy lowered the cat into Dawn's outstretched hands. Peebles purred loudly as Dawn hugged him to her chest. 'I'm *so* glad that you're OK!'

The cat's claws pricked her skin as the door of the north porch creaked open and, with a woof and an ungainly bound, Haltwhistle entered the church followed by an out of breath Felix.

'I thought I told you to stay put,' said Trudy frostily.

Felix pulled a face. 'We were far too worried about Dawn,' he said. His eyes lit up when he spotted her halfway up the nave of the church. 'Yahoo!' he yelled, breaking into a run. 'You're safe, Dawn! Thank goodness for that!'

'Out!' said Trudy, slapping Haltwhistle lightly on his behind. 'You, too, Felix. Murdo Meek is at large in this church. It's not safe for you to be here.'

'Stop ordering me about,' said Felix. 'If it wasn't for *me*, you wouldn't have found Dawn at all. It was *my* dog who picked up her scent.'

'And it was *my* idea to get Peebles to search all the buildings in this area,' snapped Trudy.

'So that's how you tracked me down!' said Dawn. She squeezed Peebles in her arms. 'I'm so glad that everything worked out. Where's Clop?' she said airily.

There were blank expressions all round.

'Clop's the name of my donkey,' she reminded them. Dawn wondered if all the excitement had addled everyone's brains. 'That's how you knew where to find me,' she said. 'I tied my donkey to Peebles's back ...'

Wordlessly, Felix reached into his pocket, withdrew his hand and opened his palm.

Sitting in its centre was a little, pleated tail.

Chapter Twenty-two

Mission Accomplished

The strands of wool which Dawn found scattered at the base of the gravestone were so few in number that they wouldn't have filled an egg cup. She picked them up carefully, one by one, and when she had finished she looked at the pitiful heap in her hand, which, together with the pleated tail, was all that was left of Clop.

Dawn bent her head, and did what spies were not supposed to do.

Poor, brave Clop. Even though she hadn't witnessed it, Dawn was certain that she knew what had happened. Guessing that Peebles stood very little chance of out-running a pair of nippy terriers, Clop had decided to distract them by throwing himself from the cat's back. He had hoped that this would give Peebles the head start he needed to dash away to safety.

Somehow, Clop must have wriggled free of the harness, but Dawn had knotted his tail so tightly to the rope that it had been left behind when he leaped. She pictured her donkey's dear, earnest little face, and knew that he would have shown no fear when he was snatched out of the air.

Dawn's fingers closed over the scraps of wool in her hand. She felt as if her heart would break.

To the sound of the church clock striking the hour, Dawn scrabbled in the dirt. She was making a hollow in the ground, between the roots of a yew tree. It took her until the very last strike to bury Clop's woollen remains. Then she bowed her head respectfully.

When she heard a scuffling sound, Dawn looked up. Coming down the path leading from the church, flanked by Red and Socrates, was Larry Grahams. His clothes were rumpled, his hair was unkempt and his scowl was so hostile and threatening that she could not bear to look at his face for very long. Behind the three men came Jagdish, who was holding Larry's revolver. At his side, with a ripped sleeve and a swollen lip, strode Philippa. Unlike her father, she showed no trace of bitterness at having been captured by P.S.S.T. Neither did she cower or hang her head in shame. Flicking back her shiny tresses, she carried herself with dignity and poise, which, reflected Dawn, was the appropriate sort of behaviour for a Chief, albeit a rather traitorous one.

Emma came next, with Trudy and Peebles a few paces behind. The cat seemed thoroughly worn out. He had settled himself comfortably in Trudy's arms and did not look as if he wished to be disturbed for several days. Bringing up the rear were Felix and his hairy hound. For a split second, Dawn wondered if she had been wrong about Haltwhistle. Was he, as Felix had always maintained, a dog of staggering intelligence? *Had* he picked up her scent at the duck pond and tracked her all the way to the graveyard? And if so, had his keen sense of smell been demonstrated before? *Did* his nose lead him to the door of the Dampside Hotel and, a few days later, through the thicket of birch trees on the trail of Angela Bradshaw? *Could* it be possible that Haltwhistle had lured her into Charles Noble's garden with the sole purpose of guiding her to the lard-smeared rung on the ladder?

Haltwhistle let out a booming bark when he spotted Dawn crouching beneath the yew trees. He hurtled towards her, his ears flopping up and down, skidded to a stop and lathered her knee with his slimy tongue. Then he sneezed twice before sitting down to scratch himself.

'No,' said Dawn, dismissing the notion that Haltwhistle was a great deal smarter than he looked. 'It's quite unthinkable. I was right about you the first time.'

A small group of villagers approached Red and Socrates as the two men frogmarched Larry down the path. Dawn identified Charles Noble among them and realised that they must be the genuine band of bell-ringers. When Charles began to address the Head of P.S.S.T., she left her position beneath the yew tree and moved closer so that she could hear what was being said.

'He may be your neighbour,' said Red, gripping Larry's arm tightly, 'but he also happens to be a criminal mastermind.'

'Thanks for your help,' said Socrates, doffing his peaked cap and returning it to Charles. 'We've been after this bloke for years.'

'I can't believe it,' said Charles in a stunned voice. 'Are you sure you haven't made a mistake? This man's a respected member of the community.'

'We couldn't be more certain,' said Red. 'Now, if you'll excuse us ...'

'Hang on a minute!' shouted Dawn. She glanced warily at Charles. 'I think he might be involved.'

'What do you mean?' said Charles, regarding Dawn with a startled expression. 'The idea that I could be mixed up in anything underhand is totally ridiculous! I'm a law-abiding citizen. How dare you cast aspersions on my character, you young monkey!'

'What makes you suspect this chap?' asked Red. 'Enlighten us, Dawn.'

'I overheard him talking about Bob in the pub,' she said.

'Utter claptrap,' said Charles. 'I don't know anyone

called Bob! This child is obviously lying through her teeth.'

'I'm telling the truth,' protested Dawn. 'You called him "Little Bob"!'

To her dismay, Charles began to laugh, and the rest of the bell-ringers followed suit. '"Little Bob" isn't a *person*,' said Charles when he had managed to straighten his face. 'It's the name of a *round*.'

'A round *what*?' said Dawn.

'It's a bell-ringing term,' said Charles. 'A round … a series of notes rung on a set of bells … a tune, if you like.'

'Oh,' said Dawn, feeling rather stupid. She was relieved when a smart, black estate car drew up beside the lychgate of the churchyard, and everyone's attention was diverted. The car's engine was turned off and somebody opened the passenger door. It was a middle-aged woman with long, straight hair and a pale, troubled face. Dawn had never seen her before.

Felix had, though.

'GRANNY!' he cried, running down the path towards the new arrival. He spread his arms wide and gave her a big, chest-crushing hug.

'John! My Long John Silver!' said the woman, calling Felix by his preferred name. Her voice shook with emotion as she asked him if he was all right.

'I'm super, thanks, Granny,' said Felix with a grin. He

led her through the lychgate. 'There's someone I'd like you to meet.'

'Hello,' said Dawn, shaking the woman's outstretched hand. 'You must be Angela Bradshaw.'

'I am indeed, my dear,' said Angela, smiling, 'and you're Dawn Buckle. I've heard quite a lot about *you*.'

They drove back to London in two fast cars, an ice-cream van, and the elderly white hatchback which rattled a bit when it tried to do more than sixty miles an hour.

Larry had been handcuffed and sandwiched between Socrates and Red in the back seat of a BMW, with Philippa in the passenger seat and Emma at the wheel; Jagdish had ridden with Nathan in the ice-cream van, which, owing to some sort of malfunction, played its melody whenever Nathan depressed the brake; and Edith acted as chauffeur in the smart, black estate car whilst Felix and his granny lounged in the back with an arm each around Haltwhistle. Dawn had guessed, quite rightly, that Trudy would like some company in the hatchback. On the outward journey they had sat together in the two front seats and on the homeward stretch they did the same but, this time, the cardboard box had been abandoned, and Dawn held Peebles in her arms.

During the sixty-mile drive, Trudy talked non-stop

and Dawn was content to nod intermittently and ask the odd question whenever she could get a word in. Before they had reached the outskirts of London, Dawn had learned how Trudy had spotted Philippa Killingback lurking in the background on one of the microdot photographs. Realising that the Chief of S.H.H. had been present at the Garden and Allotment Show on the day, that Angela went missing, Trudy had known, instantly, that something very odd was going on. She had alerted P.S.S.T. immediately, and, when Dawn had not returned from her night-time mission, she had scoured the village with the help of Felix, Peebles and Haltwhistle. A little later Nathan had joined in the search, having been parked only a few miles away.

According to Trudy, the rest of P.S.S.T. had not been sluggish either.

Firstly, they had descended upon Philippa's London residence in Belgravia, past which Dawn had probably sailed in Emma's MG on that memorable Tuesday morning just over a week ago. Finding no one at home, they had searched the building from top to bottom, coming across Angela behind a locked door in the attic. With confirmation that Murdo Meek was definitely alive, they had left a reluctant Izzie in charge at the Dampside Hotel, and raced to Cherry Bentley.

To Dawn's bewilderment, their small convoy of vehicles (with the BMW at the front and the white hatchback in last place) did not proceed to the head-quarters of P.S.S.T. in Pimlico. Instead, they made their way to Crouch End, parked in a street called Farthingale Row and walked round the corner to a sec-ond-hand bookshop. It was a run-down place called Endpapers and, by the look of the items displayed in its window, it appeared to favour books with dull jackets and even drearier titles.

Philippa crossed the threshold first, and, behind her, Red guided Larry over the doorstep. The notorious spy had a hat pulled down over his eyes and was wearing a pair of earplugs, presumably so that he had no idea where he was being taken. The rest of them followed the Chief into the shop in dribs and drabs.

'Got anything by Florence Lawrence?' said Philippa to the bespectacled girl behind the counter.

This was obviously some kind of password, because the assistant gave her a furtive wink before saying, 'Yes, indeed, madam. Right over here.' She walked to the back of the shop, did a sort of tap-dance on an oriental rug, and stepped neatly to one side.

Dawn watched as the rug began to wrinkle. Then it disappeared through a hole in the floor. She saw a flight of carpeted stairs leading downwards and waited her turn before stepping on to them. At the very bottom was a priggish-looking man with a propelling pencil wedged behind his ear. He was sitting behind a desk, and rose swiftly to his feet when he spotted Philippa Killingback.

'Ma'am,' he said civilly.

She nodded at him. 'Good afternoon, Tarquin. I need you to issue some passes.'

'Certainly, ma'am,' he answered, opening a drawer in the desk. He took out two handfuls of badges which, because they were round and attached to silver chains, looked a little like sink plugs.

'S.H.H. VISITOR', read Dawn, before hanging a badge around her own neck. She felt a thrill shoot through her. Glancing at the others, she saw Nathan with a big grin on his face and realised that he was equally as excited to be allowed inside the nerve centre of S.H.H. Nathan nudged her arm.

'Good this, isn't it, Dawn?' he said. 'A week ago, I was a probationer ... and now, Red says that I've been such a help with Operation Question Mark that he's going to take me on at P.S.S.T. permanently!'

'That's great,' Dawn said warmly.

After everyone had been given a pass, including Peebles and Haltwhistle, they all trooped along a maze of corridors. Dawn noticed that all the doors which they went by did not have any handles. Instead, there were strange pieces of flared metal sticking out of them, which looked like trumpet-shaped flowers.

Philippa stopped outside a door marked 'Deputy

Chief', leaned close to one of the 'flowers' as if it were a microphone and said, 'Tiddly-om-pom-pom.' Then she swallowed hard and straightened the torn sleeve of her jacket. 'This is it,' she said to the surrounding group. 'I'm going to give myself up.'

Dawn appreciated that Philippa must be feeling a fair amount of trepidation. When the rest of S.H.H. found out that their Chief was the daughter of Murdo Meek, and that she had lied and connived for him, there would be an almighty uproar.

'Don't forget to mention all the good things you did,' said Dawn, remembering how Philippa had done her best to keep Angela safe from Meek, and how she had risked her life to allow Dawn to escape. 'Good luck,' she added, and she reached out and squeezed the Chief's hand. (Just a normal squeeze – no message in Morse code this time.)

A man with wiry black hair and perfect teeth opened the door and looked, with some astonishment, at the mob in the corridor.

'Hello, Mike,' said Philippa. 'Do you mind if I have a word?'

'Sure,' said Mike, staring with bafflement at Haltwhistle and Peebles.

Philippa turned back to the others and suggested that they might like to proceed to the visitors' lounge. Then she entered the Deputy Chief's office, followed by Red and Larry (whose hat and earplugs had, at last, been removed).

'Cor, what a spread!' said Nathan, sinking into a leather armchair. In his lap he rested a plate piled high with food.

'Rich pickings, indeed!' said Jagdish, crunching a chocolate finger with relish.

Dawn nibbled a vol-au-vent and looked for somewhere to sit. There were several sofas and armchairs in the visitors' lounge but, with so many people converging on the room, an empty seat was not easy to spot.

'Over there, below that oil painting,' said Edith, her sharp eyes locating the only available space.

'Thanks,' said Dawn, heading over to the vacant chair.

'I'll tell you one thing about S.H.H.,' said Socrates, chomping his way through a large pork pie. 'They really know how to treat their guests.' He took a few more bites, then frowned and shook his head. 'Murdo Meek, eh? Thought he was as dead as a doornail these past ten years and all the time he was living it up in a little Essex village. I wouldn't half like to know how he did it.' Socrates gazed expectantly at Angela. 'Well?' he said.

'If you're asking me how he managed to get out of that freezing cold river,' she said, 'you're going to be disappointed with my answer. I don't have the faintest idea.'

'Er ... I think I can help you,' said Dawn. 'Philippa explained it to me.'

Every face in the room turned towards her (except Haltwhistle's, which was buried in a bowl of cocktail sausages).

'Out with it, then,' said Socrates.

Dawn took a deep breath. 'They planned it between them,' she said. 'When Meek realised that he couldn't shake off Angela, he rang his daughter and asked her to help him.'

'Ordered her, more like,' growled Socrates. 'Knocked me for six when she told me that old ratfink was her dad.'

Ignoring him, Dawn continued. 'When Philippa –'

'She was "Pip" then,' said Socrates.

'All right.' Dawn sighed. 'When *Pip* got to the warehouse, she volunteered to guard the back entrance. Meek was waiting for her there. He told her that he'd been thinking of retiring and that if she helped him to escape, just this once, he'd promise to disappear for good.'

'So, how did they do it?' asked Jagdish.

'Pip put on Meek's scarf and overcoat,' said Dawn. 'Then she fired her gun at the lamp behind the warehouse, so that it would be too dark for anyone to see properly.'

'The gunshot!' said Angela. 'Yes, I remember that. Then she phoned us to say that Meek had overpowered her and was making for the footbridge across the Thames.'

'Pip ran to the footbridge, dressed in Meek's clothes,' said Dawn. 'Then she took them off, wrapped them round a block of concrete –'

'That makes sense,' said Socrates. 'The bridge was being repaired and it was like a minefield to cycle across. Buckled my front wheel and almost went over the handlebars.'

'Shh,' said Edith.

'Pip dropped the whole lot in the river,' said Dawn. 'The concrete block hit the water with a mighty splash and sank to the bottom, but the coat and scarf floated in the water so that when Red shone his torch on them, you all believed that Meek had drowned.'

'When, in actual fact, he'd sneaked back into the warehouse and left by the front door,' guessed Angela.

'Clever,' said Socrates. 'V-e-r-y clever.'

'Yes,' piped up Felix, helping himself to a handful of grapes, 'but I bet *I* would have figured it out.'

At the headquarters of P.S.S.T., a party was in full swing in the Top Secret Missions room later that afternoon. What had started out to be a debriefing session had descended into a celebratory shindig. Having been promised a substantially higher budget for the rest of the year by Mike Lejeune, the new Chief of S.H.H., Red had stopped off at a posh patisserie on the way back to the Dampside Hotel and bought a selection of their finest cakes.

'If I could have your attention,' said Red good-naturedly. With a handkerchief he wiped the remnants of a cream puff from his lower lip, and rose out of his chair. 'Button it, please, people,' he said more sternly, and the chattering and laughing gradually ceased.

'Be upstanding,' said Red, and chair legs scraped as everyone got to their feet. 'I'd like to propose a toast,' he said, raising his teacup. Bone china cups were lifted all around the room. 'To a courageous young lady who has not only completed her first mission successfully – and bagged the most elusive villain of them all – but has saved our beloved P.S.S.T. from being disbanded.' Red cleared his throat. 'To Dawn,' he said.

'To Dawn!' said everyone, after which they took a noisy gulp of tea.

Nobody had ever toasted her before. Dawn was quite overwhelmed.

'Thanks,' she said, her cheeks flaming. 'I've loved working with all of you.' Her eyes roamed around the room, moving from face to face. Finally, her gaze rested on Haltwhistle. 'Well … *almost* all of you,' she said, and grinned.

The merrymaking continued until every crumb of cake had been eaten. Then Emma produced her car keys and jingled them.

'I think it's time we got these kids home,' she said.

Declining a lift, Felix and his granny explained that they would much prefer to walk. Angela had been cooped up in Philippa's attic for several weeks and she was looking forward to giving her legs some exercise. Before they left, Angela invited Dawn to tea on Saturday afternoon, to which Felix and Haltwhistle were also invited. Touched that Felix actually appeared quite pleased at the prospect of seeing her again so soon, Dawn offered him her hand.

'Goodbye, brother Wayne,' she said. 'I couldn't have wrapped up my mission without you.' (She *could*, of course – and would probably have done it an awful lot quicker if Felix hadn't been there, but Dawn was too nice to ever admit it.)

'No problem,' said Felix, looking very pleased with himself. He shook her hand and Haltwhistle licked her knee, in perfect unison. 'So long, Kitty Wilson,' he said.

A little while later, Dawn said a final farewell to Kitty Wilson, too, when she gave back the sky-blue suitcase which she had taken to Cherry Bentley and retrieved her red case from the bottom of the wardrobe in room four. She opened it and smiled when she saw her name drawn in felt-tip on the inside of the lid.

'I'm me, again!' she said.

There was a small space next to her mushroom-coloured knee socks which caused her quite a bit of heartache. Dawn paused for several minutes before putting some of Kitty's clothes into the case, which Izzie had insisted she should take with her. Alongside these, she squeezed a cheque from P.S.S.T. presented to her by Red for 'a job well done'.

Before she closed the lid, Dawn put one more item inside it: a gold-plated fountain pen which Socrates had given her as a parting gift. She had found his last words to her slightly hurtful.

'I dunno quite what's happened to you, Dawn,' he had said, 'but you seem to have lost your knack for going unnoticed. If you want to be accepted for another P.S.S.T. mission, you'll need to undergo some *serious* retraining.'

Dawn shut her case and thought about what Socrates had said. She realised that he was right. Somewhere along the course of Operation Question Mark, she had ceased to be invisible – and, unlike Socrates who had deemed this development to be rather disappointing, Dawn found that she was secretly thrilled by it.

Hearing Emma calling her from the corridor, she hurried towards the door, and in less than a minute they were stepping out of the lift and walking over to the reception desk. Edith's piercing eyes watched them draw nearer.

'Goodbye,' said Dawn politely.

Edith nodded. 'I hope you've had a pleasant stay,' she said – and smiled for almost a tenth of a second.

Peebles was sitting on the hotel guest book, with his paws tucked underneath him. A rumbling noise emanated from him when Dawn began to stroke his head. It was the loudest that she had ever heard him purr.

'Jump to it,' said Emma pleasantly, 'or we'll hit the rush-hour traffic.'

Dawn gripped the handle of her suitcase and followed Emma outside. Parked in front of the hotel was the two-seater sports car, its dark green bonnet glinting in the sunshine.

'Hello-o!' hollered Dawn through the letterbox of number eight, Windmill View. She pressed the doorbell for the second time, and before she could press it yet again, the door flew open.

'Have a bit of patience, can't you?' said Dawn's mother, wiping floury hands on her apron. 'I'm in the middle of baking a cake. My daughter's coming home today. Good heavens, Dawn, is that you?'

'Of course it's me,' said Dawn, grinning broadly. 'Hello, Mum!'

Beverley Buckle put her head on one side. 'Your hair's all short … and your clothes are new … and there's something else different about you.'

'I'm still the same old Dawn. Are you really making me a cake?'

'Mmm,' said her mother. 'It's called a devil's food cake. My boss gave me the recipe. Keeps asking me if I've tried it out yet. When I got the phone call saying that you'd be home tonight, I thought I'd give it a whirl … as a welcome home sort of thing.'

'Can't wait to taste it!' said Dawn. Even though her stomach was filled to the brim with tarts, scones and buns from the patisserie, she was determined to force down a slice of her mum's cake, somehow or other.

'Wotcha, kid,' said Jefferson Buckle, appearing at his wife's shoulder. 'Get on all right, did you? Good. When you've dumped your bag, why don't you pop down to the cellar? I've got a new cuckoo clock that'll take your breath away.'

'Great,' said Dawn. 'I'll be with you in a minute but first I want to say hi to Gramps.' She squeezed past her parents and went into the living room, expecting to find her grandfather sitting in the dark in front of his favourite electrical appliance. 'Where is he?' said Dawn, her voice stricken with panic. The curtains were pulled back, the armchair was empty and the television set was switched off. 'Where's Gramps?' she said, returning to the hallway. Tears sprang to her eyes.

Her mother seemed reluctant to meet her gaze.

'Something … hasn't happened to him, has it?'

'No, no … nothing like that.' Beverley gave an exasperated sort of groan. 'He wanted it to be a surprise.'

'Pardon?' said Dawn.

'Your grandfather's gone to buy you a present.'

She tracked him down outside the toy shop. He was wearing a vest, tatty old cords and a pair of carpet slippers. His forefinger kept jabbing at the windowpane, as if he were trying to decide which of the toys to choose.

'Hello, Gramps,' said Dawn, slipping an arm through his.

'Oh, darn it,' he said. 'You've gone an' caught me in the act. S'pose your mother let the cat out o' the bag, did she?'

'Yes,' said Dawn. 'You really don't have to get me a present, Gramps.'

'Well, I'm goin' to … see?' he said. 'So, what do you fancy, Dawnie? That tiger isn't bad … but I was sort o' leanin' towards the elephant.'

Dawn bit her lip. 'Would you mind ever so much if I didn't *have* a toy, Gramps?'

'Not want a toy?' said Ivor, staring open-mouthed at his granddaughter. 'Why ever not?'

She wanted to tell him that no other toy could

possibly replace the one she had lost – but she didn't.

'Because,' said Dawn, looking desperately around her, 'I'd rather have a … a *pet*, if that's all right.'

'A pet? Where'm I goin' to get one o' them?'

'From over there,' said Dawn, pointing to a shop called Bertha's Beasties which was situated across the road.

Dawn chose a rabbit. Not a cute, baby one with snowy fur and droopy ears that her grandfather was besotted by – but a half-grown, brown buck.

'What d'you pick him for?' said Gramps.

For a moment or two, Dawn wasn't sure why that particular rabbit had caught her eye. He was rather a plain fellow with ears that didn't seem to know at which angle they should be pointing. Halfway through a shrug, Dawn realised what it was about the rabbit that she'd found so arresting.

There was something distinctly Clop-ish about the way he looked at her.

Afterword

A soft-hearted judge presided over Philippa Killingback's trial. She was given a big slap on the wrist and a colossal fine but escaped a prison term.

Murdo Meek was locked up for an impossibly long time. His jailors were told to throw away the key.

And Pilliwinks was sentenced to life in a tortoise sanctuary in Cornwall.

Glossary

Acronyms

S.H.H.	**S**trictly **H**ush-**H**ush
P.S.S.T.	**P**ursuit of **S**cheming **S**pies and **T**raitors
A.H.E.M.	**A**cquisition of **H**ugely **E**nlightening **M**aterial
C.O.O.E.E.	**C**overt **O**bservance and **O**bstruction of **E**nemy **E**spionage
P.U.F.F.	**P**rocurement of **U**seful **F**acts and **F**igures
C.L.I.C.K.	**C**reation of **L**udicrously **I**ngenious **C**odes and **K**eys
P.I.N.G.	**P**roduction of **I**ncredibly **N**ifty **G**adgets

The Cumberbatch Alphabet

(Conceived by Stanley Cumberbatch in 1981)

Armpit	**F**lip-flop
Bungalow	**G**unk
Chutney	**H**urrah
Doodah	**I**diot
Egghead	**J**ellyfish

Key-ring	**S**ausage
Leotard	**T**racksuit
Muesli	**U**nicorn
Nasturtium	**V**oodoo
Onion	**W**ednesday
Puddle	**X**mas
Quicksand	**Y**o-yo
Roundabout	**Z**ilch

Morse Code

(Invented by Samuel Morse in 1872)

· = dit (short signal)

– = dah (long signal)

A	· –	**N**	– ·
B	– · · ·	**O**	– – –
C	– · – ·	**P**	· – – ·
D	– · ·	**Q**	– – · –
E	·	**R**	· – ·
F	· · – ·	**S**	· · ·
G	– – ·	**T**	–
H	· · · ·	**U**	· · –
I	· ·	**V**	· · · –
J	· – – –	**W**	· – –
K	– · –	**X**	– · · –
L	· – · ·	**Y**	– · – –
M	– –	**Z**	– – · ·

Full stop (AAA)	. — . — . —
Apostrophe (AMN)	. — — — — .
Question mark (IMI)	. . — — . .
End (AR)	. — . — .

Some Codes and Ciphers

Clown	a cipher involving the repeated juggling of letters
Ditchwater	consisting of such a dull letter that the person reading it gives up long before the end and therefore misses the message concealed in the postscript
Easy-Peasy	in which the message is hidden letter by letter in front of every 'e'
Noah's Ark	conceals the message by writing the letters two by two in each consecutive word
Shopping List	in which shopping items represent particular words
Tornado	a cipher that turns letters back to front and upside down

Spying Terms

Agent	another name for a spy
Assignment	another word for **Mission**

Briefing	a meeting where instructions for a **Mission** are given
Cipher	a secret way of corresponding where letters are swapped with other letters so that the message is impossible to read without the aid of a **Key**
Code	a method of writing where words are replaced with other words so that the message's meaning is hidden
Dead letter box	a concealed place where messages can be delivered and collected
Espionage	another word for spying
Forger	someone who makes false documents
Gadget	a small, cunning device
Key	a piece of information which enables someone to work out the meaning of an enciphered message
Legend	a false name and life history
Microdot	a minuscule photograph, the size of a dot
Mission	a job which a spy is sent to carry out (see also **Assignment**)
Morse Code	an alphabet which swaps letters for dots and dashes
Quarry	the person or thing a spy is pursuing
Rendezvous	a meeting at an agreed time and place
Sleuthing	another word for spying/detective work

Surveillance	keeping a close eye on a suspect
Tradecraft	the skills needed for a career in **Espionage**
Traitor	a treacherous person who is disloyal to his country
Undercover	assuming another identity in order to observe others

Useful Books

Keeping to the Shadows by Anonymous
C.L.I.C.K.'s Compendium by Various
The Hugger-mugger Handbook by Sue de Neame
A Pocket Guide to Gadget Repair by Arnold Twitch
Hot Pants Are a No-no: What Not to Wear Undercover by T. Ward and S. Caldicott
White Lies and Whoppers: A Spy's Guide to Fibbing Convincingly by Amelia Punch
They Were Jolly Brave: Wartime Spies of Yesteryear by Sqn Ldr Stodgy Washington

Anna Dale

Anna Dale was born in 1971 and has lived in various counties in the south-east of England. She spent most of her childhood in a village called Writtle, and attended the local grammar school there. At the age of seven Anna gained her writer's badge at Brownies, and from that moment she secretly dreamed of becoming an author.

Anna has an MA in Writing for Children, and she wrote her first novel *Whispering to Witches* in two months as part of her MA. Anna lives in Hampshire where she divides her time between working in a bookshop, writing and roaming the countryside with her dog, Bess.

www.bloomsbury.com/annadale